Chapter
The girl on

Jack's journey to work had ......ventful as usual, he noticed the girl on the train, he had seen her before and wondered where she worked? Could it be the same building as him? She seemed to be on the same train at the same time every day, she caught his eye that morning because she seemed to be upset. But then Jack was a bit of a people watcher, he often looked at people and wondered about their lives, what they did for a living, what sort of car they drove, it was a sort of game he played in his mind to pass the time.

The train came to a halt and the mass exodus for the doors began, even before they opened people were pushing and shoving, Jack remained quietly in his seat, he didn't want to be part of the rat race, he didn't need to fight for a taxi outside the station as work was a five minute walk away.

It was raining, not cold, just a gentle warm summer shower, they never last long, Jack stepped inside the newsagent's doorway and waited for the rain to ease, "Can I help you sir" a voice called out, Jack turned to see a shop assistant standing there, Jack simply shook his head "Well you can't stand there sir, you're obstructing the exit, it's a fire hazard" explained the shop assistant, Jack said nothing, he thought how petty and unhelpful people were becoming in modern life, years ago he would have been welcome to step inside, out of the rain, Jack emerged from the doorway and walked straight into the girl from the train, she dropped the book she was carrying under her arm, Jack could see she was struggling, she had a bag in one hand and two more in the other, "Here let me help you" Jack said after apologizing for the collision, He picked up the book, glanced at the cover and as he carefully tucked it back under her arm said "Good choice", the girl smiled and replied, "Thank you, Have you read it?" Jack paused for a moment, wondering if he should claim to have read it but then said "No but I like the author, I have read a few of hers".

Jack then began his short walk to work, he turned left out of the station doors and found the girl was still right behind him, Jack slowed his pace and when she caught up he asked if he could help with her bags, she agreed and the two of them walked together, the rain had stopped a minute or two earlier and the sun was now shining, " I'm Jack by the way" he said, "Carol" she replied, She asked if jack worked near by, he told her he was at the Old corn exchange building, he nodded forward as if to point as his hands were full, surprised, Carol replied "really? I'm just over the road in the travel agent's" Jack made a joke about knowing where to come to book his holiday, as if he ever went on holiday, it'd been many years since Jack had ventured abroad and it'd been a disaster, his mind briefly wandered back to that holiday, He suddenly snapped out of it when Carol chirped "This is me! Thanks for the help." Jack handed back the bags he'd been carrying and after a simple "bye" stepped out into the road, spotting a gap he made a run for it.

Jack's job was pretty boring, he sat in his office arranging meetings for other people, people from upstairs, people with careers and shares and their own parking spaces in the company car park, parking spaces with their names on, Jack thought how he would love his own reserved parking space with his name on, even though he didn't own a car at the moment.
He was envious of the people upstairs, jetting off around the world to exotic locations, eating in fancy restaurants, staying in luxurious hotels and being waited on hand and foot, all Jack had was a small rented flat and an ageing TV. He hated his life and the constant shouting and screaming from the flat next door, he struggled to understand why people who obviously hate each other choose to stay together, was it purely to annoy those who live around them with their constant foul language, fighting and throwing things?

Lunch time was approaching, Jack usually sat outside with his sandwiches rather than go to the canteen, it was far more entertaining to watch people going about their daily routines, he sat on the polished marble wall around the raised garden because the bench was taken. He thought "I wonder what delicacy awaits me today" as he unwrapped the tin foil from his sandwiches, "oh Cheese and pickle" he thought, pretending to himself to be surprised, he knew what they were as he had made them himself the night before.

Jack was watching the people walking past wondering if their lives were any worse than his when he happened to glance over the road and in the window of the travel agents he could see Carol behind her desk talking to a couple, he waved to her but she was engrossed in her work trying to find the scruffy pair a budget holiday for ten quid, he thought. Jack liked to imagine strangers and their lives, he'd pick someone or maybe a couple like those in the travel agent and imagine them as secret agents or maybe professional burglars robbing diamond necklaces and tiaras from safes in top class hotels in Monte Carlo, but then he thought the obese slobs in the travel agent's would never get down that air duct or climb the drainpipe to the twenty fifth floor, that would be ridiculous.

Jack finished his lunch, rolled up the tin foil and put it in the bin before slowly and unenthusiastically heading back inside. He stepped into the elevator and found himself surrounded by executives in hand tailored suits talking about multi million pound investments, the smell of their cologne made the air in the enclosed space hard to breathe but it didn't seem to bother them, he wondered if he should fart, would they even notice above the scent filled air?

On the train at the end of the working day Jack found himself standing very close to Carol, the train was packed out like the inside of a sardine can, he could feel her firm breasts pushing into his chest every time the train moved from side to side, Jack tried not to think about it, he was worried he might start pushing into her if he got too excited but it was impossible not to have thoughts of her naked, they were just too squashed together and she was so pretty, he tried to think about other things, like football, that's supposed to work, he'd heard somewhere, a distraction is good in these situations, but that wasn't going well, he could feel himself getting aroused and was sure that any second now Carol would notice.

The train pulled into a station, seats were suddenly available, jack grabbed one and pulled Carol along with him, they sat together side by side, Jack had his briefcase on his lap covering his embarrassment, "I saw you today" he said, "Oh really?" Carol replied, Jack explained how he was outside eating his lunch and he saw her through the shop window, he didn't mention the fat couple as he didn't want to appear judgmental or offensive, "That's embarrassing, you saw me

in my uniform then?" she said "No" replied jack, "I could only see your face there were people sitting between you and the window"
Carol seemed relieved that Jack hadn't seen her in her uniform, Jack thought "does this mean she's interested in me? Na! She probably has a husband or boyfriend at home," He thought about her in a uniform, he wondered why it would be so embarrassing, uniforms are generally quite sexy, Jack had often fantasized about a police woman and how he would like to have one from behind in uniform bending over the bonnet of a police car, screaming harder! Harder, or I'll arrest you! He smiled at that thought as he gazed out of the carriage window, he saw a familiar car sales yard and realized his stop was coming up, Jack said goodbye to Carol and as the train slowed he stood up and headed for the door.

That evening Jack couldn't keep his mind off Carol, his thoughts were ranging between how lovely her personality was, how pretty she was and how horny he felt being so close to her on the train, in fact he was still feeling aroused, Jack thought about taking a cold shower, then he toyed with the idea of drawing the blinds and relieving himself by hand, but then decided fantasizing about her and acting on it in that way would make him feel it was all a bit sordid and cheap, like he was seeing her as flesh and nothing more which wasn't the case, jack felt there was something more, he desperately wanted to get to know Carol so he decided he would risk embarrassing rejection and ask her out.

Jack phoned the takeaway and ordered food, showered and changed into his robe as he had no plans to go out that night, the food arrived and Jack sat watching TV with a tray on his lap, The news started, without looking up Jack listened as the news reader told of how the police had chased a blue Mercedes after an undercover drug sting had gone wrong, two police officers had been shot dead, it was interesting to Jack because it had occurred close to where he worked, a back street a couple of hundred yards away, in the six years Jack had been doing his mundane job at the corn exchange building nothing exciting had happened, not even a minor car crash on the busy road out front, nothing.

Jack thought about how boring and uneventful his life had been, here he was in his early thirty's and living in a cheap apartment with rubbish neighbours in a cheap part of town, buying cheap off the peg suits, it was all very depressing, Oh how exciting it would be to be like James Bond, a secret agent, dicing with death, always getting the girl and living the life, Jack drifted off to sleep.

He woke up with a chill, it was one twenty in the morning and he was still sitting in his chair, the heating had gone off, Jack got up and slowly made his way to the bedroom.

The following morning He was all hyped up, today was the day Jack was going to ask Carol out, for the first time in years he felt nervous as the train pulled into the station, he boarded the train and looked for Carol but she was nowhere to be seen, he made his way through the busy carriage to the next and there she was, "Good morning" said Jack "Morning" replied Carol with a smile, Jack thought about the question, he worried it may cause a problem with their friendship but that was a risk he'd decided to take because a friendship with her would always be a disappointment when he wanted so much more, he decided not to ask her on the train as it might be embarrassing with all those people around for one or both of them if she turned out to be married or spoken for, rejection worried Jack, it wouldn't have normally but this girl seemed special, "Join me for lunch?" asked Jack, quietly, without hesitation Carol responded "yes, what time? Where?" Jack suddenly felt good, this was exciting, "The Café?" he suggested, Carol thought about that and said "I have sandwiches, couldn't I join you on your bench?" Jack laughed "Yes of course, one pm OK?" She agreed.

The morning dragged, it felt like lunch time would never come around, eventually it did and Jack eagerly grabbed his lunch and headed for the elevator, when he got outside Carol was already there, reserving his seat, they enquired what each other had in their sandwiches, Jack was a little embarrassed to show his drying cheese

sandwiches with their turned up corners because he'd run out of pickle and forgotten to wrap them the night before, "Oh dear", said Carol, "would you like one of mine?"
Jack being polite said, "No it's fine, this is how I like them" they both laughed. He finally got up the courage to ask Carol if she was alone and after her little joke of "No I'm with you eating lunch" she confessed she wasn't living alone, after a pause and the disappointment clearly showing on Jack's face she said "I live with my mother"
Jack gave a sigh of relief, "How about dinner?" he asked, "Now just slow down Jack, we haven't finished lunch yet, I won't be hungry for hours" said Carol laughing, then she said "Yes of course I'll have dinner with you" they made their arrangements and Jack watched as Carol walked back across the busy road to the travel agents, he liked the little wiggle she did as she walked, it was so feminine.

Jack was home about six fifteen, he tidied up a bit, unloaded the dishwasher then the phone rang, Jack answered it only to find Carol was canceling the date, she said her mother wasn't well and she had to reschedule, Jack was sympathetic but skeptical, it seemed like some coincidence that on their first real date her mother gets sick, He wondered if it was an excuse, maybe Carol had got cold feet, maybe she wasn't as free or single as she made out, all the possible reasons he could

think up went through Jack's mind, he thought it was all too good to be true, maybe it was.
On the train the following morning Carol looked upset, Jack thought he was about to get dumped but still had to know, he asked "are you ok? You look a bit upset," Carol said "do I ?, I'm sorry, Let's talk at lunch" Jack agreed, they walked together in silence from the station to work with a casual "see you at lunchtime" as they parted to go to their respective places of work.

Jack was not happy, he was not concentrating, in fact he booked Robert Wiseman onto a flight to Zurich instead of Brussels, it's a good thing Mr Wiseman's secretary spotted the error or Jack would have been in a lot of trouble.
This was the longest morning Jack could remember, he was sure he was going to get bad news at lunchtime, Carol was going to tell him she wanted to drop him, or maybe she was going to confess to being married, Jack really didn't have a clue and was dreading it.

Eventually the hour arrived, Jack with a face like a boy about to be spanked made his way outside, totally forgetting his lunch, he sat on the bench for nearly the whole of his lunch hour until with ten minutes to go Carol appeared, "So sorry I'm late Jack, I couldn't get away, I do wish people would have some sort of idea where they want to go before they come in." Jack looked her in the eye and said quietly and calmly "Shall we get it over with then?" "What do you mean?" asked Carol, "You're going to dump me, aren't you?" said Jack, Carol looked surprised "Good grief Jack, no, whatever gave you that idea?" "It was just that you broke our date, then this morning you were upset and didn't want to talk, what else could it be?" Jack said,

Carol remembered how she'd felt in the morning, and realized Jack had put two and two together and made five, Oh don't be silly! It's my mother, about eight thirty last night, after the restaurant booking had come and gone she made a miraculous recovery, I should have known it was sabotage!" she said quite angrily, it became obvious to Jack that Carol was being kept prisoner by her mother to some degree, he'd heard of this sort of thing before when mothers are afraid of being left alone because their daughters fly the nest, in a way he felt relieved, he wasn't getting dumped but by the same token a great big uphill had presented itself, how could he get past Carol's mother without going to war because that would surely alienate Carol too.

Over the following weeks Jack and Carol dated regularly, Carol was fast getting immune to her mother's tricks and demands, She wanted a life without being tied to mother's apron strings, her mother was the reason Carol had never had a lasting relationship.

In the restaurant one night Carol completely out of the blue said "Let's go away for a week or so?"
Jack thought about that for a moment and said "OK, why not, oh, but what about" and before he could finish Carol butted in with "The wicked witch of the west?" Smiling, Jack said he would never have referred to Carol's mother in such a way, they laughed about it. "Where shall we go?" asked Carol, Jack immediately responded by saying "You're the travel agent!" "Oh yes" she said, laughing, "leave it with me, I'll see what offers we have at work."
Carol had never been to Jack's apartment, he was too embarrassed to take her to the apartment block from hell, the elevator rarely worked and there was always rubbish in the corridors, oh and the stairwell had a distinct smell of urine about it, as did the elevator when it worked.
Jack had never dared to venture into Carol's home either, he had visions of an eighty year old Rambo running at him with a pitch fork as he entered the front door.

Chapter Two
The holiday

It was Tuesday lunchtime, they had met in the café next to the travel agents because it was raining, "I got us a great deal on a holiday" Carol chirped, Jack was a little apprehensive as he asked "Where are we going?" "Kenya!" came the reply, a little stunned, Jack thought for a moment, "isn't that really expensive?" Carol explained it was a last minute cancellation so she'd got it really cheap. When Jack heard the price he reached into his pocket, smiling, wrote a cheque for half the cost and handed it to Carol, "Bargain!" he said, "I always wanted to do a safari, do I have to wear the silly beige jacket and trousers?" He said, she laughed.

A week later the tickets arrived, it was Sunday and the couple were walking together in the park, Carol said, "I noticed last night the flight is from Glasgow", "No problem" said Jack, "I bought a car yesterday from the police auction down on Hambly Road"

Jack was starting to get a little impatient, they'd been dating for nearly two months and no sign of getting together physically, Jack thought he'd better mention it as they'd be on holiday together in the same hotel room.

"What about sleeping arrangements?" Jack asked, Carol smiled, "That took you long enough" she said, Jack replied " I didn't want to appear pushy," Carol laughed and said "I was wondering if you were ever going to ask, how about Thursday night?" Jack looking a little puzzled said "Thursday night?" Again carol laughed "You did mean sex didn't you? Well we'll be in a hotel Thursday night because we fly out on Friday morning." Jack trying to remain calm and appear totally cool said, "OK, good point".

Thursday morning arrived, Jack picked Carol up at the station car park just after eight in his blue Mercedes, "Nice wheels" she said, they loaded her two enormous suitcases, one in the boot and one on the back seat, Jack made a joke about bringing an elephant along in one of them to return it to the wild and they set off.

An hour or so up the road Carol said "Can we stop? I need a wee" Jack agreed and decided to stop at a transport café and get a coffee at the same time. They were only there for about twenty minutes, then as they pulled out onto the main road Jack spotted a Black Jaguar S type in the mirror with two men inside, he thought he'd seen it in his street and again at the station, he dismissed this as it's not an uncommon car and anyway why would anyone follow them, especially all the way to Glasgow. He kept an eye in the mirror anyway, it was gone, lost in the two long rows of traffic behind them.

It was mid afternoon when Jack and Carol pulled into the hotel car park, they checked in and headed straight up to the room, Jack was nervous, he thought Carol would be too but she seemed to be taking it all in her stride. There was nothing really to unpack as the bags would be going with them on holiday, Carol could see he was nervous so to try to lighten the mood she said quite openly "Well do you want to eat then fuck or fuck then eat?" Jack looked shocked by the language she'd used, he'd never heard Carol use a four letter word, He went a little red then carol headed to the en suite bathroom saying "fuck then eat it is then," she was laughing as she left the room, it was some time later when Carol emerged, "off you go then, your turn, I'll be ages with this hairdryer" she said, and without a word Jack headed for the shower.

When he returned Carol was tucked up in bed, waiting for him, he still had on his boxers but she said nothing, Jack wanted to make this good, fumbling and thrashing about the first time in bed together wouldn't win him any brownie points, the light was dim, Jack climbed into bed beside Carol, she immediately snuggled up to him putting her head on his chest, they lay there for a moment or two then Jack felt her hand on his erect manhood, this was probably not the best plan because it had been a long time and he was likely to blow early, Jack started to work his way down in the bed so she couldn't reach, he rolled Carol over onto her back, he gently kissed her neck, then her shoulders, she was already making little noises of pleasure, the he worked his way down, her nipples were rock hard as he took one in his mouth and sucked a little before flicking it back and forth with his tongue, Carol's hands were now both on Jack's back, Jack threw the covers off the bed onto the floor, he admired Carol's perfect body for a brief moment before kissing and licking around her smoothly shaved pussy being careful to avoid the most sensitive areas, she was writhing in ecstasy and pulling his hair, trying to direct his mouth but Jack was making her wait.

He gently licked the soft white flesh of her inner thighs, Carol was on the verge of screaming, her moans were getting louder, her breathing heavier, then it was time to strike. Jack held her open with his fingers so he could delve his tongue as far as he could reach inside her before gently sucking the wet from her, then he began licking her, he had barely touched her clit when she started pushing her groin hard into Jacks face, he could feel her orgasm as he put a finger inside, there was a distinct throbbing and then a flood of moisture, Jack tasted her, she was sweet nectar, at that point Carol was begging him to stop, she couldn't take any more, Jack moved back up, he laid on his back listening to Carol still enjoying

the moment, they lay side by side for several minutes.
Then Carol took Jack in hand, he was rock hard with excitement, she slid down in the bed, she put her mouth over his hard cock, then further deep into her throat, Jack knew this wasn't going to last long and sure enough after just a few strokes he could feel the overwhelming urge, his muscles tensed up there was no way he was going to penetrate Carol this time, it was already too late, Jack came deep in Carol's throat, she didn't make a sound, she simply stopped and let him, then as Carol released him, Jack was feeling a little guilty but a lot satisfied he looked at Carol who made it very obvious that she had all Jack's seed in her mouth, she opened her mouth a little so he could see then in one she swallowed it all and smiled cheekily at him.

Morning came early, there was a plane to catch, Jack and Carol packed up what they'd used last night and headed down to the restaurant for breakfast, The hotel and parking for the holiday were all part of the holiday package and there was a minibus organized to take them to the airport.

With breakfast done and luggage loaded they set off in the minibus to the airport, The minibus pulled into the drop off zone and Jack went to get a trolley, as he returned he once again saw the Jaguar, he was sure it was the same one he'd been seeing all the way there, a heavy set man in need of a shave got out and the Jaguar drove off, Jack thought it must be a coincidence, maybe someone on the same holiday, Jack loaded the trolley with his rucksack and Carol's mountain of luggage, thanked the minibus driver and headed inside. He thought as he trundled this trolley along the tiled floor "Why do I always get the one with a wonky wheel?"

Sitting on the plane, Carol was gripping Jacks hand tightly, he asked her if she was afraid to fly. "No" she replied "I'm afraid to crash, Oh god, I wish I hadn't said that, now I'm thinking of an uncontrollable dive all the way down to the ground!" Carol gripped even harder, Jack could feel her nails digging into his hand, he thought "and this is before we start moving!"
Once in the air Carol settled down although the stewardess wouldn't or couldn't give her as much alcohol as she'd have liked, and an hour later Jack was sleeping soundly, Carol wondered how he could do that, she could never sleep anywhere with an impending threat of death and doom lurking.

Chapter Three
Africa

After landing safely much to Carol's relief they had a connection to make but it was from another airport so they collected their luggage and caught a taxi, the heat was intense, fortunately the taxi had ice cold air conditioning which was something of a relief, being able to breathe again without inhaling hot air, the taxi pulled into a much smaller airfield on the other side of town, Jack paid the driver and the pair headed into the building, not really a terminal, more of a hall with a few tables scattered around, Carol spotted a sign with the holiday written on it in marker pen, tapped Jack on the arm, they headed over to the table, at the table there were two rather large middle aged women in traditional brightly coloured African dress, One woman examined the tickets and passports while the other stood looking at Carol's luggage, tutting and shaking her head, "This gonna fit?" she said bluntly to the other woman, who replied "How da hell is me supposed to know dat?, it is da pilot's problem!" the luggage woman looked at Jack and Carol and quite rudely said "come on den, move it along"

There were several people ahead of them who were now heading for the wooden shed style doors at the back of the building so Jack and Carol followed them through the doors to outside.

Once outside in the blistering heat they saw to their horror an old, scruffy light aircraft sitting with it's twin propeller engines already running, it was already pretty full and after struggling to get Carol's enormous suitcases into the hold the couple took the last seats, there were fourteen seats and fourteen passengers, Jack had counted them on the way in, he thought if Carol was that nervous on the commercial flight from Glasgow this was going to be a whole new ball game.
The pilot didn't fill them with confidence, a worn out T shirt with some long expired seventies rock band printed on it, a pair of shorts and flip flops on his feet, Jack wondered if this guy even had a pilots license, there was a degree of muttering going on behind from the other passengers who were anything but satisfied at being squashed into this relic of a plane which looked like it should have ended up in the scrap yard years before.

Once locked in, the pilot put on a dirty pilot's cap he'd probably found, pushed the throttle forward and the engines revved up, the noise was deafening as the plane taxied towards the runway, Carol sat quietly, again gripping Jack's hand with such force he was hurting, he could tell she was way beyond nervous, bordering on terror.

Jack tried to console Carol by saying " the pilot probably does this trip every day," but that didn't help.
Jack was wondering if they were ever going to get off the ground, they used all the runway, the engines were screaming as they hurtled along the tarmac, it felt like they were trying to win the formula one grand prix in a bus, finally they were up, after a few minutes Carol relaxed her grip,

Jack could see the deep nail marks in his hand, then after another fifteen minutes or so she got up enough courage to look down at the ground, the view was breathtaking, she could see herds of some sort of cow like creatures running together leaving a huge dust cloud behind them, "Look Jack, there's a Giraffe" she called out excitedly, Jack was too busy thinking about weight limits, turbulence and the mountain up ahead to take too much notice, he'd been a rock for Carol because she was so scared but now he was getting a little worried, especially when the pilot began banging on the top of the dashboard and tapping gauges.

Eventually they landed on an earthen landing strip in the middle of nowhere, the plane bounced along the dirt track until it finally came to a stop, several land rovers were waiting for them, the passengers all took their luggage and mounted up, the track was rough, the seats were hard and Jack started wondering about the cost of spinal surgery they headed at speed along this assault course of a road, then suddenly the convoy came to a halt and the driver jumped out, walked back a little way and picked up one of Carol's cases which had bounced off the roof rack and almost got run over by the vehicle behind, while they were waiting she leaned towards Jack and whispered "never again."

They finally reached the hotel, well hotel it certainly wasn't it was a compound, quite military looking, there was a high wire fence all around and armed men in camouflage gear standing by the gate as they drove inside, Once inside things started looking up, the group was greeted by an Englishman sporting a large handlebar moustache and wearing a safari suit, "the only thing missing was the monocle" thought Jack. "Welcome, welcome, welcome my friends" he shouted in a rather well spoken English accent, Jack was now beginning to think this was all some television prank show as it seemed so far removed from reality. "Please settle yourselves in and then join us in here," said the host pointing to an open sided building with a grass roof and wooden rail around the perimeter.

Everyone picked up their bags and headed off to a row of motel style chalets, all white walls and in a single row, "which one?" asked carol, Jack replied "does it matter? They're all the same" the couple entered number seven, there was a double bed, and en suite bathroom, a dresser, mirror and a television, everything you'd expect in a hotel and surprisingly clean even though it looked as if it had been put together in the nineteen seventies.

After dumping their bags in the room they went over to the meet and greet as instructed, here the Englishman introduced himself as Mr Sykes and explained the rules and safety procedures, He told the guests that no one should venture outside the camp alone, especially at night, and if during the daytime they did want to go out and about they should take one of the armed guards with them, One of the other guests raised a hand, "Is that because of lions?" he asked, Mr Sykes responded with "Good question, Yes partly but generally lions are not too much of a problem, it's the poachers, they are armed and dangerous, but our men are all trained ex soldiers and they will look after you"
Jack turned to Carol and whispered in her ear "Now you know why you got this cheap, we're all in prison here for two weeks then we have to survive the return journey" Stop it!" she whispered back, "he's probably exaggerating, it can't be that bad or surely they wouldn't be able to sell it."
Dinner was quite pleasant it was a buffet with all sorts of local fruits and a good choice of dishes, not all identifiable but then they were on holiday and that's the time to try new things.
Entertainment in the evening was traditional African drumming and dance, Carol was

exhausted, she nudged Jack and suggested it was time to turn in, so they discreetly left the proceedings and went back to the room.

Jack switched on the TV while Carol was in the bathroom, he flicked through the local channels, none of which he understood so off it went, Carol emerged from the bathroom and climbed into bed, Jack, whilst in the bathroom was hopeful of finishing what he'd failed to in the Glasgow hotel the night before but when he came out of the bathroom after only a few minutes, Carol was fast asleep, he climbed in behind her, snuggled up, kissed her shoulder and drifted off.

Morning arrived with a loud bang on the door and a man's voice shouting "Breakfast is ready!" the same could be heard over and over again as he walked along the row of chalets, banging on each door in turn, Jack leaped out of bed, Carol opened one eye and said "you making coffee?" Jack stopped in his tracks, he was heading for the shower, "Really?" he asked, "there'll be coffee at breakfast, we better hurry." Carol propped herself up in bed on her elbows, "do we have to dress?" she asked, Jack pulled the curtain aside to see a few of the other guests walking over, "Looks like it" he replied and with that Carol climbed to her feet and pulled on her jeans and t shirt, "Ready?" asked Jack, "No, I need a wee before I go anywhere" Carol said as she headed for the bathroom.

Jack was anxious to get the day started, he was looking forward to exploring the wilderness, he'd brought his new Nikon along and was itching to use it.

Carol seemed to be spending a lifetime in the bathroom, when she did finally emerge she was in full makeup, showered and ready for the day, Jack thought that was one elaborate wee, no wonder she took so long.

After breakfast Jack returned to the chalet to shave, shower and get appropriately dressed for the day's adventure while Carol went to watch some orphaned lion cubs being bottle fed by the game warden at the other end of the complex.

By eight thirty they were ready to set off on their adventure, Jack had secured two seats in a land rover along with another couple and a guard and off they went, they traveled for well over an hour along dirt tracks, there was no sign of human habitation anywhere, no power lines, no houses, not as much as a grass hut, this really was nature at it's raw, eventually the land rover came to a stop, the guard gestured the guests to follow him quietly, they all carefully walked up a small hill covered in long dry grass, once at the top they could see a pride of lions lazing in the sun, several cubs were play fighting each other, Jack grabbed his camera from his rucksack and began snapping.

As the group returned to the land rover they could see other vehicles stopped around it, the guard told them all to get down, so the five of them were crouched down in the long grass watching quietly, "What's up?" whispered Jack to the guard, the guard put his finger up to his lips and sad "shhhh, stay here," he left the group and sneaked forward towards the men at the land rover, Jack heard him cock his rifle as he went, "I'm scared" whispered Carol, there was a commotion down the hill, the guard had been spotted, the men panicked, gunfire rang out, the men jumped into their vehicles and drove away, quickly. The four guests, stood up once the men were out of sight and headed down the hill, Just before the long grass ended they came across the guard, he had been shot several times, he was obviously dead, there was blood everywhere,

Carol screamed, Jack quickly put his hand over her mouth, "Shhh" he said, they might be close, we don't want them coming back. Jack began searching the dead guard's pockets, Carol looked shocked, "What are you doing?" she said with clenched teeth, "Looking for the key" said Jack, he found it and they all ran for the land rover, jumped in, inserted the key and it wouldn't start, nothing! Not even a dashboard light, Roger, the other guest who was with his wife Sue, opened the bonnet, then he could be heard saying "No, no, no oh NO!" "What's up?" called Jack, "they've taken the battery" replied Roger, "What the hell are we going to do now?" he said, Jack thought for a moment, "we'll have to stay here and wait to be rescued" said Jack, "if we lock ourselves inside the land rover we should be safe enough" "Oh yea, until the damn poachers come back" said Roger.

Sue finally spoke, she had been crying although quietly, she was obviously very scared, "Do they even know where we are?" she asked, Jack tried to reassure everyone by saying "the guard must have filed a route plan or something, they wouldn't just let people wander off anywhere."

The four of them sat inside the land rover for hours, no one came, it was getting late, it looked like they would have to spend the night there, Carol checked for supplies, she found five bottles of water one of which was half empty, the only food was a packet of crisps and half a packet of biscuits.

It was getting darker, Sue was still sobbing on and off, Roger was trying to console her, then there was a noise, a rustling sound coming from outside, it was too dark to see what it was, there were shadows moving silently then a roar, it was obviously lions, the group was surrounded, "Just stay quiet, they can't get in here" said Roger quietly, they sat there terrified, all night, occasionally someone would be startled by a noise as something brushed by or was rubbing itself against the land rover,

"I have to go" whispered Carol, "No one is going anywhere" Jack whispered back, Carol whispered "No, I need to go, I need to wee!" "Me too said Sue" Roger said to Sue "You do pick your moments" Sue then replied, "its OK for you, you can stick yours out the window, Roger looked at Sue with a shocked expression "What! And get it bitten off? No way!" He said. Jack meanwhile unable to believe this was the conversation while they all stared death in the face, responded with "just go on the floor for Christ sake."

After what had seemed an eternity daylight broke over the horizon, the question still remained how were they going to get out of this situation, would they be found if they stayed where the were or should they try to walk out of there, Jack said "I'm going to get the rifle" the lions seemed to have gone, and Jack stepped carefully and quietly out of the land rover, he cautiously made his way back to the long grass where the guard had been shot, there was a lot of blood but no body, he figured the lions had dragged the guard's body off in the night, so where was the rifle? He wondered whether or not the poachers had taken it but then thought there was a mad panic going on so it was doubtful.

Jack decided to follow the blood trail for a way, the others soon lost sight of him, Jack was finding bits of green fabric, here and there obviously from the guard, he kept walking,

quietly and carefully, he knew he could never out run a lion so he had to remain unseen.
He was almost halfway up the hill when he found it, along with a leather strap and the guard's hand held radio, the lions must have stopped there to feed, Jack picked up the rifle and the radio, he checked the rifle was intact, it seemed to be, not that Jack knew anything about guns, again, slowly and quietly he made his way back to the others.
The radio was useless, chewed beyond repair, so jack dumped it on the wet floor of the land rover,

Carol was in floods of tears as Jack climbed back into the driving seat, "Whatever is the matter?" he asked, "I thought I'd lost you, you've been gone ages" she sobbed, Jack calmed her down then put the question to the others, do we stay here or try to walk out?
"How far?" asked Roger, Jack thought about how long it had taken them, maybe and hour and a half, maybe closer to two, they couldn't have done more than thirty miles per hour on that track so at most it was going to be fifty or sixty miles.
"Fifty miles maybe" said Jack, that started another panic, there was no way they could walk that distance in that heat and survive the lions, especially at night because they certainly wouldn't do it in a day.
"How far do you think that mountain is?" said Jack, Roger looked, "maybe fifteen or twenty miles, certainly closer than the hotel" he said,

no one wanted to spend a second night in the Land rover which was now starting to smell and that would surely attract predators come nightfall, the decision was made to head for the mountain, they figured there would be less wildlife there and maybe they would be able to see some sort of civilization from a higher point and possibly find shelter.

Chapter Four
The walk

It was about eight am, they left the stricken land rover after scratching the word "mountain" on the bonnet, there was a concern over water as much of it had been used up over night and the heat was already scorching, there was no track towards the mountain, so they had to trek across countryside where only the wild things roam.

Everyone was keeping their eyes peeled, Jack knew it would be pointless because there wasn't much they could out run but maybe a shot from the blood stained rifle he was carrying would possibly scare off an attacker, only one problem, no more ammunition and Jack had no idea how many bullets were in the magazine.

"What about water?" asked Carol, Jack said "I don't know but don't rivers begin in mountains? Anyway what about water if we don't go? What we have left won't last us."
They'd been walking for hours, the mountain was getting closer, luckily the only wildlife they'd seen so far was a Giraffe ripping the leaves off a tree, but animals could be heard howling in the

distance, Sue started falling behind, she couldn't go much further in the scorching sun, Roger was wearing a baseball cap which saved him to a point but Jack's forehead and face were getting really burnt, the girls were almost as bad, their longer hair protected them a bit but Jack, poor Jack was really starting to suffer, Roger was now helping Sue, she was exhausted, at last they made it to the mountain, the ground was getting more and more covered in stone as they approached, Sue went to sit down on a rock but Roger walked her on "You can't sit there" he said, "Oh god Roger, please just leave me to die quietly" said Sue, "Come on," he insisted, almost dragging her along, "We need shade more than rest" he told her, shade there was precious little of, every inch of the mountain which was now towering above them seemed lit up with cruel baking hot sunshine.

They stopped, not knowing what to do next, no shade, no water, Jack stood looking up at the mountain, "Look!" he said, the others looked but couldn't see what Jack could, "Look! There! About a hundred feet up near the ledge, is that a cave?" Carol agreed it looked like a cave, it was dark so it was shade if it wasn't a cave, "we'll never make that" said Roger, "Sue can barely stand up and you want us to go mountaineering?"

Jack decided to go up himself to check it out, he had only climbed about twenty feet when he came back down, Jack then walked fast, almost ran, he would have if he had the energy, a few minutes later Jack returned smiling and soaking wet, the others realized he had found water and headed that way to, there was a watering hole there surrounded by some green trees, the water looked good, it was clear and cool, they all fell into it, splashing about like children, suddenly hope and energy had returned.

The water bottles refilled it was decided they needed to rest for the night as they were still lost in the middle of the wilderness and there was no way they would make civilization by the end of that day, everyone made it up the mountain, it wasn't a difficult task as it had a path, maybe from years of use by mountain goats or something but it definitely looked like a trail, and yes it was a cave.

Sue sat in the mouth of the cave scanning the area for any signs of civilization, nothing visible anywhere, but then she saw a cloud of dust, it was in the direction they had come from, maybe they were getting rescued, the rescuers had found the land rover and the message left scratched in the paintwork, now they were heading for the mountain, she ran inside, excited, shouting "We're saved, we're saved!" suddenly hope appeared on the faces of Roger and Carol but Jack wasn't so sure, "I think we should wait here in the cave" he said cautiously, "Why?" asked

Roger, Jack looking very serious replied, "Roger, what if that's the poachers who shot our guard? They wouldn't want any witnesses would they?"

Roger said "I'm going, It has to be our guys, bloody poachers will be miles away by now," and with that, Roger began walking down the path, "Stay here Sue" said Carol, "what if Jack is right?"
Sue replied, "But what if he's wrong?" "Then Roger will bring help, won't he?" said Carol, Jack meanwhile had positioned himself outside the cave on the ledge, laying face down aiming the rifle towards the oncoming vehicles, Roger was now almost directly below him on the path down the mountain which zigzagged back and forth.

Chapter Five
The fight

All of a sudden gunshots rang out, it was the poachers, the first couple of shots just ricocheted off the rock, then Roger got hit.

 He was alive, Jack could hear him moaning below him, he'd managed to get into a lying position on the mountain path, the poachers had stopped below, two vehicles, a jeep and a truck, they were standing out in the open until Jack took one out with his first shot, a head shot, he felt sick as he watched the blood and fragments of shattered bone spray away from the gunman but Jack knew that everyone was depending on him to keep them alive.

It must have been quite a shock for the poachers when Jack opened fire, initially they were not taking cover, they must have thought the group was unarmed, now all of a sudden they were running round and getting behind their vehicles, the shooting had stopped, it seems the poachers didn't know what to do next, there's no way they could have known how many guns they had pointed at them. Jack realized this and held his fire to see what they would do next, he could hear them shouting to each other, they seemed to be confused and in a panic, maybe the one Jack had shot was the leader, just maybe he'd cut the head off the snake.

Roger was about twenty or so feet below Jack, on the ridge, Jack called out "are you OK Roger?" There was no reply, he could hear him quietly moaning every now and then, "Keep still and keep low," said Jack whilst trying to sound calm and in control. The poachers hadn't moved, it seemed to be a sort of stalemate. Maybe they were just going to wait until the water had run out, maybe they were waiting for darkness to fall. "Surely someone must have heard the shooting?" said Carol, she was trying to keep Sue calm, Sue was crying and worried about Roger, wounded and stuck on the ledge below, "I doubt it, not out here" said Jack, nothing was happening. The poachers were still hiding behind their vehicles, occasionally they could be heard talking but it wasn't in English so Jack couldn't make out what was being said.

"This is all my fault" said Carol "I wish I hadn't booked this stupid holiday." Jack who was still watching down below said "Don't be silly sweetheart, no one could have predicted this."

It went very quiet, no one was talking, even Roger was silent, then Carol said quietly "How many are there Jack?" "I counted five but one's down, so four I think, we have one advantage though, there's no way they can know how many

people we have or how many guns so I don't think they'll try to rush us."
The stand off continued, it was getting dark, Jack thought that would be the time the poachers would try something but he didn't say anything because he didn't want the girls to worry.

It was cooling down, soon it would be cold, the girls were at the back of the cave huddled together, Jack was tired, all of a sudden there was a sound from the ledge below, "Roger?" Jack whispered, slow movement could be heard, again Jack said quietly "Roger? Roger are you OK?" Still no reply but Jack could hear Roger moaning in pain, it was too dark to see anything.

Another hour passed, in the little moonlight there was Jack could make out the poacher's vehicles and occasionally see them moving around, It had been over an hour since he heard movement from Roger, surely he should have made it back here by now, he thought, Jack peered around the corner, nothing but darkness, one of the poachers must have seen Jack moving and a shot rang out, a crack sound as it hit the rock, nowhere near, Jack not knowing how many bullets he had didn't return fire, he didn't want to waste them or give away his position, he returned to where he had been and continued watching.

Then in an afrikaan accent one of the poachers started shouting "Come down, come down and

we won't kill you! We have your friend," Jack thought it highly unlikely they wouldn't kill them all, they knew the group had witnessed them killing the guard, so there was no way they were going to let them leave alive. Sue however protested "They've got Roger, we have to give up!"
Then the poacher shouted again, "I will give you ten minutes then your friend will pay."

Jack knew if they really did have Roger there was nothing they could do, surrender would have been certain death for them all. Ten minutes passed, then Roger started screaming in agony, Sue ran towards the cave entrance, Jack grabbed her, "He'll kill you" he said and he explained why, Sue was crying uncontrollably, then the voice from below shouted again "If you don't come down we will come up and after we kill the men we will do as we want with the woman before we kill her too!" Jack thought about his choice of words, of course it may be just bad English but it sounded like Roger either hadn't talked or he had told them there were more men than there actually were in the cave.

Again an agonizing scream from Roger and once again Sue reacted but this time Carol held onto her, "we have to save him, we have to!" Cried Sue. Jack was tense, he snapped at her "exactly what do you think we should do?" Carol responded "Jack! She's understandably upset, please calm down," Jack apologized, they were all in a desperate situation, their only hope seemed to be from a rescue but that was not going to happen in the dark.

They tortured Roger throughout the night, none of them had ever heard anything so barbaric or as horrible as his screams of pain, they had no idea what the poachers were doing to poor Roger.

It had been quiet for a couple of hours, as the dawn broke, Jack who had been awake for two days and two nights had finally fallen asleep, he had an imprint of part of the rifle on his face where he'd laid on it, Jack woke with a start, he hadn't realized he'd fallen asleep, it was more like passing out, instantly, now wide awake and feeling alert Jack peered over the edge, They'd gone, the poachers had gone but where? They could be hiding, after waking the girls Jack sneaked quietly out of the cave, carefully peeped around the corner to the path, nothing, he could see the foot of the mountain and quite some distance but not around the other side, He went back into the cave and whispered "stay here, I think they may have given up and gone, I won't be long."

Jack cautiously made his way down the path, there was blood where Roger had been hit, but where was Roger? maybe he was alive, maybe the poachers still had him he thought,

Jack checked out the area, tracks from the vehicles led off back the way they'd come.

Satisfied the poachers had gone Jack went back to the cave for the girls, eventually they all got to the ground, Jack said "we can't stay here, they may come back with more of them, we must move on," they went to the water hole to fill the plastic water bottles for the impending journey that's when the grizzly discovery was made, Roger's body was laying face down in the water, they dragged him out, he had been cut to ribbons, the poachers had spent the night slicing into Roger with a knife just to make him cry out, eventually realizing their plan wasn't working they cut his throat and watched him die, gasping for air in the African dust.

Sue demanded they bury Roger but common sense prevailed, they had no tools, the ground was hard and if they were to survive they had to get going, it seemed so wrong to fill the water bottles from the water where poor Roger had been laying and even harder to drink it but it was survival and maybe that thought would make the water last a bit longer.

"What I wouldn't give for a crusty dry cheese sandwich" said Jack as they set off. "Which way are we going?" asked Carol, "towards that green area, there must be water there and if there's water maybe there's people" Jack said pointing, they set off.

Chapter Six
Greenery

It took about four hours to reach the green trees, the sun was scorching, their lips were cracked and peeling, clothing ripped and dirty, insect bites had taken their toll but they were still alive.

What they'd found was the beginning of a dense forest with thick undergrowth, thankfully it was a little cooler below the trees but it was also steep and humid, the further into the trees they went the muggier it got, Carol nudged Jack, "Shhh" she said "What? Replied Jack nervously, "What did you hear?" Again Carol said "Shhh, Listen, can't you hear that? It sounds like water." Carol led the way, the noise grew louder and louder, as they got nearer it was so loud the only thing they could hear above it was Jack slapping his neck swatting the odd bug that was feeding on him.

They came to a clearing, there was a thin tree line beyond the clearing and then nothing but that was where the noise was coming from, they stepped up the pace, almost running as they reached the tree line then stopped dead, there was a sheer drop, rocks below and a river, to the left a waterfall which was where the noise was coming from.

It certainly wasn't home, or by any means safety but this breathtaking sight was paradise compared to what they'd been through so far.

By hanging onto tree roots protruding from the cliff face the three of them managed to climb down the rock to the river, it was difficult but determination and finding the odd rock to put a foot on they all made it down and the next hour was spent sitting in the shallow cool water which was rushing over the smooth rocks, not much was said except a very upset Sue saying they should have done something with Roger's body instead of just leaving him there, what they didn't know was the search party had found the land rover and the clue scratched on the bonnet, they had then recovered Roger and found the wasted bullet cases where the poachers had been.
They were now tracking the three but were still some distance behind.

After resting for a while it was decided to follow the river downstream because they thought the bigger the river gets, the more likely it would be to find people living by it, Carol was concerned

about trekking into the jungle "People have been lost, never found in places like this, don't you think we should wait for help?" she said,
Jack thought, then said, "I know what you're saying but if we go back we'll probably get killed by the poachers, if we stay we'll never be found here, I wouldn't find me here and I know where I am! Well sort of," trying to make some sort of joke which no one found at all funny.

Carol said "I really don't want to get lost in the Jungle, I vote we go back to the land rover, we have no idea what's in here!" Sue was nodding in agreement as Carol spoke, "OK, OK, we'll head back, but first we need to find some food, I'm starving" said Jack, at that moment a sudden loud roar of an engine broke the peace and a small aircraft flew over, they all started waving and shouting but it was too late, the noise from the waterfall had masked the engine sound until it was too late and even though it was overhead they couldn't be seen through the thick canopy. "That's it! See I told you we wouldn't be seen in here, if we were still out there they'd have spotted us!" shouted Carol at Jack.

Jack sat down for a moment, "If I'm right" said Jack this is the Tana river and if it is then there's a bridge, the Tana river bridge, that means there's a road, we need to find that bridge" "Where's all this coming from?" Asked Carol, "I saw a map on the wall back at the compound, I was interested to see where we were" said Jack, Carol seemed a bit more interested in following the river now, the thought of a road, with cars on it sounded like the solution, Carol said "which way then, Tarzan?" Smiling as she suddenly had a glimmer of hope, Jack looked at the river and said "I'm not sure but I remember it's narrow at the bridge, I think It's south There's a lake past the bridge"

"Looking at the position of the sun and the time of day would make south-ish, that way" said Jack pointing up stream, everyone agreed a road was the most attractive option so they set off, at least this way they wouldn't be exposed to the sun and water wasn't an issue, to start with their progress was slow, they were climbing over rocks and boulders along the river then the surrounding woodland cleared and the river sides became muddy. Off to the sides of the river were more plains, an easier walk but they'd be more visible, Jack knew they had to stay away from cover and long grass because that's where the lions would be and the thought of getting ripped apart alive was not a good one, of course he kept this to himself, he didn't want the girls any more scared than they already were.

It was hot, the sun was merciless as it fried the sweat on Jack's face, he kept wiping his burning face with his hand, that made his raw skin sting! The two girls were faring no better, the pace was slowing, A distant gun shot rang out and echoed,

the Jack instinctively ducked down out of reflex then searched the horizon, every now and then wiping the sweat away from his eyes, he could see nothing, "Which way was that?" he asked, Sue and Carol shrugged and Carol said, "I have no idea" It was still a long way off, believing the shot to be the poachers they all kept looking for signs of movement or dust clouds as they walked slowly onward, but nothing, no movement anywhere.
Meanwhile the rescue team had lost their tracks due to crossing the river and walking in the water, They were at the waterfall firing a shot in the air now and then to try and let Jack and the girls know where they were.

Jack and the girls came across a part of the river bank that was sloping, muddy and full of footprints, lion's foot prints, this was all the encouragement they needed to step up the pace a little but it didn't last, "I can't go on" said Sue "can't we rest a while?" "If you want to get eaten!" snapped Jack. "It can't be much further" Sue had stopped crying a while back, although she kept thinking of Roger their own survival had taken priority in her mind.

The sun was starting it's descent in the sky as they spotted a bridge up ahead, Sue suddenly sped up, she had been the one holding them back up till now, she cried "There's the bridge! There it is, come on" almost running, Jack had his

doubts, this certainly didn't look like a major road bridge and sure enough, as they got closer it turned into a rusty relic on what used to be a dirt trail, hopes shattered they all sat down on the river bank by the old bridge, "do you think anyone uses this bridge?" asked Carol, "Doubt it" replied Jack, it was obvious it wouldn't take much weight now, maybe the odd wild animal but even the Elephants would know better than to try this one,
They had some bananas they'd grabbed from the edge of the Jungle and Jack started ripping the hard skin off one of them, "It's green!" said Carol, Jack explained they only go yellow long after they're picked and for now a green one would have to do, time was moving on, there was no sign of shelter anywhere, this old decrepit bridge provided some sort of cover, the worry was come nightfall what would visit the river, which was now looking more like a stream, this was their third night in the wilderness and the only people they'd seen were trying to kill them.

The three went in search of wood to start a fire in the hope it would deter predators, well it did in the movies, there were a few trees by the riverside, Carol picked up a large rotting branch and as she did a snake lunged at her, she fell backwards onto her back, scrambling on all fours and trying to get up all at once, she hadn't seen the snake withdraw in the other direction and had visions of it recoiling at her, she didn't want to die from a snake bite, she didn't want to die at all.

She was scared for a moment and then, once she realized it hadn't bitten her she headed back to the others, she told Jack about the snake, "best not tell Sue" he said as he screwed up some dry grass into knots to start the fire.
The fire was down the bank by the water at the edge of the bridge so as not to be visible to the poachers who may or may not be following them.

As the three sat by the fire, still very wary of what may be sneaking up on them, Jack said "I can't believe Roger didn't tell them we were just two women one man and one gun, the man's a true hero" Sue replied, "he was a true hero, Roger was in the army, he would have died rather than give me up, I don't know what I'm going to do without him, assuming we get out of this alive." "Of course we will" said Jack but in his mind he had serious doubts, he had been thinking about all the ways they could die out there, none were particularly pleasant.

Despite being tired and exhausted no one wanted to sleep, they were all too scared, adrenaline was running them like petrol runs an engine, things were moving in the night, mostly small creatures, maybe rats, Jack was sure he could see the outline of a big cat drinking from the river, the fire provided heat and light but it also made it very difficult to see far into the darkness, that may have been a good thing, maybe it was better not to know.

First light and everyone was scratching, something had been eating them in the night, Sue jumped up and started dancing around brushing herself down with her hands. Carol soon joined her, Jack smiled as he watched the two jigging about then suddenly he was up doing the same, Ants, they were all covered in ants they had not felt them crawling on them, despite not sleeping they were all suddenly covered in the tiny critters, or maybe they had slept a bit, it was impossible to say, they were all tired and confused.

Once free of the pests which left them all covered in itchy bites, as if they didn't have enough to contend with. Jack climbed up the bank, it wasn't far, just eight or ten feet, once up he looked around for signs of human habitation, he was still smacking the odd ant here and there.
Jack could see something down the track a little way, the track which went over the bridge, it was a straight pole sticking up in the air, a bit further down the track there was another one, and another, he suddenly realized they were old telegraph poles which once carried power or phone lines, well if there was power or phones there had to be civilization, maybe there was still something there? He told the girls and off they went, it was decided that whichever way they went there'd be either the source or the

destination of the wires which were once there so they set off.

Carol was limping a bit, she took off her shoes, her blisters were bleeding and so sore, Jack said "I wouldn't do that if I were you, there may be snakes and scorpions about" "I don't care said Carol, if I'm going to die it's not going to be from blisters!" she said, Jack sort of half laughed, something none of them had done for a while, "you can't die from blisters!" "No" said Carol "these blisters are worse than death!"

There was a feeling of new hope as they staggered on down the barely visible track, Sue meanwhile had removed her blouse and wrapped it around her head, they had been walking for about another two hours then Sue said "Sod it!" whipped off her bra and threw it aside, Carol smiled, took her T shirt off wrapped it around her head and threw her bra away too, Jack said "You'll get sun burnt" Sue looked at him and replied "can't be any worse than my face!" Jack was sweating too but kept his shirt on, it was soaking wet but he didn't want to fry his back as well as his face which was blistered and peeling.

Another two hours or so and suddenly smoke ahead, black smoke, now that had to be people, barely able to walk, the three staggered on slowly towards the smoke, "What if it's those gunmen?" asked Carol, Jack didn't answer he just kept going, more on determination than strength, again she asked "Jack, what if" he interrupted her "I don't know but right now I just want to see a human being preferably one who has access to a pint of ice cold beer, the devil would do!" Jack obviously wasn't thinking straight.

They were close to the smoke, the girls put their tops back on, their bodies were burnt and red so it was a bit painful but with the possibility of rescue it didn't matter. An old wrecked car became visible as they approached, the paint had been scorched off due to years of sun beating down on it, there were no wheels, it just sat on the dirt, then a roof line, it was a building, at that moment it was the most beautiful thing any of them could think of, it soon became apparent that they'd stumbled into a village, it was run down, the house had several windows boarded up and there were holes in the veranda floor, a few other makeshift buildings were dotted about, kids could be heard playing.

A beaten up old leather football rolled out in front of them closely followed by a boy of about eight years old, he stopped in his tracks, then suddenly ran away shouting something!
It wasn't long before a few adults showed up, fussing and trying to help the three but they had no idea what was being said, it seemed English hadn't reached this village and it's population of about a dozen, then the small boy took Sue by the

hand and led her to one of the houses, Jack and Carol followed, once inside they were all beckoned to sit down, the village women dressed their wounds, and gave them water and some indescribable food which they ate, they were being signaled to slow down, it was difficult as they were all starving.
Three days they spent in the village, mostly sleeping, the locals were brilliant, unfortunately there was no phone or any means of communication, no one spoke English so they couldn't even ask where they were.

Recovered to a point it was time to go, a skinny boy of about ten years old was leading them out of the village down a track, this one had obviously been used a bit more, the track was a bit more shady than they'd endured with high hedges on either side, it was rutty where vehicles had been and occasionally wet and muddy but it was the best conditions they'd experienced for what seemed like an eternity, after walking behind the boy for most of the day they came across another village, the boy was talking to a tall thin man, explaining what had happened at his village it was assumed, the thin man then took them to a wooden hut with a tin roof, inside was another man, he was much younger, probably about thirty years and in broken English said "welcome to my home" he dismissed the boy who ran away in the direction of the track they had just walked, after being offered water they explained what had happened, the man listened with interest, he explained there was no electricity or phone in the area but he would send a runner to bring help, meanwhile he said he would arrange accommodation for the group.

As the four of them walked to another building Jack noticed a stack of tusks by a small shed, there also seemed to be a lot of guns about, once they were shown into their accommodation Jack said to the girls "I don't like this, something stinks" Jack decided to take a look around the village, once outside he noticed a high aerial protruding from a shed, he carefully, without being seen got to the shed where he could hear the man they'd just been talking to speaking in his native language on a radio.
Jack sneaked away and returned to the girls, "We have to get out of here now!" "Why?" came the reply from both simultaneously, Jack picking up the rifle said He's lying to us, I just heard him on the radio he said they didn't have, I'm sure he's calling those poachers and telling them we're here!"

In something of a panic the three left quietly by the back of the hut, Sue grabbed a long silky looking cloth which was hanging up outside "I'm having that!" She said as they hurriedly made their way out of the village.

Chapter Seven
Hide and seek

As the only way in or out of the village it was obvious the bad guys would be coming on that track, there was no point in going back to the previous village so they went in the opposite direction, this part of the track seemed much more used, there were fresh tyre marks. "We have to get off the road" said Jack, there were hedges either side, tall thick spiky hedges, they found an opening and got through, there was a small foot path along the back side of the hedge, it didn't look like it had been made by people but more likely animals so keeping an eye out whilst listening for vehicles they continued.

It was going to get dark soon and they had to find shelter, there could be no lighting fires tonight, they were too close to those who were trying to kill them.

They'd been walking for over an hour, still no sign of any sort of shelter and luckily no one shooting at them either, the hedge between them and the track was getting patchy, if the bad guys turned up now it'd be difficult to hide, there were trees off to their left, more chance of hiding there than in the open so they made for the trees, they hadn't got very far when the sound of vehicles could be heard, the they were close to long grass, not ideal because you never know what's lurking in there but there was no choice, they ran as fast as they could, eventually ducking down and laying in the grass, although the vehicles were noisy and the track was some distance away no-one dared to breathe or make a sound, they all lay perfectly still, Carol was actually holding her breath, the trucks passed, the engine sound was getting further away, it wouldn't be long before they reached the village and found they were missing, then there would be hell to pay!

As soon as the engine noise could no longer be heard, Jack called to the girls "Run!" they got up and ran but so did the lion which was also in the long grass, Jack found himself running towards it, he stopped long enough to take a shot, he missed but fortunately the lion was scared enough to run away, then they all ran into the trees. Out of breath, panting hard there was no time to rest, they walked quickly through the trees until they could no longer see the track or the long grass, it was getting dark, nowhere to hide, they had to keep going as long as they could see because their enemy certainly would.

Eventually they came across a tree stump laying over a small gully, Jack told the girls "Go and find sticks and branches" Sue said "surely we're not lighting a fire?" "No of course not" said Jack "but we need to build some kind of hide" they all collected as many sticks and bushy branches as they could find and piled them up either side of the tree stump, before climbing inside, now it was pitch black, the noise from the insects alone seemed deafening.

It was a long night, they sat there silently, throughout, they saw nothing and only heard an occasional rustle as something unknown moved around outside their makeshift den, Jack thought about sitting in his nice safe, clean office doing his nice safe job and wished he was there, Carol was thinking about holidaying in good old Skegness, lying on the sand listening to families bickering about lousy service and the rain which was bound to come, Sue remembered good times with Roger.

It wasn't even light when they moved on, there was no way they were going to let the killers catch up with them if they could help it, the trees seemed to go on forever but there wasn't much cover below them, they were too spaced out and the stony ground only had clumps of long grass here and there, the sun was already getting hot and it'd only just popped over the horizon, Jack had a plan, if they could stay far enough away from the track but follow the same direction it must lead somewhere, hopefully somewhere safe.

Some distance off to the left was what looked like thicker growth, it's what they needed, more cover. As they were they could be seen from some distance away, the only problem was it took them further from the track they were following but between them they decided lost was better than dead so they headed for the tree line, Jack thought they could make cover in about an hour or so, they walked quickly, although tired the few days rest they'd had at the previous village helped a lot, their burns had been treated to a point but were still sore and the sun beating down mercilessly certainly wasn't going to help, another reason to find cover,
Sue stopped "Listen" she said, carol said "yes, I here it, where can we hide?" they'd heard the distant sound of an engine, "Lay flat on the ground" said Jack which they did, the noise got a little louder, In the distance the green canvas canopy of a truck could be seen on the track, it was moving slowly, it was too far away to make out any details like people in it, and Jack reasoned that if he couldn't see them, then maybe they couldn't see him, they laid flat for a few minutes until the truck was out of sight, Jack got to his feet, Sue got to hers but Carol stayed down and still, "come on Carol" said Jack, "I can't" she replied quietly "there's something on my back" she said, Jack carefully walked over, to see, "What is it?" Carol asked nervously, Jack said just keep still, Jack picked up a stick which was

laying nearby then carefully and slowly placed the point of the stick on Carol's back close to the critter, then in one quick flick whacked it off her and away, Carol jumped up, "What the hell was that! She cried, "Oh just a scorpion "said Jack trying to be a totally cool dude.

Carol wasn't a fan of insects, at home she'd totally freaked out and fetched a neighbour to deal with a spider once but this was a whole new league, after several minutes of going on about the little orange scorpion Jack commented "Well look on the bright side, it's not everyone can say they've had a huge deadly scorpion attack them, is it?"
This freaked Carol out even more, "Huge! Deadly!" she cried, Jack had to calm her "It was tiny and harmless" he said, calm down, Jack had heard that the small scorpions were more venomous than the big ones but he kept that particular piece of information to himself.

They had just reached the edge of the tree line which turned out to be a forest much like the one they had briefly visited before, thick dense undergrowth, masses of trees and plenty of shade, there was a whack sound as something hit a tree trunk close to Carol, she jumped and screamed, then immediately a shot was heard in the distance, what had hit the tree was a bullet, the poachers had abandoned their vehicle and were pursuing them on foot, they were still some distance off,

Jack Carol and Sue ran into the forest, towards the deepest darkest part they could see, there could be anything lurking in there but they knew there was definitely something bad chasing them from behind.
After running with them for a while, Jack stopped "I've had enough of this" said Jack suddenly getting all Rambo, "you two hide" the girls ducked down under the green cover, Jack ran back towards their pursuers, once near enough to see but still under cover Jack found a hiding place, next to a tree crouched down in the leafy undergrowth, by now Jack had learned quite a bit bout the rifle he was carrying and knew how many rounds he had.

Jack carefully took aim, he counted four armed men, they didn't seem at all cautious, they were walking together in a group, Jack knew once he fired they'd scatter but just maybe they'd give up and leave, he aimed for the middle of the group hoping he could hit just one, the telescopic sight on the rifle was good, Jack could see like he was standing right in front of them it was time, his intention was to shoot and run, Jack took his shot, the telescopic sight on the rifle was set spot on, there was absolutely no breeze, he slowly squeezed the trigger, felt the impact as the rifle kicked back into his shoulder, his bullet flew straight and true and hit not one but two, Jack didn't understand but wasn't complaining, how can one bullet hit two targets? One of the men dropped lifeless to the ground, another put his hand up to his neck then fell to his knees, screaming out in pain, the remaining two dived down and began returning fire, Jack stooping low ran back to where he'd left the girls "Come on!" he shouted, the girls suddenly appeared out of the bush and all three ran together into the forest, "What happened?" called Carol, "I slowed them down" shouted Jack as they ran on.

After a while the greenery was so thick that any sort of progress was incredibly hard work and slow going. They were dehydrating, sweating profusely the humid air felt like they were breathing water,

"I have to stop" said Carol, it was like climbing through a wall, the dense foliage was unforgiving and was taking it's toll, "Should we go back?" asked Sue, "I don't see how we can, they'll be following us" replied Jack. They were trapped in a place where going forward seemed impossible, going back would surely be suicide, they didn't have the intense sun beating down on them but it was so hot and unbearably humid which seemed just as bad, not to mention the insects which were constantly feasting on all of them.

Exhausted and barely able the three battled on through the obstacles ahead, every now and then there was be a clearing and finally an earth footpath, it looked as if it had been recently used, there were fresh footprints in the muddy bits, Jack thought about that, how was the ground muddy? Everything else in Africa seemed bone dry but there it was a footpath with mud on it. It was only after walking the path for some time Jack realized it was a dry stream, they weren't the only ones to walk it recently, he wondered whether or not it could be the bad guys who'd somehow got ahead of them.

Anything was better than climbing through that stuff they'd just had to contend with. All the time they were in there Jack was having visions of a huge silverback gorilla popping up and ripping his arms off, he didn't even know if there were any gorillas in the region.

Chapter Eight
Signs of civilization

Suddenly there was noise up ahead, mechanical noise, a familiar smell filled the air, Jack knew it but couldn't place it, they moved onward, following the stream which now oddly had a couple of inches of water in it which was stinging their broken blisters and soaking their feet but it didn't matter, it was such a relief to feel something cool, the noise was getting louder, much louder then voices, in English, proper English with an American accent, They were all getting happy, ecstatically happy, Carol had tears flooding down her face, Sue was smiling from ear to ear, Jack was still apprehensive, they'd had their hopes dashed too many times, although hopeful and almost bursting with excitement inside he kept his cool expression and plodded on.

Ragged, bleeding and exhausted the three of them staggered into a clearing, there they found construction machines, a huge caterpillar, logging machines, there were men with chainsaws cutting trees, diggers getting roots up, fires burning and all of sudden a voice from behind said in an American accent "What the fuck!"
Carol thought she had never wanted to hear a swear word as much as she did then, it was like poetry, "What the fuck!" she thought, it's a poem, or maybe one of those phrases which become

famous like "Doctor Livingstone I presume" of course she wasn't thinking rationally,
Sue was on the ground, she had fainted at the sight of all these Americans, of course she would have fainted had it been a group of any sort, certainly not because these were muscle bound lumberjack types in construction clothes and work boots.

When Sue regained consciousness she was being carried in the arms of a huge man wearing a hard hat, Jack and Carol were walking behind with their arms around each other, they were led to a trailer kitted out as a medical unit where they received treatment from the team's doctor, they were all handed a bottle of water, Jack barely able to speak because his throat had dried up and he was too overcome with emotion to say anything, tried to explain what they'd been through but doc said to wait, first thing was to get them fixed up.

Sue asked "What are you people doing here?" the medic replied "Isn't it obvious? We're building a road" Jacks ears pricked up "A road, a road, they are building a road!", He thought, a road was to jack what a lottery win would be to anyone at home, this road a flat smooth surface was the most wonderful thing Jack could imagine, he spoke, he started saying it over and over, almost like he was singing "A road, a road, we've got a road!" tears of relief were starting to appear in

Jack's eyes, the girls were still amused by his "road" song, All Jack wanted to do was to kneel down and kiss the beautiful tarmac.

Later that day Jack was taken to the crew boss in his trailer office, "I can get you some clothes, the women will have to make do with what we have here, it's all men's stuff I'm afraid, doc tells me you've all had it a bit rough?" He said, Jack sat down and told the crew boss everything that had happened to them.
The crew boss who's name was Bill said "Doc says you all need to rest for a few days before we get you back home or to your hotel or wherever the hell it is you came from, we have a supply truck due then, you can get a ride back with that guy"
Bill arranged some bunks for the three in a converted truck " you can sleep in my place" he said, "What about you?" asked Jack, Bill replied, Now don't you go worryin' yourself about me, I'll throw up a hammock in this here office, I'll be just dandy here."

One thing about Americans, when they go to work abroad or go to war they seem to take entire towns with them, these guys had everything and it was all on wheels, parked up back along the tarmac they'd already laid, that night Jack and the girls walked into the bar, the one thing he had been craving was a long cold beer and there it was, in the middle of a savage jungle an

American bar, Jack discreetly pinched himself just to make sure it wasn't all a dream, they sat down and were served drinks like they were celebrities, Jack sat looking at this tall glass filled with ice cold beautiful golden lager with a fluffy white head thinking "I don't want to drink this, I want to frame it and keep it forever" but then he picked up the glass and savoured every last drop.

It seemed strange sitting down at a table with a plated cooked meal, something they all thought they'd never do again, simple things were so important, just washing with soap and water over a sink or a shower, yes these guys even had showers with them, with hot water.
A few days later as promised the supply truck arrived and Jack, Carol and Sue climbed aboard and headed back to the holiday compound, a few hours later they were back in familiar surroundings,
Mr Sykes was there waiting at the gate to greet them, his face changed when he saw them, battered, bruised, covered in cuts and scratches, skin peeling off their faces where they'd been so burnt, he kept apologizing over and over again.

Jack and Carol were in their chalet, they'd been in less than an hour when there was a knock on the door, Jack opened it to find Sue standing there, "I'm afraid of being on my own, can I stay with you two," this was understandable because despite the high wire fence they were still in Africa, miles away from civilization.

Another knock on the door, again Jack opened it to find Mr Sykes and two African guys in camouflage uniforms carrying guns, Mr Sykes said "Sorry to disturb you, these two gentlemen are police officers and would like to talk to you"

"Sure" said Jack and asked them in, one of the policemen said "No, you are all to come with us to the Police station," Jack protested "Oh come on, we've only just got back and we're the victims here!" again the policeman spoke "No matter, you still have to come with us," the three of them were bundled into the back of a van, well it was a sort of van body on a land rover chassis, there was a small window on each side with bars on it. The wooden benches down each side were hard and uncomfortable, one policeman sat in the back with them and there was a third one in the front. Jack kept asking the policeman in the back with them "What's this all about? Why couldn't you talk to us there?" he said nothing, he just sat there holding his rifle pointed to the floor.

Eventually they van stopped outside a small stone built police station on the edge of a small town, the doors opened and they were escorted inside, once inside the building their names were confirmed and the officer on the desk checked them against their passports which they had obtained from Mr Sykes.

Once their identities had been confirmed all three were taken through a door and locked up in separate cells, the heavy metal door slammed closed and the key made a loud clunk as the door was locked, Jack couldn't understand what was going on, they had been the victims so why were they being treated like criminals.

Carol was calling Jack, Sue was crying again, Jack called back to Carol then a policeman could be heard shouting "No talking!"

It must have been several hours later when the door opened and Jack was taken roughly to another room, a grim looking place with grey peeling walls and a table with three chairs, Jack was handcuffed and the chain between the handcuffs was fed through a large metal ring on the table.
Two men entered one introduced himself as a policeman and introduced the other as Mr Okembu, Jacks lawyer. "Am I under arrest?" Jack asked, "Just a precaution" came the reply, Jack was asked all about the events of the past few days, he answered honestly and accurately, the girls had been asked the same and their account had tallied with Jack's,
 Jack was told this, he then insisted he and the girls be released, the policeman said "Yes of

course the two women are free to go but you my friend have charges to answer, Jack was then arrested on multiple counts of suspected murder, and locked back in the cell.

He could hear a commotion at the desk in the front of the police station, it was Carol, shouting, he couldn't make out what she was saying but he had a pretty good idea.

Chapter Nine
Detained

Within a few hours Jack was taken out of the cell and back to the interview room, "I want to go over this statement again with you" said the policeman who from his accent was obviously South African, he spoke good English, Jack looked him in the eye and said "Again?" "Yes again", he said, "You said the men you shot were shooting at you?" "Yes they were, ask the girls" replied Jack, then the policeman said "Well, I have several statements here saying the men you shot were trying to rescue you, they said they could see you were in trouble and were only trying to help, they also said you concocted your story to shift the blame from yourself" Jack protested, That's rubbish, what about Roger? They shot and tortured him!" According to their statements you did that, You were having an affair with his wife weren't you and you killed him and tried to make it look like a lion had attacked him by cutting him, I suspect you hoped the wildlife would get rid of the evidence for you? Didn't you?"
"That's ridiculous! OK, so what about the guard? Why would I shoot him?" Shouted Jack, then the policemen started to put his paperwork in order as he said "Well you wouldn't want any witnesses, would you?"

Jack was then taken outside in handcuffs and loaded into the same van he had arrived in, the girls were still there, sitting on a step out front, Jack spotted them and shouted to Carol "Contact the embassy Carol, contact the embassy and tell them what's happened!", Jack was almost thrown into the van, the doors slammed and the van drove off.

Jack had no idea what to expect, they drove for hours, Jack said to the guard "Where are you taking me?" he replied "You're going to Jail my friend until your trial, this will teach you not to come to my country and start shooting my brothers, I have heard about you white racists and how you see black men as a lower species," Jack reacted by shouting loudly "White racist? You think I'm some kind of racist? Some sort of neo Nazi Fascist? I am nothing of the sort, I hate racists!" The guard responded with "Well you would say that wouldn't you, now shut up unless you want my boot up your white racist backside!"

On arrival at the prison Jack was dragged out of the van, he didn't even get to his feet, two of the policemen dragged him through the huge metal gate and into the yard, Jack was terrified, he expected to meet the governor and be familiarized with the rules and routines, it never happened, he was now on his feet, "They're going to love you in here, black man killer!" said

one of the prison guards as he shoved Jack along a long corridor only stopping to unlock the barred metal gates along the way.
Eventually they reached what looked something like a shower area, Jack was ordered to strip, when he was naked one of the guards turned a high power hose on him which forced Jack up against the wall, he couldn't breathe, the water was spraying in his face, he was sure the bastards were enjoying his humiliation and suffering. Jack was thrown a rag and told to dry and get dressed which he did, then again roughly pushed and shoved through a gate into a dusty yard then into another gate and eventually ending up in a large room full of prisoners, it was so crammed in there he could hardly move, no one spoke to him, Jack had no idea where to sleep or even if he was safe, he felt he could be murdered at any moment.

There were wooden bunks three high and so close to each other there was barely standing room between them, there must have been thirty or more ragged rough looking men in the room, the walls were high, the old paint was peeling off the walls and ceiling and the smell took Jack's breath away, a stench of shit, piss and sweat filled the air, "You wouldn't keep animals in a place like this" he thought, he seemed to be the only white man in the room, somewhere over the back of the room somewhere he could hear arguing going on, Jack just stood there silent, this wasn't hell, it was worse than hell.

At the end of the day the bunks were all taken so Jack grabbed a dirty piece of foam from a stack in the corner, threw it on the floor and sat down, he wanted to cry, he felt so miserable but he also needed to stay strong as the others would consider him weak and would no doubt target him, there were rats running around, there was dirt all over the floor and Jack thought he'd be better off dead than live like this.

It was pitch black, Jack had no idea what the time was, then suddenly he made out the shape of someone standing over him, in broken English the man quietly said "why you here?" Jack said nothing, again "Why you here?" this time there was a gentle attention getting kick with it, Jack sat up, the man crouched down, once again "Why you here?" Jack replied, they say I murdered people" The response to this wasn't as Jack had expected, he thought it might be "Black man?" but it wasn't instead he heard "Did you do it?" Jack said "It was self defense" the man didn't understand "What is this self defence?" Jack said "I had no choice" the man then said "So da police lie?" Jack thought about it for a moment, he could try to explain but it seemed like a lot of work so he simply said "Yes, the police lie" The man said "yes, da police always lie, I am Kimbo, my name Kimbo, you stay with me, I take care"

Jack really didn't understand what Kimbo meant so he just said "yes, thank you" then the man was gone into the darkness.

There were things moving around on the floor all night, jack grabbed something as it ran across his face, cockroaches, loads of them, they were making a racket all night, he hardly slept.

The morning sent a dusty shard of light through the window, a window without glass, a window with just bars, people began stirring, there was a queue for the half of an oil drum which was the toilet, the stink got worse if that was possible, banging and shouting could be heard outside as the guards unlocked the doors. Jack needed to pee, it was his turn, the smell was making him wretch, he needed to wash, he felt dirty after spending the night in that shit hole.

Jack hoped he would be released today, someone must have the power and the truth is out there, alas it was false hope, the reality of his situation was dawning on him, Jack started thinking about how to escape, he thought about suicide, then he thought about Carol, he knew she would be doing all she could but did she even know where he was?
The door opened and the mass exit began, not wanting to upset any of these tough looking hardened criminals Jack stayed back until the masses had gone, he followed behind, it was the

same shower block he'd been hosed down in the day before, the prisoners were all taking showers or washing at dirty sinks, all cold water, no soap, Jack washed the best he could then followed the others out into the yard, there was a long table and food being dished out, Jack joined the queue, when he reached the table it wasn't food but some sort of barely edible grey slop, no utensils, the prisoners were eating with their hands while sitting on the ground.

Jack was amazed he'd not been beaten up or raped so far, he was dreading the conflict which was bound to happen sooner of later, Jack was trying to keep himself to himself in the hope they'd leave him alone.
He sat there eating his disgusting slop whilst looking around for weaknesses in the security, if he could find a way out he would surely take it. Across the yard there were two white men so when Jack finished eating he made his way across the yard, he kept looking around in case he was doing something wrong but nobody batted an eyelid, he stood next to one of the white men and said "English?" "No" came the reply, "Scottish and my friend here is a yank, how are you settling in to this lovely hotel?" "I hate it, I hate this country, I just want to go home" said Jack, he felt like crying but again held back, he wondered how the Scot could be so cheerful, and in his strong Scottish accent said "Hi, I'm James, this is Ralph and you are?" Oh, sorry, I'm Jack,"

Jack replied, "Hi, jack" said Ralph, "Hey, you're not a Hi-Jacker are you Jack?" laughing, Jack replied, "No, I'm apparently a mass murderer" Ralph looked at James, James looked at Jack then Ralph said "You got a trial date yet buddy?" "No said Jack, have you?" again they looked at each other then James said "No laddie, and no sign of one either, "How long have you been here waiting?" Jack asked, Ralph said "I'm not quite sure, a year maybe" Jack was shocked, "A year!" Ralph went on, "Yea, I reckon about a year, there was a fella here waiting for his trial, think he said he was from Utah back in the states, he was here for over two years, but he didn't make it," Jack said "you mean he got found guilty?" "No I mean he died before he got his trial date" said Ralph.

Jack was feeling even more disheartened, the three men talked throughout the morning, Jack learned he could sleep in any of the rooms so decided to stick with his new found friends, he also learned there was nothing to do all day but stand or sit around in the yard, Jack was gazing up at the high walls and the guards up there on top. James said "Forget it, those bastards will shoot you before you touch the wall.

He thought if he could find a way to escape how would they know he was gone, there didn't seem to be any head count or checks but then he didn't relish the thought of being shot while trying to escape, that was nearly as bad as the thought of spending years in this hell hole.

Jack had survived nearly three weeks with the help of James and Ralph when he was told he was getting a visit from the British consulate, he was taken to a room, a room a world apart from his living conditions, a room which actually resembled some sort of civilization, there were curtains, a clean tiled floor, comfy furniture and even a picture hanging on the wall, a man in a suit carrying a briefcase entered, he introduced himself "Hello old chap, I'm Howard Johnson from the embassy, how are you holding up?"

Jack again almost broke down, just the glimmer of hope at seeing this posh bloke and hearing his queens English introduction sent emotions running wild, Jack was so pleased to see him, he'd have been thrilled to see anyone who wasn't a guard or a dirty disheveled crook.
"Can you get me out of here?" was the first thing that came from Jack's mouth, Howard sat down, opened his brief case and threw a carton of cigarettes on the table, "I don't smoke" said Jack, "Those my dear friend are not cigarettes, they are currency in here, now then to the matter in hand, I have managed to get hold of all the statements and the evidence and the short answer is yes, probably but it will take some time" Jack looked confused "Which is it? Yes or probably? And how much time?" Howard replied, "the law here

is very different to the law you and I know, also it would be very difficult to get the witnesses to tell the truth as they would then become the guilty so you see we have a bit of a dilemma, our best course of action is to go through diplomatic channels, after your trial we can apply to have you returned to the UK to serve your time there and then we can look at the case under British law"

Jack was horrified "You mean I have to be found guilty in order to get back to England?" well it's not quite that simple because with a criminal conviction of this kind you may be sentenced to life and then not extradited, there are some political avenues we can explore but that has to be authorized through high government."

Jack said "that could take years!" Howard then looking down at his papers said "Yes, in all probability it would, I must go now, I'll pop back in a month or two if there's any progress!" with that Howard left and Jack was taken back to the yard.

Jack was now thoroughly depressed, he didn't care at this point whether he lived or died, so if anyone wanted to fight him he would have told them to bring it on, Jack told James and Ralph what Howard had said, they were sympathetic but not surprised.

Chapter Ten
The Trial date

Jack had been incarcerated in this filthy dump for nearly nine months when he received word his trial date had been set for next Thursday, he didn't know whether or not this was a good thing or a bad thing, he was sure he wouldn't be going home any time soon if ever, Howard had made that perfectly clear.

Thursday morning came around, Jack had nothing to wear for court just the dirty ragged remains of the clothed he was wearing on the day he arrived, the same ones he'd worn every day since, four men arrived in camouflage army gear which seemed the norm throughout the police and army alike, these men were big, scary and carrying automatic weapons, Jack was escorted out to a van and loaded into the back, as he left the main gate one of the guards said with a grin "see you later boy!" Jack thought the guy knew he'd be back like every other poor sod before him.

The van set off down the road, Jack could see the town through the small tinted window, it was horrible but to Jack it looked like paradise simply because it was outside the prison walls,
They turned into a gravel covered yard and the van came to a halt, the doors opened and the men got out, as Jack stepped out into the blinding sunlight he realized they were no longer in the

town but somewhere remote, two men also in military gear and armed took Jack by the arm and put him in the back of a car, the two soldiers got in the front, one threw a bundle of clothes tied with a string to Jack and ordered him to get changed and the car sped off immediately, as they pulled out of the car park a green land rover followed them, it was the men who'd picked him up from the prison and within seconds they were on the tail of the Mercedes Jack was in.
Jack stripped and was struggling to get dressed quickly in the limited space he had, he guessed this wasn't going to end at the court room, the soldiers in the front seats were calm but driving fast to get as far away as possible, the Land rover stayed with them for a while then turned off down a dirt road.

Jack said "What's going on?" the front seat passenger said "best you don't know the details but we're getting you out of the country, hopefully" Jack now getting very excited said "But, but who? What? But was met with "shhh" the car drove on fast for over and hour, all of a sudden up ahead there was a road block, one of the soldiers said "That may be coincidence" the driver said "No such thing!" he put his foot down "Get down!" he snapped at Jack, the car accelerated towards the wooden barrier, the men at the barrier opened fire on the car, One of the soldiers wound down the window and returned fire with his machine gun sending the men in the road running for cover, the barrier shattered into matchwood as the car hit it, cracking the windscreen, the driver said "we have to ditch this car" the other soldier said "not much further," Jack noticed they didn't use names and hadn't introduced themselves but hey, if this was the path to freedom who cares, The car suddenly left the main road for a dirt track, a few minutes later it stopped, all three of them got out, there were two cars waiting for them, Jack was told to get in the black BMW and the soldiers ran for the land rover parked by a tree, as the BMW drove out one soldier tossed a grenade into the Mercedes from the land rover as they left, the merc exploded, now back on the main road Jack found himself being driven by a middle aged Englishman in a beige suit and a trilby hat, the land rover with the soldiers in was behind them, "Good morning, My name is Robert, You're Jack I presume, well I hope you are or there's been something of a cock up," he smiled,

 They drove at a steady pace and Robert pointing to the glove box said "In there you'll find your identity papers, passport, British driving license and so on, get them out and learn them, learn them well.

During the long journey Jack learned his new name, date of birth, home address etc and kept saying them all over and over again in his mind. Eventually the car pulled up outside a hotel, Jack was booked in under his new name, handed in his new passport at reception and was shown his room, Robert went in with him, he handed Jack a phone and said, if you have a problem and you feel you're in danger just call mother in the contacts list, Jack asked who had arranged all this and Robert said I don't know, he said they don't tell us anything apart from who, where, and when, ours is not to question why! You'll be contacted by phone in the morning, I would suggest you stay in the room until then," with that he left.

Throughout that night Jack sat on the bed, he didn't get undressed or sleep at all. Every sound worried him, maybe it was the police, maybe he'd been rumbled, he imagined hundreds of officers and soldiers surrounding the hotel, blocking off his escape, then a siren broke the night silence, it was approaching, Jack peeped out of the window just pulling the curtains aside enough to see with one eye, the siren passed, he could breathe again.

It was about eight in the morning when the phone rang, it was mother the display said, so Jack answered "Hello It's mother here, collect your papers and meet me out in front at nine sharp", the phone went dead before Jack could reply, at ten to nine Jack went to reception and collected his passport and checked out, once outside a woman in a small red sports car pulled up, she reached over and opened the door, Jack got in and they drove off, about ten minutes later they arrived at a transport depot, jack was told to get into the back of a truck, he did so and then a fork lift stacked a load of pallets inside after him, within half an hour Jack was on the road again, no idea where he was or what was happening, the truck drove on for quite some time, then it stopped, Jack remained silent and still, he could hear voices, barking orders, the doors of the truck opened allowing light to flood in, Jack couldn't see anything except the light over the top of the cargo, the doors remained open for some time then to Jack's relief they closed, within a few minutes the truck was on the move again.

It seemed like an eternity, Jack was getting cramp in places he didn't know you could get cramp, he was hoping this journey would stop soon, he needed a pee and it was getting desperate, just about bursting point the truck stopped, Jack still couldn't get out because of the cargo which was now being unloaded, once the last pallet was removed and Jack saw the outside world he was greeted by a big fat jolly looking man who said in a booming voice "Welcome to Uganda!" he started laughing like he'd just heard the funniest joke ever.
"Jack responded immediately with, " I gotta pee!" which the fat man thought was hysterically funny and began laughing again.

Chapter Eleven
Welcome to Uganda

"Am I safe?" Jack asked the fat man, he replied "you are for the moment my friend but Kenya and Uganda security services cooperate with each other so we must be careful," he said still chuckling away, there seemed to be nothing in this world which wasn't funny to the fat man.

The two of them drove to the airport, as they arrived the fat man handed Jack an envelope which contained some cash and a plane ticket to Cairo, Jack thanked him and headed inside, he was very nervous, there seemed to be armed security everywhere, Jack wondered if they were looking for him, he tried to act normal, he felt everyone was looking at him, but they weren't, He thought he looked conspicuous as he walked through the airport, he had no luggage, he was limping, the shoes he'd been given were tight, he was terrified someone might recognize him and he'd be carted off back to prison, Jack was sweating, he was sure someone would take him aside and discover his documents were fake, there was a TV on, it was showing the news, standing at a distance he looked discreetly at the screen, looking to see if Kenya's most wanted was going to have his photo broadcast but nothing, so happy that he apparently hadn't gained such celebrity status he nervously walked on.

As Jack handed in his ticket and passport at the check in desk he felt the attendant was scrutinizing his documents much more than usual, it seemed to be taking ages, "No luggage?" he was asked, Jack simply replied "no," he didn't want to draw attention by making unnecessary explanations or making this last any longer than it absolutely had to, finally a bit of paper stamping and Jack was handed his boarding pass and passport, breathing a sigh of relief he headed for departures, this was probably the more likely point to get caught as these guys weren't just checking paperwork they were security forces, Jack casually walked through, he got called aside, the guy wanted to double check his documents, Jack was sure he was about to get arrested, the security guy made a phone call whilst holding Jack's documents, then he put Jack's passport on a scanner, there was a pause, all of a sudden the light went green, Jack was allowed through.

Sitting on the plane was tense, at least there was air conditioning, Jack thought he must stink, he had been sweating in the truck and right up to the airport, even inside the terminal but that may have been nerves, it seemed ages before the plane finally moved, it even seemed to taxi at a snails pace, Jack wouldn't feel any safer until they were in the air, he had no idea what treaties or arrangements existed between Egypt and Kenya, and hopefully he wouldn't need to know.

Once in the air Jack could breathe again, he had a few hours respite, he thought about seeing Carol, he hadn't heard from her or been able to contact her in the best part of a year, maybe she's given up on him, maybe she's met someone else and moved on he thought, this made him sad but the overwhelming thought of getting his feet on British soil was the uppermost priority now.

Jack was not so nervous now, the landing was fine, and despite getting a bit twitchy going through customs Jack felt this was the home run, and then, as he was almost to the main hall he got stopped. "Where are your bags?" he was asked by a rather mean looking officer, "I lost them", said Jack, "How can you lose your luggage?" asked the immigration officer, Jack, quick as a flash said, "the taxi drove off with them in his boot, at the airport," he was asked if he'd reported it, but Jack was ready for that one and said there was nothing of value and he didn't want to miss his flight, unbelievably he was allowed to continue, Jack couldn't believe his luck, he had managed to get through two airports, even had his fake passport scanned and verified without getting caught, he was thirsty so Jack went to a coffee bar and using some of the cash he'd been given ordered a coffee and a sandwich, He had just picked up the cup and his phone rang, it was mother again, "Hello darling where are you?" she said, Jack thought this was a different voice, but it was the same phone she had called, he was amazed at how coordinated and well executed his escape had been, so far at least, "Hello mother, Jack replied "I've Just arrived, "I'm waiting for you at the pick up point" she said

Jack put down his coffee and taking the sandwich, looked around for the drop off and pick up point sign and headed out.

Looking up and down the waiting row of cars he saw a hand come out of a window beckoning him, he walked cautiously over to the car, inside was a woman nowhere near old enough to be his mother but nevertheless he got in and the car drove off.

As they drove through the streets of Cairo, Jack had endless questions running through his mind but had no idea how to ask so he simply said "Where are we going?" the woman paused for a moment then said "a safe house, I'm Carla by the way", "Jack," Jack replied, "I know said Carla", Jack just had to ask, "who has done this for me? Is it the government?" once again Jack got the same reply as before "I don't know, I just do as I'm told and that's it," Jack looked puzzled, "Told by who?" He asked, Carla said, "Like I said, my instructions come through channels and that's all I know, I expect someone will contact you once you're home," Jack looked a bit worried for a moment then thought whoever was behind this obviously wouldn't go to all this

trouble if they intended him harm, he was sure it was to do with the bloke from the embassy,
The car stopped, Carla went inside an apartment block with Jack, showed him to a door on the second floor, "Someone will be in touch soon. Stay indoors and make sure the phone is on and charged" she said, Jack thanked Carla as she left, Jack turned the key and went inside.
Once inside he plugged in the phone and switched on the TV, still worried he may be on the news, but the news still had nothing, it was hard to believe someone wanted internationally for multiple murders and an escape from prison wasn't even mentioned, maybe it was too soon to reach this far but Jack believed it was only a matter of time,
There was a sound by the door, it made him jump, Jack carefully walked to the door and found a large brown envelope had been pushed underneath, he picked up the envelope, there was nothing written on the front, he could feel papers inside so he opened it as he sat down, inside was another passport with Jack's photo and yet another name, and a load more information to learn, new UK address, new date of birth, parent's names, their birthdays and so on, now he was a Brian, he'd never imagined himself as a Brian but whatever it takes he thought.

About seven thirty that evening the phone rang, this time the display said "Dad" so he answered with "Hey Dad!" "hello son" came the reply, the man on the phone then said "I'll pick you up at your place in ten minutes," Jack waited, exactly ten minutes later there was a knock on the door, "It's dad" said the voice from the other side, Jack opened the door to find a middle aged man with a beard standing there, "You got everything?" he asked, Jack said he had, they went outside and climbed into a waiting taxi, the man said "Give me the old stuff" Jack had already put all his old documents in the envelope the new ones had arrived in, the man took them and put them in his inside jacket pocket, he didn't introduce himself as anything other than dad.

The taxi driver already knew where they were going but that was more than Jack did, he was happy to go anywhere as long as he was free of that jail.

They stopped at a taxi rank at the railway station, Jack was handed a ticket and told to catch a train, without another word the two men parted company, the taxi drove off, once again Jack was standing alone in a public place and that was quite frightening,

Once Jack had identified the train he was to catch he went to the appropriate platform and waited, again feeling like everyone was watching him, how should he act so not to draw attention to himself, he was even conscious of how he stood or walked, Jack was one of very few non locals, then it happened, Jacks, greatest fear, a man had been looking at him from further up the platform, the man looked at a paper he was holding, then back at Jack, the man began walking towards him, Jack knew he'd been recognized but before the man reached him the train pulled in to the station, in a moment of hesitation, should he board or should he run, Jack decided to board the train, once inside he felt trapped the man would obviously be on the train too, maybe he wasn't after Jack, maybe there was someone beyond Jack the man was running towards, all these thoughts were running riot in Jack's mind, he was scared.

Minutes passed, no sign of the man from the station, Jack began to calm down, thinking it was all his imagination, it must have been something else.
The carriage jolted a bit then began to move, Jack was feeling relieved, then he saw him, the man was walking down the carriage, Jack looked around, there were few people in the carriage and the nearest one was a few seats away, Jack wondered if he should go and sit with someone else, maybe this guy would leave him alone if there were witnesses, Jack was undecided, he was still thinking about what to do when the man sat down opposite him, he put his folded up newspaper on the table.
For a while there was silence, then the man spoke quietly, "we have been looking for you Jack" emphasizing his name as if to confirm he knew Jack's real identity, then the man said "Don't

think about running, we are being met at the next stop," the next stop being some time away Jack considered Jumping from the train, it was an option to be seriously considered, there was nothing else said for quite some time, the train had slowed a little and Jack thought he would seize the opportunity to get off, He knew once he jumped he would be on his own because his rescuers wouldn't know where he was, Jack went to get up, the man put out his foot, "tut tut" he said, tapping his newspaper, Jack sat down again, he could make out the barrel of a gun in side the newspaper, there was no way this guy was letting him out of his sight, when the next stop was about five minutes away, Jack considered making a run for it,

Just then a huge black man in typical local dress sat himself down next to the man from the station, he spoke quietly too but with an American accent "Do you have business with my young friend here?" he said to the man from the station, "what's it got to do with you he replied"
"Oh nothing" he casually replied, then the American said Come with me Jack, the man from the station reached for his newspaper then before his hand got anywhere close his expression changed, he seemed to slump like he'd simply fallen asleep, The American took the newspaper, he took the gun from inside it and put it in his pocket, glancing around briefly to make sure he hadn't been seen, with one hand he picked up the

paper laying open on the table and as he got up he pulled a big bowie knife from the man's side and put it in his jacket, then he put the newspaper there to hide the blood and wound, in a casual movement that Jack hardly noticed, the American closed the man's eyes so he looked asleep, he and Jack then headed back up the train to the luggage car.

"This is something we didn't expect" said the American as he looked around, there was a huge trunk, it was brown leather with straps and buckles, the American opened it and started dragging out the content, "Hide this crap!" he ordered, Jack started gathering the clothes and effects from the trunk and stuffed them down behind a stack of wooden crates, once empty the American stabbed some air holes in the sides of the trunk with the knife he'd used on the man from the station, Jack climbed into the trunk the American did up the straps and buckles then went to the next carriage and sat down.

The train stopped, the American got off the train, he stepped into the café, he sat by the window and watched for the trunk to be unloaded, all of a sudden there was a lot of activity, the body had been found, the police were all over the platform and the train, the American made an exit in case he'd been seen.

Chapter Twelve
The trunk

The train left the station, Jack was locked inside the trunk, too scared to make a sound, he could hear the clatter of the train and feel the bumps now and then but apart from the odd couple of shards of light from the air holes the American had made he was completely in the dark.

The journey seemed to go on forever, Jack had no idea where the trunk was headed for, he was hoping it wasn't Kenya but he thought that unlikely as he had been traveling in the opposite direction.

Everything went quiet, then a loud scraping noise as the sliding door on the side of the car was opened, Jack could hear voices, banging, lots of commotion, he gritted his teeth, had he been discovered? Luckily it seemed not, the trunk was being unloaded, Jack found it hard to stay silent as the trunk was dropped heavily on the floor. Jack could feel the trunk was being barrowed along and then loaded into or maybe onto a vehicle, he felt a degree of relief as the vehicle drove off, what would happen when the owner opened the trunk to find Jack inside and all their possessions gone? What if the trunk was being taken to a storage facility? Jack realized he could die in there but still he had to hold on until he knew he was safe.

The vehicle stopped, the trunk was unloaded, at one point Jack was completely upside down, standing on his head then on his back again, the trunk was then put in an elevator, Jack could hear people pressing buttons and the familiar sound and motion as the elevator rose,
Finally he had been delivered to the owner of the trunk, it went quiet, Jack could hear water running, it sounded like a shower, then the fiddling sound of the buckles and latches being undone, finally daylight as the lid opened, a woman screamed and jumped back, Jack could hardly see, the sudden light had all but blinded him, the woman started to scream louder!

Jack waving his arms gesturing to be calm and saying "sorry, sorry, it's OK, it's OK" whilst trying to escape from the trunk had some effect, the shocked woman had backed off across the room and was clearly frightened by Jack's unexpected appearance, "Who are you? What are you doing in my trunk?" she demanded, at least she had stopped screaming, Jack said he had been mugged and locked in the trunk whist traveling on the train, of course it was a lie but he couldn't tell her he was wanted for several murders, that really would have freaked her out.
 Hearing the excuse Jack had concocted seemed to change things dramatically, She had gone from hysterical screaming to sympathy, "Oh you poor thing" she said, "Are you hurt?" Jack replied, No, I'm fine but I have no idea where I am," "You're

at Minya" she said, now she had calmed down and regained her composure, she said, "would you like some tea? Before Jack could answer there was banging on the door, the screaming had been reported and the staff were coming to her rescue, the woman opened the door just a little and told them it was nothing, just a small Gecko, but it's gone now,

Jack noted the woman was not a local, she was more European and as she was about to take a shower when she discovered Jack she was barely dressed, this was a woman in her fifties, very well to do, the apartment was furnished in only the very finest antiquities which must have been imported as they were certainly not of Egyptian styling.

"If you don't mind me asking, where are you from?" Jack said, the woman replied "Oh I'm so sorry, we have not been properly introduced, I am Sophia de Marco, I am originally from Spain but now I spend my time between Paris and here, and you are?" Jack recalled his most recent papers, "Oh, I am Brian Jackson from England" he said, Sophia thought about her time in London and asked, "London?" "No," said Jack "a bit further North, but I work, well worked in London."
Sophia then asked "so what brings you to Egypt?" this was a question Jack had not prepared for, he thought for a moment and then

said, "I got a little lost and wound up here" "In my trunk" said Sophia laughing, "here is your tea" they talked for ages, Sophia seemed interested in Jack's life and Jack was being very careful what he revealed.
Jack was fascinated by this woman, she had to be twenty years older than him but he found her strangely attractive, everything she did, everything she said was with such grace and class,

She may have been in her fifties but she had the perfect figure, he could almost taste her expensive perfume in the air, he had to ask, Jack just blurted out "So where's your husband?" that was all Sophia needed to hear, she moved closer to Jack and said, "Oh he passed away a long time ago, I have been alone since then," Jack's thoughts momentarily went to Carol, he hadn't heard from her in nearly a year and was convinced she had moved on and forgotten him.

As Sophia's hand touched Jack's knee He turned his face to meet her kiss, it was warm and deep, even her kiss had class, like a kiss you would see in the movies, in that moment nothing else mattered, his desperate fight to get home, the danger pursuing him, nothing, it was as if time had stood still, Sophia took Jack by the hand, she moved so gracefully he was mesmerized, she led him to the bathroom, slowly Sophia started to undo Jack's buttons, he was soon naked, standing in front of her, There was no way Jack could hide his excitement, it stood up like a rod of steel, Sophia dropped her flimsy lace negligee to the floor, she then turned the shower back on and stepped inside, Jack instinctively followed her into the amply sized cubicle.

 Sophia washed Jack all over using a foaming soap and her bare hands, sensual hands, hands that knew exactly how to please a man, she reached down and fondled Jacks genitals, then she turned around and pushed her firm buttocks against Jack's hard cock, the water and soap made their bodies slippery which added to the sensation, Sophia pressed harder against Jack, he then took hold of his proud cock and pushed up gently between her legs, she moaned and put her hand down her front and guided Jack into her warm welcoming wet pussy, he thrust forward, deep inside her, she made a little sound of ecstasy and bent over further, Jack thrust deeper inside her body, thrusting harder and harder, again and again, the water from the shower was making lines on Sophia's back as it ran down, Jack watched them, he was trying to make this last because but he desperately wanted to cum, she knew this, she could feel he was getting close, she stood up releasing him, then she turned to face him, "you mustn't" she said, "you really mustn't, naughty boy", Jack was confused, he thought maybe she was worried about getting pregnant, Sophia continued to soap Jack and Jack in turn ran his wet soapy hands all over her body, he was still so hard, was this encounter over?

Sophia turned off the shower, stepped out and handed Jack a towel, they both dried themselves, then Sophia left the bathroom without saying a word, Once Jack was dry he didn't know whether or not he should put his clothes back on, he decided to put on his boxers and carry the rest into the lounge, as he entered, Sophia was nowhere to be seen, Jack noticed an open door and quiet music playing beyond it, he walked over to the door and peeped inside the room, there she was, laying naked on the bed, Sophia looked at Jack's boxers and gave him a puzzled expression, he dropped the bundle of clothes and removed the boxers and laid on the bed beside Sophia.

"Do you want me?" she said softly in her sexy Spanish voice, Jack said nothing, he began to touch her, he put his hand between her thighs, she moaned and moved her legs apart, Jack could feel she was already excited, his fingers were covered in her juice the moment he pushed them inside her, "Kiss me, Lick me" she said, Jack moved down the bed and positioned his face between her thighs, his tongue soon found her clitoris and as he gently licked he could feel her moving, wriggling and moaning, she was getting so wet he just had to taste her, Jack placed two fingers either side and gently pulled her open revealing her wet pink inner flesh, he pushed his tongue as far as he could inside and sucked the nectar from her, she seemed to love this, so he continued, licking and occasionally sucking, then all at once an explosion of wetness, she had soaked him ,Jack had never experienced this before, her orgasm was squirting from her, Jack took it all in his mouth and swallowed, Sophia was saying "sorry, sorry!" As she continued to cum intensely, then as she calmed , Jack emerged from between Sophia's legs, grabbed a tissue or two from the bedside table and went to wipe his face, Sophia put her arm out and stopped him, she rolled Jack onto his back and began licking her cum from his face, then she went down on him, this woman was insatiable, Sophia took Jack's hard cock in her mouth, she licked the length of it from his balls to the tip then she slid it deep into her mouth until she started to gag, She turned around to get astride his face, Jack obliged her with his tongue as Sophia continued to slide her mouth up and down his eager cock, once again Jack was getting close, Sophia knew this, she stopped, she climbed off his face and lay on the bed beside him, Jack was frustrated, he was starting to wonder if she would let him cum at all, Sophia laid there just long enough for Jack's urge to pass, then she turned onto her back and beckoned Jack to get on top of her, He did so, still worried she might stop him as the eruption was imminent but this woman he could not resist, he could feel her ample breasts against his chest as he pushed his erection up inside her soaking wet pussy, it was so warm and she knew exactly how to excite him, Sophia grabbed Jack's buttocks and pulled him inside, deep and hard, she wrapped her legs around his so there was no escape, She cried "I want it, I want it, Give it to me!" Jack needed no encouragement, he had been passionately making love to this beautiful woman for over an hour and the time was approaching, they were both breathing heavily, Jack muttered "Can I ? Can I?" as he pushed trying to get deeper that ever before, "Can I?" Sophia replied "Oh god yes! Do it! Do it!" and he did, Jack's orgasm had such force he could feel every muscle in his body tense so hard it almost hurt, he came so much he wondered if he was ever going to stop, Sophia was crying "Yes! Oh Yes!" which excited him even more, Jack stayed inside her as long as he could, his arms were hurting where he'd been propped up on them, he finally withdrew, rolled over and then it was all calm, the two of them lay on the bed in an embrace for ages, both exhausted and contented, Jack fell asleep only to be woken shortly afterwards by Sophia gently sucking on his now embarrassingly limp member, she wanted to taste his cum, or what remained after he had filled her, this awoke his sleeping phallus but despite getting hard again Jack was too tired to act upon it, he soon drifted off to sleep once more.

It was early evening when Jack woke, he was alone, he could hear noises from through the bedroom door, Jack got up, got dressed and went through, "Oh Hello, you naughty boy" said

Sophia, "I am making a meal for us, Oh and your mother called, I answered your phone, I hope you don't mind but she didn't want to talk to a strange woman, so she hung up,"

Jack grabbed his phone, he had forgotten he had mother's number in the contacts, he dialed, nothing, it didn't ring, he just got the unobtainable tone, he tried dad's number, that was the same, he felt abandoned and alone again.

Sophia was in the kitchen, Jack sat in the lounge and assessed his situation, he was still in Egypt, where exactly he was unsure, his phone was useless now, and he had very little money, he did have a dodgy passport, unsure what to do Jack had to make a decision,

Sophia put their food on the table and they both sat down to eat, "What will you do now?" Sophia asked, after a moment of thought Jack said "I don't know, the muggers took my wallet, and I have to get to England" he said
Sophia casually said, "maybe I can help?" Help? How?" said Jack, Sophia looked at him across the table and said "I have a house in Paris, I could take you there with me if you want, I will be going in two days"
Jack could see no other option, he accepted Sophia's offer but suspected she would want more than a traveling companion but that was no bad thing.

That night they went to bed together and slept soundly in each others arms, both still exhausted from earlier.

Chapter Thirteen
Paris

The next day was mostly spent packing ready for the journey, "How will we travel?" asked Jack, Sophia replied "We will fly, my baggage will follow by train" Jack wondered if his identity had been compromised, would he be able to get on the plane? Well there was only one way to find out.

The courier collected the heap of bags and the infamous trunk which was now full once again with more of Sophia's possessions and then it was time to head for the airport.
Jack and Sophia arrived at Cairo international after a long ride in a taxi, with only a couple of carry on bags, there was no baggage to check in, Sophia went to the desk and picked up the two tickets she had ordered over the phone and then she and Jack walked to the departure lounge, Jack didn't feel at all worried, this time he felt as safe as anyone else, like he'd been on holiday perhaps, he was blending in at the airport among the many tourists,
Sophia insisted they walk with arms linked together, Jack had no objection to this as his enemies would be looking for a man traveling alone and this definitely didn't look like that.

Sophia had a presence which got her all the right sort of attention, airport staff couldn't do enough for her, it was almost as if she had celebrity status. Jack went walking onwards towards the allocated gate but Sophia pulled him back, "It's this way" she said, She led Jack into the first class lounge, "much nicer than sitting in the normal departure" lounge Jack thought, "I could get used to this," he smiled.

First class flying was something Jack had never experienced, in his job he had booked people onto business class but never flown that way himself, he had always gone budget, knees cramped up against his chest and surrounded by the riffraff of society heading for Benidorm or the like for a piss up they could have had at home, now this was something else, there was a bar, you could lay down, choose your own entertainment, the flight crew were at you beck and call, Jack was in a different world.

Sophia however took it in her stride, this was a woman who had everything, Jack knew he was just a temporary plaything to her but he was enjoying the moment.

They landed in Paris, even exiting the plane and the airport was a pleasant experience, a limousine was waiting for them, the driver opened the door, and called Jack "Sir," he was impressed by this.

Sophia's house in Paris was something else too, it was huge, she had staff tending the garden, cleaning, cooking, Jack was surprised she didn't have someone to dress her too.

They were treated like royalty, the staff were on hand all the time, "Wow!" Said Jack, "you live like this?" Sophia smiled, it gets a little tiresome sometimes" she said and then added "and a little lonely" "Lonely!" Jack gasped, "Yes" she replied "I don't have friends like you, I live here all alone in this house which is far too large and I don't see anyone for ages, everything has to be so formal, it's all about appearances."

"When do you intend to leave?" she asked, in a very neutral manner, "I don't know" said Jack, he had handed control over to Sophia, she had taken him home like a possession and now he didn't know what his next move would be, he missed his life in England, it'd been so long but he also loved what he had with Sophia.

"Will you stay for a few days?" she asked like it was a favour, Jack felt he owed her his life, she had got him back close to home and relative safety, "Yes of course I will" he said, the next three days were spent showing Jack the sights from the window of a limousine, running through water fountains which rose up from a paved courtyard, hand in hand they walked together under the Eiffel tower and along the banks of the

Seine, by night they would make passionate love in Sophia's bedroom, they were so happy together but still Jack's heart yearned for home.

The day came and Jack had to say goodbye to Sophia, "Will I see you again?" she asked, obviously upset at his leaving, "Do you want to?" Jack replied, "Very much so," she said, Jack looked back at Sophia as he climbed into the limousine, "soon," he said "you will see me soon," Sophia's limousine took Jack to the airport, Sophia had arranged a first class flight to Heathrow in London, Jack felt a sensation of freedom as the plane touched down on British soil, he felt he could breathe again, he was still thinking about Sophia, he had told her she will see him again soon but the truth was Jack had no idea what was to become of him.

Everything went smoothly until immigration control, Jack's dodgy passport which had been fine at Paris when he boarded the plane suddenly threw a red light and set off an alarm at the automatic passport control, He panicked, he had nowhere to run, he was grabbed by two uniformed police officers then another arrived, an armed one. Jack expected to be taken into one of the rooms where you get strip searched or interrogated but no, the police took him straight out of the airport, into a police car and drove towards the city.

Awful thoughts were running through Jack's mind, was he to be taken back to Kenya to stand trial, was he going to be arrested in the UK and charged with murder?
Despite his repeatedly questioning the police officers, all he got was silence.

The police car stopped outside a very familiar building, it was the old corn exchange where Jack worked or used to before he vanished for nearly a year, he was escorted inside and handed over to a familiar face, Mr Gordon, he held the post of operations manager, Jack had worked there for years but never knew what they did, his job was simply booking flights and sometimes arranging train tickets for people within the company, and sometimes not, but he had only clapped eyes on Mr Gordon a few times, Mr Gordon took Jack to the top floor of the building and into his plush office overlooking the city, "Take a seat, Jack," he insisted, Jack sat down on a big leather sofa, Mr Gordon took his place at his desk.

"You've had quite a time of it haven't you Jack?" said Mr Gordon, Jack was impressed by the fact the head of the department even knew his name, but still very confused by all this. "You could say that" replied Jack, "What's going on sir?"
Mr Gordon then said "What I'm about to tell you must never leave this room, "On my life," said Jack, "Exactly" replied Mr Gordon with a very serious look, before I tell you anything you do

remember signing the official secrets act when you first started working here, don't you?" Jack agreed that he had but thought nothing of it at the time. Mr Gordon asked, "do you know what we actually do here Jack?"
"Not really," said Jack, "I just do my job, I was only ever told I was a cog in a machine."

"Exactly and you're about to be offered a job as a bigger cog in this machine. OK, you do know what we do because we did it for you" albeit we did lose you in Cairo," " Jack said" prison breaks?"
Mr Gordon laughed, "Not really son, we arrange all sorts of logistics, we get people and things where they need to be, political extractions, we're in the business of doing what her majesty's government can't be seen to be doing, how do you think countries like the Ukraine get their soldiers trained? Or how do you think we get weapons there on the quiet? Who do you think makes coups in unstable countries possible?"
Jack sat there totally stunned by all this, then he asked "What about my escape?" well he said, a young lady came to see us and said you wouldn't be back to work for some time, she explained why, we did some legwork and got you home, well as I said, we lost you part way but you're home now, we couldn't let one of our own rot in that place so I authorized a sort of non sanctioned rescue, but! And I mean this! You can never tell a

soul what happened over there, none of it, you get me?"
"Yes sir!" said Jack as if he was in the army.
Mr Gordon then went on to say "Truth is we didn't know how much you knew about what goes on here so we couldn't take any chances, so we either had to kill you or rescue you, and when an Englishman gets killed abroad it makes news and people start digging, so welcome back, take a month off on your new pay rate and see you on the third floor."

Mr Gordon then threw a wallet to Jack, "here, this is yours, inside you'll find a card for expenses, I don't suppose you have anywhere to live so get a hotel room for now, We'll sort something out later"

"One more thing sir" said Jack, What about the trumped up murder charges in Kenya? "
Mr Gordon said, Don't you worry about that, they'll be dropped soon, you can't charge someone without witnesses can you?" he winked, stood up, and showed Jack to the door, as Jack was walking away Mr Gordon said "your expenses card is also your elevator pass, just hold it up to the plate, Goodnight son!"

Jack checked into a hotel near the old corn exchange building that night and the following morning he went to the travel agents where Carol worked, Jack waited until he could see her at her desk, then walked into the shop, Carol thinking it was just another client entering looking for the world's cheapest holiday looked up and almost burst when she saw Jack standing there, the other girl in the shop nearly fell off her chair as Carol screamed "Jack!, Jack!" she ran to him knocking her own chair over in the process, she threw her arms around him, "I never thought I'd see you again" she said through floods of tears.

Just then a customer walked in before the gent even opened his mouth Jack said "I wouldn't, last holiday I booked from here was a disaster," the customer turned and walked out, Carol laughed, her colleague who had only recently started work there had a puzzled look on her face, Carol said she'd explain later.

Jack and Carol married the following spring, Jack jets off all over the world as part of his work, he sees Sophia occasionally when he can, Sophia is happy with their arrangement, it does make Jack feel a bit like James Bond, Carol knows nothing about Sophia but she is happy in her life with Jack
The remaining two murdering poachers were "accidentally" shot dead whilst hunting elephants for their tusks.

No one knows what happened to Jack's car which was left at the hotel in Glasgow.

Chapter Fourteen
Mission One

There was very little space, Jack was sure people could hear from outside the door, Bianca was being quite noisy, she moaned and squealed almost continuously. She had her face in the tiny plastic sink, bent over at an awkward angle with her knickers round one ankle laying on the floor, her other foot up on the toilet and her skirt high up around her waist as Jack pounded her from behind, he gritted his teeth so as not to make a noise as he came deep inside her, Bianca reached out and pulled some tissue off the roll and started to compose herself, Jack gave her a brief kiss on the lips, opened the door to make a discreet exit only to be was greeted by the passengers in the nearest four or five rows looking at him, cheering and clapping, Jack took a bow then made his way back to his seat, a very red faced Bianca made her escape to the Galley to resume work.

Jack had joined the mile high club but now he had he didn't understand why it was such a big deal to some people.

It had been two years since Jack had been promoted to special operative, a hard two years, mostly training with ex special forces guys, he was now getting the good jobs instead of just taking papers from country to country, he thought about his first job with the company, sitting at a desk booking people onto flights, now he was the one being booked onto flights by some poor schmuck sitting behind a computer screen getting bored stiff. This was his first job after being transferred last week to special ops.

The plane landed at Warsaw international and Jack disembarked, he took a taxi to his hotel and checked in. Later that evening Jack met with his operations coordinator in a restaurant in the city, Jack was handed some paperwork, which he put in his Jacket, it gave him a feeling of pride as he sat eating his meal opposite the guy doing the job he used to do, Jack had always wanted to be his on screen hero James Bond and now he was as close as it gets, obviously he would have liked the classic Aston Martin with the pop out machine guns behind the headlights and ejector seat but this was real life, not the movies.

Morning arrived, it was cold and wet outside. Jack was up early, there was a long drive ahead, he checked his papers were all in order then hired a car, "Do you want the extra insurance cover?" the girl behind the desk asked, it didn't really matter to Jack and as he was only going to pick someone up, it was basically a taxi job for some civil servant, he declined, took the keys and left.

Jack's first stop was Terespol, some hundred and twenty miles, Terespol was a check point between Poland and Belarus, Jack could have flown directly to Belarus but it was better not to leave a trail if possible, it was just the way it worked, no problems at the checkpoint so Jack drove on, he could have taken a route through the Ukraine but because of the war he could well have been watched as there were very few foreigners landing there and tensions were still high.

Once through the checkpoint it was off to Minsk, Jack was running a bit late now as traffic had built up before the border so he put his foot down, this proved not to be the best course of action as he had only gone a few miles when he got pulled over by the police for speeding, they wanted to know a lot, they asked where he was going, and as he had crossed the border what was his reason for traveling to Minsk.

Naturally this eventuality was all pre planned for, Jack gave the police officer a number with a Minsk area code to verify he was visiting family, of course the number went to another operative who backed him up, the downside was the local police now had the registration number of the hire car so he was leaving a trail.

Jack was a little suspicious because the cops usually want a back hander then just let you go on your way, but this one seemed to be asking a lot of questions and was scrutinizing Jack as he was verifying his story and details, then the cop seemed quite nervous after he had spoken to someone else he called on the phone, all these

little signs put Jack on his guard, he drove off, still thinking about the encounter, then maybe he was being paranoid.
Jack was driving on his wits, he kept checking his mirror to see if he was being followed, alarm bells were still ringing, but why? Something just didn't feel right, eventually Jack put it down to the cop being probably the only straight cop in the country, no one was following him, maybe he was taking the Bond thing a bit too seriously.

Jack parked close to a restaurant in Minsk, he went inside and ordered some food and a coffee, the police stop was still on his mind so he was still being careful, He ate his meal alone and in silence, he was being vigilant except for the moment a long legged attractive girl entered to restaurant, one thing Jack had a weakness for was women, she walked to the counter, ordered a coffee and left, as she was leaving her and Jack's eyes met and as usual Jack was picturing her without the fur Jacket, hat and everything else she was wearing.

The street outside was quiet, Jack had left the cold rain some distance behind, now it was just cold, there was snow here and there on the ground, Jack paid for his food and left, as he approached the car he noticed two men walking away from it, this added to his suspicions that he was being followed, but why? As far as Jack was aware this was a simple job, a taxi run as the guys would say.

Chapter Fifteen
Nikki

As Jack was leaving Minsk he saw the girl with the legs again, she was trying to hitch a ride, thinking he might be able to mix business with pleasure he stopped and picked her up, "Where are you going?" Asked Jack, The girl replied in English but with an accent, "Orsha, and you?" " I'm actually going through Orsha" said Jack, The girl climbed in, "I am Nikki" she said, Jack replied "Jack, pleased to meet you Nikki." They had been on the road for over an hour when Jack's phone rang, it was mother, Jack held the phone up to his ear, when the call was finished he said to Nikki "I'm sorry I have to make a detour to Mogilev," " that's fine, I am in no hurry" she replied, "I mean it's an overnight delay, would you like me to drop you off?" said Jack, She didn't hesitate, she put a hand on Jack's knee and said "Overnight is good, but I have nowhere to stay in Mogilev," at that moment Jack knew he'd scored, this was definitely against procedure but if he was going to spend the night in a hotel why do it alone? He thought, Jack smiled at her, one thing Jack was good at was making the girls melt with just a smile, of course his rippling biceps and six pack helped a bit too.

Jack checked into the hotel, then the two of them went out clubbing. Nikki seemed to know people in the nightclub, Jack saw her a couple of times talking to some men who were sitting around a table in a separate area, he assumed she had been there several times before as she was fairly local and thought it rude to ask, anyway Jack was only interested in getting one thing from this girl.

The drinking and dancing over, they walked arms round each other back to the hotel, in the elevator Nikki was getting very friendly, she was feeling Jack through his trousers, as she pinned him against the wall, the doors opened and both slightly drunk they almost fell into the hallway, Jack opened the door and they both went inside the hotel room.

Jack went to the bathroom and as he returned he could feel the cold, the patio doors were open and Nikki was on the balcony, it was quite windy, her long hair was blowing around, Jack saw a trail of clothes along the floor, the fur Jacket, then her jeans, it was when he got closer he realized Nikki was stark naked in the bitter cold, Jack reached out and grabbed her hand, he pulled her back inside and closed the door, she was laughing, her nipples were rock hard from the cold, Jack thought he had better help so he began warming them with his mouth.

Nikki walked away, she was going to the bathroom, as she walked Jack watched her, she was tall and extremely thin but with all the right curves in all the right places, Jack poured some drinks while he was waiting for her.

Nikki returned, she was happy and playful, Jack asked her if she was cold, she said she liked the cold, it made her feel fresh and alive, he handed her the drink he'd just poured, she put it down and leaning forward she whispered in his ear, do you want to play now?
Jack without replying went to draw the blinds, Nikki said "No, leave them!" Jack said "but we're visible," Nikki laughed and said "Good, I love the idea of being watched" as she pulled him on to the bed,

Jack was trying to get intimate but Nikki was way too playful, she was making it fun, teasing him, rolling away, brushing his hand aside, Jack was wondering whether or not she actually wanted this and eventually he gave up playing her games and just lay on the bed, it was then Nikki got real, she wasn't interested in foreplay, she straddled him and immediately lowered herself onto Jack's erect penis, she was so tight it was almost painful as she started riding him, he reached out and felt her small breasts, he nipples were still hard like little pink bullets, he felt like she had taken the lead, not something Jack was used to, he had always been the dominant one, this was something different.
After a while Nikki climbed off Jack, she took him in her mouth, he was getting wet, she was deliberately soaking him with her saliva, it felt nice, then Nikki looked up at Jack and said "Do you want to get kinky?" Jack without thinking

simply nodded, he had an idea what she meant but he was happy to do whatever she wanted, Nikki got back into her previous position and lowered herself onto him again, his soaking wet slippery hard cock was now entering what his wife Carol referred to as the forbidden zone, for the first time in his life Jack was getting what he had only ever fantasized about, Nikki was pleasing herself with her fingers as she slowly moved up and down, Jack was getting close, the thought of what she was doing was driving him wild, he tried to hold on long enough for Nikki to get hers but it wasn't to be, all of a sudden Jack shot his cum forcefully up inside her, pushing up with his hips as he erupted, he moaned as waves of pleasure ran through him, Nikki felt it, this turned her on and she orgasmed too, Jack was getting sensitive he needed her to stop but like some kind of pleasurable torture she kept riding him slowly, drawing every last drop of semen from him, when she finally sat still, Nikki remained there with Jack still inside her, she leaned forward so she was face to face with him and said, "Good? Da!" Jack didn't need to answer, it was written all over his face.

Jack woke up in the early hours, he could see Nikki moving about in the dark, he stayed still as if asleep, maybe she was looking for money? He wasn't bothered by that as he had very little cash, he knew people in that particular area weren't well off by any means, she only had to ask and he would gladly have helped her out, this didn't make her a prostitute, just needy, she got back into bed, Jack said nothing.

Jack was woken by his phone, it was mother, he put the phone to his ear and the voice simply said "OK to proceed" then hung up, he was used to these odd calls, it was better never to discuss details, just enough to get things moving. He woke Nikki who was still sleeping soundly, he really didn't want her to get dressed straight away but he had work to do and they had to get going. Jack got dressed, while Nikki was in the bathroom he checked his wallet, the little cash he had was still there so maybe she had thought better of it.

They were both up and dressed, nothing was said about the night before, they just sat together drinking coffee before checking out. Jack was still thinking about last night's kinky sex with Nikki and couldn't help smiling a little as he finished his coffee, he thought about offering her some money but then didn't want her to be offended so decided she'd ask if she wanted some.
They drove off, Jack stopped the car in Orsha and let Nikki out, she thanked him for the ride, he smiled at her and said "thank YOU for the ride" with that Nikki laughed and walked away, Jack still smiling drove off, not far away was his destination, a place called Horki, close to the

Russian border, Jack watched his mirrors as he approached the rendezvous point, it seemed safe, there was a car waiting for him, in the car was a man and a woman, the man got out, approached

Chapter Sixteen
Ingrid

Jack and asked for the code word, Jack responded with "Truffles" then the man went back to his car, got the woman and whilst looking around in all directions walked her quickly over to Jack's car, she got in and the man threw her bag on the back seat before returning to his car and driving off.

As Jack pulled out, the rear side window of his car exploded into millions of tiny pieces of glass, Jack knew that was a shot, he changed direction and drove fast up a narrow hilly street which eventually led out of town, in the mirror Jack could see a car in the distance also traveling fast, the woman sat silent, gripping the side of her seat, the road became twisty and covered in loose gravel, the car was sliding around but Jack knew whatever the road threw at him those behind would have to deal with too, so he kept his speed up.

A truck appeared coming it the other direction, Jack positioned his car on the wrong side of the road, he was playing chicken with the truck, fearing a head on collision the woman started screaming "What are you doing? You're going to kill us!" Jack said nothing, he sped up, he was concentrating on the truck, he could see the driver, the truck horn sounded continuously, Jack didn't back off, at the last possible moment the truck swerved to avoid Jack, the rear quarter of Jack's car hit the side of the truck as they passed each other ripping the plastic rear bumper off, Jack was hanging on to a car almost out of control, he got it straight again, and just before he went over the brow of the hill he caught sight of the truck Jackknifing in his mirror.

Knowing the road was now blocked and would be for some time Jack slowed down,
He looked across at the woman who then introduced herself as Ingrid, Jack could hear the Russian accent in her voice, she was a woman in her mid thirties, quite attractive if you look beyond the frumpy dress sense, she was a little shaken by the recent encounter with the truck but was obviously getting over it, she didn't say much. Jack had a problem, he had no idea where this road went, he had just gone for a street to get them away from the shooter, they kept going, there was obviously no turning back now. Jack's sense of direction was telling him they needed to turn left but this road was just going on and on, no junction anywhere to be seen, then the car started making a familiar noise, "Flat!" thought Jack, he pulled over and got out, sure enough among the damage to the rear of the car the tyre had gone, a piece of torn bodywork had punctured it, Jack grabbed the spare and with the wheel wrench banged the bodywork out away from the wheel, this had cost him time, he was on

the wrong road, going in the wrong direction and he was going to miss the next rendezvous.

Jack tried to call mother but there was no phone reception, finally there was a turning on the left, he took it, the road was narrow and looked as if no one had traveled that way for a long time, the further they drove, the worse it got, at one point the greenery on the banks was brushing the sides of the car, the tarmac had become loose gravel and frozen puddles.

Ingrid finally said something, "Have you got any idea where we are? Why have you brought us down this farm track of a road?" Jack ignored her and continued slowly, the road widened a little, Jack thought this was only going to get better, then they came across a bridge and obviously the reason this road hadn't been used for years, the bridge was down. There was no going back because they were being chased and this wrecked car would only draw attention if they drove into a town, so only one option, continue on foot and find another way.
They had to get off this road, it was only a matter of time before the bad guys figured out where they'd gone and the only option was to get across the river, it wasn't that deep, but it was cold, if they waded it they'd have to deal with wet clothes in sub zero temperatures, Jack searched the nearby hedgerows and field, he came back with a long branch, long enough to reach across

the broken bridge, it didn't look that strong but it would have to do, Jack laid the branch in place, while he steadied it Ingrid did a careful walk to the other side, she looked like a Gymnast on a bar, she was steady and confident, Jack however didn't feel quite so secure, Ingrid tried to hold the branch in place from the other side but it was thinner there and harder to grip.

Jack tried to walk across like he was on a tightrope but the branch rolled a bit, he lost his footing and fell, he managed to grab hold and ended up crawling across but just over half way his phone, his lifeline, fell from his pocket and plunged into the water, he didn't realize until he was up on his feet on the far side of the bridge, he reached for his phone to see if there was any signal yet but it was gone!
Jack didn't say anything about it, he didn't want to tell Ingrid they were now on their own because she was in a bit of a state already after recent events, Jack kicked the branch into the river and it vanished downstream on the rushing water.

"What now?" asked Ingrid, Jack looked around, there was a woods on the other side of the field and needing to get out of sight Jack said to head that way, they both set off.
It only took about ten minutes to reach the woodland and it didn't take long to find a well worn path which they followed, hoping to find a town or even a village.

All the time they were walking Jack was trying to figure out how they had been compromised, he had kept an eye out all the way there, he was sure he hadn't been followed, it was unlikely to be the operative who did the hand over because the shooter only showed up after Jack had arrived, they would have made a grab for Ingrid sooner, nothing was making sense.

Thirty minutes later they came across a car park and a main road, a sign outside said Lenino so they walked in that direction, Lenino turned out to be a large village, Jack needed to get to a town to hire a car, there was nothing here. He stopped at a cash point and put in his bank card, he drew out enough money for something to eat and get change for a bus to the nearest town, there was a café so they both went inside and ordered some food.

"Do you have a change of clothes in that bag?" Asked Jack, Ingrid replied "yes but I've worn them already, they'll be a bit dirty now", Jack suggested they get her something more practical to wear when they get to town and do what they can to change their appearance, they left the café and headed to the bus stop, Jack was trying to fathom out the timetable, he couldn't read it so Ingrid did, "The next bus is in twenty minutes and it goes to Horki" She said, Jack thought about that, maybe that was good, the shooter would never think they would go back to there.

They had only been at the bus stop for a few minutes when a car came speeding down the street, the racing engine sound caught Jack's attention, he saw a gun barrel protruding from the passenger window, Jack Grabbed Ingrid and pulled her to the ground just as the gunman opened fire, the glass around the bus shelter shattered, the few people in the street ran for cover. Holding onto Ingrid's hand Jack ran into an alleyway.

The car had turned around and as it passed the end of the Alley, Jack and Ingrid ducked down behind a commercial bin, just then a police car stopped at the end of the Alley, Ingrid went to get up, Jack stopped her, "But why?" she said, Jack pulled Ingrid further under cover and said "I have no idea how they're tracking us and I have no idea who's involved but I wouldn't trust anyone at the moment, no one!" The police drove off.

Music was playing not far away, Jack and Ingrid made their way carefully towards it,
It was a taxi, the driver was sitting there smoking something he shouldn't and listening to the radio which was way too loud, Jack and Ingrid kept low and got into the back seat of the taxi, this startled the driver who said he was on his break so they'd have to find another cab, Ingrid spoke to the driver and offered him a good sum of money to get them to Horki, they set off, Jack and Ingrid were laying flat on the back seat

which amused the driver until he asked quite seriously, "Are you hiding from the police?" Ingrid replied "No we're hiding from his wife!" pointing to Jack, of course Jack had no idea what was being said as he didn't speak the lingo, but it made the taxi driver laugh.

The taxi dropped them off in the main shopping area, this was good as they could mingle among the crowd, they went into a big clothing shop and bought some practical clothes for both of them, then they booked into a nearby hotel, they needed to lie low for a while to try and figure out what was going on, once in the room Jack suspected Ingrid may have a bug on her, so the first thing he did was to tip her bag out on the bed, Jack searched it thoroughly, checked the lining, her bits and pieces like makeup mirror, Jack found nothing, he told Ingrid to strip, she guessed he was looking for something like a tracker so she didn't argue, she stripped down to her underwear, Jack searched her clothes thoroughly then told her to hand over the rest, Ingrid protested but did it anyway, first her bra, she passed it to Jack while she tried to cover herself with her arm, Jack felt all around the strap, and examined every inch of it, the same with her knickers, now Ingrid was getting embarrassed, even more so when Jack walked closer to her and began searching her hair, he pulled off the elastic ring which held it all up, Ingrid's hair fell down around her shoulders and Jack continued to search as if he was looking for head lice.

Ingrid now totally naked and feeling embarrassed ran to the bathroom, Jack noted her soft round buttocks and how they seemed to dance a little as she went, but then stripped off himself and searched his own clothes, there had to be something somewhere but no, Jack found nothing, Then he thought, maybe his card had been compromised and they're following transactions? Jack called Ingrid from the bathroom and told her to get dressed quickly, they grabbed their stuff and rushed downstairs, Jack checked out, they both ran down the street and when Jack found a cash point, he stopped and withdrew a good amount of cash, then they booked into another hotel in the same street using cash, Jack thought if it was his card the shooter would think they're in the first hotel.

When Jack and Ingrid got into the hotel room, Ingrid noticed it was a double bed, the previous one had twin beds, she thought that might be awkward but it was the least of their problems, "Can I finish my shower now?" asked Ingrid, Jack said "I guess so" and off once more to the bathroom she went, Once she had finished Jack showered and changed, he noticed Ingrid looked quite sexy in her new tight jeans and baggy sweater but Jack was on a job and one thing he was told not to do was get involved with the client.

Pizza was ordered from the local takeaway and Jack paid for it in cash, after they had eaten they sat and watched TV for a while, not that Jack understood any of it but Ingrid did, he asked her if there was anything related on the news but she said there wasn't. It looked as if they'd given their pursuers the slip, for now anyway.

About ten pm that night police sirens were howling in the street, the flashing lights lit up the room, Jack carefully looked out of the window, it was all happening at the other hotel, it looked as if he was right, it was his company card they were following and that could only mean one thing, the information was coming from his own people, what the hell was going on!

Chapter Seventeen
Temptation

Sleeping in a bed with a woman without access was very difficult for Jack, especially one wearing next to nothing, just a pair of knickers and a T shirt, he went to sleep hoping he didn't mistake Ingrid for Carol while he slept, after Jack had been sleeping for a while Ingrid was woken by Jack, not deliberately as he was asleep but she'd moved around and was now laying with her back to him and his erection was pressing against her, right between her thighs, she thought about moving away but then thought oh why not enjoy the moment, she didn't touch it or wriggle about even though she was turned on just in case she woke him, so she just lay still enjoying the attention until she fell asleep again.

Morning came bursting through the window, it was still cold outside but there was a clear sky and the sun was shining. Jack got up and went to the bathroom, as he walked past the other side of the bed he looked at Ingrid, still laying there asleep and noticed her T shirt had ridden up and he could see the curve of the underside of her breasts, such a shame she was off limits he thought.

Ingrid woke to a cup of coffee that Jack had just made, Jack switched on the TV and there it was on the news, a couple had been shot and killed in the hotel up the road, that was where Jack and Ingrid were supposed to be, the hotel must have re let the room, this may have given Jack and Ingrid an advantage, especially if the gunman thought they were dead, the heat would be off, or at least until the identity of the victims was released.

The problem of the leak still remained, if Jack got in touch with the company or used his card it would soon get back to the bad guys that he was still alive, now was the window of opportunity, now they had to vanish, They left the hotel and went to a nearby hairdressers, Ingrid had her lovely long hair cut short and dyed blonde, Jack bought a black baseball cap from a nearby shop and pulled it down at the front, even their own mother's wouldn't recognize them now, there wasn't enough cash to buy a car and they couldn't hire one because Jack would have had to provide his card for security so it was public transport from Horki to wherever they were going, ultimately England but that was going to be dangerous because the second they hit immigration they'd be flagged up at base and that's where the leak was, so where to go?

Jack thought about Paris and Sophia but did he really want to involve her? And what would she think if he turned up with Ingrid, Sophia didn't

know about Jack's work, it was all very hush hush.
Jack decided the best plan of action was to get back to the UK without going through customs, he had a sort of half a plan, first they had to get to Latvia, they were currently in Belarus which has close ties with Russia, Jack believed it was the Russians who were trying to stop Ingrid. Going via Latvia also had it's problems as Latvians were generally pro Russia and the country shares a border, the alternative would be to head south, totally the wrong direction and there was a war raging in the Ukraine, going back the way he came was not safe so it looked like Latvia was the way,

The pair stood waiting for a bus and late as they always are in that region it finally arrived, Ingrid did the talking as she spoke the language, Jack remained mute, an Englishman there would have stood out like a goose in the chicken run.

They boarded the bus which was terminating at Orsha, Jack wondered if he'd spot Nikki but Orsha is a big place so the odds were against it. The bus ride was soon over, how were they to move on from Orsha, by train may well have meant showing identification and passports if they realized Jack was a non national which no doubt they would, ideally they needed a car, Jack considered stealing one but these days it's all computer control and immobilizer, you can't just hotwire a car like in the movies, "What about hitching a ride?" said Ingrid, Jack didn't even consider it, "too risky" he said, Ingrid argued the point saying "we don't look anything like we did, so why is it too risky? Do we even have a choice?"

Chapter Eighteen
The Motel

It took most of the day to hitch hike to Lepiel even though it was only one hundred and twenty miles, no one seemed to want to pick them up, just a sign of the times Jack thought, they were tired and exhausted despite having one whole day without being chased or shot at.

They checked into a cheap motel and paid cash, it wasn't bad, a self contained chalet with a parking space out front for the car they didn't have, Jack was still feeling insecure about handing in his passport at reception but he didn't have alternate identity papers this time and no way of getting any. Ingrid was in the same situation, it seemed like she was one of Russia's most wanted and all she had were genuine documents.

They were in the chalet, Ingrid was watching the news in case anything connected came on, Jack was making coffee as it'd been hours since they had a drink.
It was quiet, the occasional vehicle moving around outside, then just after eleven that night there was a knock at the door, Jack told Ingrid to get in the bathroom, he then called through the door, "Who is it?" the reply came "Hotel manager, can I have a word?" Jack unlocked the

door and opened it just a little, there was a loud bang as the guy outside booted the door, Jack instinctively grabbed him by both ears, pulled his head downwards whilst driving his right knee hard into the guy's face, the gun he was reaching for flew up into the air and Jack caught it as the guy hit the floor, he was out cold and bleeding from his broken nose. Ingrid was already half way out of the bathroom window when Jack got to the bathroom door, there was the sound of a car screeching to a stop out front and no sooner had Jack cleared the window another guy burst in from the front door almost tripping on the first one.

Ingrid had run towards reception at the other end of the chalets, she was in the other car park behind the chalets, the second gunman was still climbing through the bathroom window when Jack ran round to the front and jumped in the guy's car which was still running and the driver's door still open wide, he drove fast back the way he'd come, skidding in the loose gravel at the end of the row of chalets, the gunman was still chasing after Ingrid, he stopped when he heard Jack coming, he dropped to one knee and began firing at the windscreen, Jack ducked down and ran the guy over with his own car, there was a sickening crunch sound as the car bounced over him, Jack stopped by Ingrid and shouted, "Get in!" Which she did, then he stopped outside the office, he ran inside, the clerk was lying dead across the desk, Jack and Ingrid's passports were on the floor, Jack grabbed them and the pair of them sped off into the night.

Jack was driving fast until he found a turning and got off the main road, "We'll have to ditch this car before too long, but at least we have our passports he said, Jack glanced over at Ingrid, she was shaken, she looked scared, How far will this car get us?" she asked, Jack didn't know, his plan was to stick to the back roads, they didn't want to get seen by the cops as there wasn't an honest one in the whole country. There was no way they were going to drive across the border and without visas they were going to have to sneak across somehow.

They drove through a small village called Okono and onward through dense forestry, there was a big tarmac yard with a row of small run down units by it, Jack pulled in, "we need to get rid of this car" he said, "it's low on fuel and we're going to get to the motorway if we keep going, the best bet now is to hide out for a while," they both got out, Jack picked up the gun and they checked the car for anything useful, in the boot there was a bag, inside the bag were a selection of weapons, ammunition, and a toolbox with all sorts of bit's and bobs in it, Jack took the bag, threw anything useful from inside the toolbox into the bag with the guns, he then tore off a piece of fabric from a seat, stuffed it in the petrol filler, set it alight and ran after Ingrid. The car didn't explode but did go up pretty impressively, there was a bit of popping and a big whoosh sound as the fuel tank went up.

Jack and Ingrid followed the path into the woods, it was pitch black in there, they could hardly make out where the sides of the path were, it was slow going. Eventually daylight started to show, the two of them had walked for miles, this massive forest seemed to go on forever, the path was obviously some sort of tourist trail as occasionally there would be a little marker with an arrow on it showing the way, it was unlikely they'd see anyone this time of year so it was pretty safe.

After walking for hours they came across a log cabin, some sort of hunting lodge Jack guessed, he jimmied a window open then unlocked the door with the spare key someone had left hanging on the inside of it. Jack gathered some logs from the stack by the cabin while Ingrid checked out the facilities.
 The place was dusty, it hadn't been used for months, there was everything they needed to hold up for quite some time until the heat died off. There were even cans of food in the cupboard, a gas cooker and two full bottles of gas, no bath but there was a sink fed from a water tank on a tower outside, and hot water once the gas boiler was started.

There was only one room in the cabin and an outside toilet but it was warm and relatively safe, they must be at least five miles from where they torched the car and several twists and turns into the forest, it was extremely unlikely anyone would find them. Ingrid cleaned up the place a bit, Jack made some wire rabbit snares, that was something he'd learned as a kid, it was comfortable, there was no phone, no TV so no outside communication at all, they hadn't decided how long they were going to be there but they were in no hurry to get shot.

After a few days the two of them were starting to relax, they'd caught up on sleep and life in the cabin was beginning to feel like a holiday, they only had the clothes they were wearing and they needed washing, so it was decided to do something about it, after all it wouldn't be the first time they had seen each other naked, Jack stripped off while Ingrid ran a sink of hot water, then she too got undressed, all their clothes were washed and hung up on a line across the room to dry, it was cold outside but they shouldn't take long indoors with the roaring fire they had going.

Jack was trying not to look at Ingrid because he knew what would happen, he tried to think about other things but Jack's one track mind came back to sex every time, so it wasn't long before the beast raised it's head, Jack thought about putting a pillow over it but that would have been too obvious, there was nothing he could do but sit there with his stiff cock pointing at the ceiling while he waited for his clothes to dry. Ingrid smiled and said laughing "Can I hang my hat on that?" Jack just smiled, he wasn't embarrassed but it did make him feel a bit awkward. "Do you want to do something about that?" She said pointing, "It's against the rules," said Jack, "No touching the client," Ingrid laughed, "OK she said, "is it against the rules for the client to touch you? Jack thought for a moment, "Not that I know of" he said, Ingrid sat down beside him and took him in hand.

Jack laid back on the bed as Ingrid stroked him gently and slowly, Jack was laying on his hands so he couldn't break the rules, Ingrid knew this was difficult for him so she deliberately teased him, she put her face close, put her tongue out and almost touched the tip of his cock while Jack watched her closely in the hope she would take him into her mouth, she was being so cruel and it was driving him crazy. She spent ages torturing him, she gently fondled his balls and again pretended to lick them, then there was a whistle, Ingrid let go of Jack and in a matter of fact sort of way said, "Kettle's boiled," Ingrid left Jack frustrated and mid stride to simply make coffee, she took the kettle off the hook where it hung over the fire and poured it into their cups and sat down again.

Jack couldn't believe it, "what!" he thought "What the hell!" Ingrid looked at him and laughed "Rules" she said "Rules! Who would know?" She did have a point and Jack thought about it then decided, to hell with the rules but the moment had passed, "maybe later" he thought.

Jack tried it on with Ingrid several times over the next week or so but all she did was push him away laughing and say "It's against the rules!"

They had been in the cabin for a couple of weeks, one day they ventured outside to check the snares, they were now running low on food and there didn't seem to be many rabbits about or at least they weren't catching many, "lucky day" Jack thought as the first snare had caught a nice big one, Jack snapped it's neck, they checked the other snares but nothing so they returned to the cabin, Jack skinned and cleaned the rabbit while Ingrid opened a can of new potatoes and a can of beans, one thing there was plenty of was beans. The rabbit was tasty although once cooked there wasn't a lot of meat on it, after dinner they sat and read one of the many magazines in the cabin, some were in English, mostly adult magazines, old copies of playboy and fiesta, the stories were still valid but mostly wildly exaggerated, some things in life just don't change, thought Jack.

Chapter Nineteen
Breaking the rules

It was late, Jack and Ingrid turned in, this was Ingrid's favorite time of night in the cabin, it was warm and cozy, in a big comfortable bed with the room lit up by the flickering firelight, she thought it was so romantic, and to top it off she was in bed with a good looking guy, to save their only set of clothes they were sleeping naked and after Ingrid had been pushing him away for over a week and now seemed interested, there was no way Jack was ready to sleep. Ingrid didn't need any encouragement either, Jack whispered, "Wanna break some rules?" "All of them" replied Ingrid, and with that Jack slid down under the covers, it took him moments to find what he was seeking among the forest of dark curly hair, Ingrid was already wet and it wasn't long before she erupted, pulsating waves of pleasure surged through her, she tensed up, Jack thought she was going to break his neck as she clenched her thighs together, as soon as the moment passed Jack continued teasing her with his tongue, rolling her clit round and round, then flicking it with his tongue, every now and then Ingrid would get close and her body would tense up, Jack knew she was about to cum so he stopped for a moment, if she wanted a second one she would have to wait for it, this game continued for a while then Ingrid was cumming and there was no stopping her, she moaned as her powerful surges took control of her body, involuntary trusting and wriggling as she experienced the absolute pleasure Jack had brought her to.

After resting for a minute Ingrid went to work on Jack, this time she wasn't teasing, she went straight onto his erect cock with her eager mouth, sucking hard while her head moved quickly up and down, her tongue wrapping around his shaft, Jack had to stop her it would all be over too fast if he didn't, Ingrid let him relax for a moment then getting out of bed she went over to the old armchair by the fire, she bent over and put her hands on the arms of the chair, Jack could see the firelight reflecting on her skin, "Come here!" she ordered, Jack obeyed, he stood behind her, she put one hand under herself and guided him inside, she was so warm, so wet and she made Jack so horny, his erection was so hard he felt like his cock was going to explode, he pushed deep inside her, she cried out in pleasure so Jack pushed harder, long slow strokes but very deep, Ingrid was loving every movement, eventually as Jack was getting close, Ingrid could feel it and hear his breathing change, she said "Don't cum inside me Jack, Don't, and as Jack withdrew, Ingrid spun around dropped to her knees and immediately took him in her mouth, within a few strokes of those soft red lips sliding the length of his shaft and with an almighty groan Jack erupted, Ingrid choked a little as he filled her throat with his cum, he stopped moving but was still cumming, Ingrid withdrew, she couldn't breathe with Jack so far in and the amount he was producing was too much to handle, finally finished Ingrid ran to the sink and was choking it all up, half choking and half laughing,

"Did you enjoy that?" she said once she had composed herself, Jack simply smiled and said "Did you?" They both knew the answer to each others question so no response was necessary, instead they got back into bed and snuggled up.

Early morning, they were woken by the sound of barking dogs, Jack jumped out of bed and ran to the window, there were people coming, he could see them on the path, still some distance away, Ingrid was almost dressed, Jack was just putting his second shoe on when the door burst open, there was nowhere to run.

Two men carrying rifles and two dogs on long leads were standing between Jack and the door, the only exit, One of the men said something in Russian, Ingrid answered, there was a short but friendly exchange between the two, the man who was obviously a hunter said something to Jack but was intercepted by Ingrid, they then obviously said some sort of goodbye and Ingrid signaled Jack to leave.

Once they were some distance down the path Jack asked Ingrid what that was all about, she said the cabin wasn't the property of anyone really, it had been abandoned for years so the local hunters fixed it up for general use, it was basically free shelter for anyone who needed it, "What a great idea" said Jack "but what about the locked door?" Ingrid explained the key is held in the shop in the village, they didn't ask how Jack and Ingrid were there while they had the key.

Jack had been expecting trouble when the owner of the cabin turned up so this was one hell of a stroke of luck. It wasn't long before traffic could be heard, the two found the main road and within a minute of sticking out a thumb a car stopped, Ingrid did the talking and off they went, she had been telling people Jack was mute and he knew not to speak but just sort of nod if spoken to, he wondered who was actually rescuing who at times.

By the end of the day they reached a village called Yarevo, this was actually not where they were heading for but just as good, the only difference was they now had to cross the nearby border into Lithuania instead of Latvia as planned, not tonight though thought Jack, they found a farm just outside the village and settled into a barn for the night, things were going well at this point, they hadn't been chased or shot at for about three weeks, admittedly most of that was holed up in the cabin in the woods, Jack wondered if the Russians who were chasing them still thought they were both dead or had they found out otherwise, Jack hadn't used his card anywhere so he felt they were still fairly invisible.

Chapter Twenty
The border

Their biggest problem was going to be the border, because of the war between Russia and the Ukraine border security between Belarus and Lithuania was very tight and there would be regular patrols along the fence, without visas getting across by road would be a non starter, especially as Ingrid was on her genuine Russian passport.

They took a walk to see what the situation was and there was no hope of crossing without some serious help, help came with risks.

After a ten mile hike to Pastavy Jack used what cash he had left to buy a cheap pay and go phone, well of course Ingrid did the talking, once he had it set up he called Carol at home, "Hi sweetheart, I need you to do me a favour, I need you to take this number to my work, ask for Sally in ops, don't speak to anyone else, when you see Sally just give her this number," Carol somewhat stunned by the lack of explanation asked, "Where are you?" Jack told her he couldn't say, it was to do with work but please hurry, Carol was used to this cloak and dagger stuff although she didn't know what Jack's job was all about, she knew not to ask.

Jack and Ingrid were sitting in a park when the phone rang, It was Sally, Jack spoke quietly so his English didn't get overheard, he explained he was stuck and needed papers and a car to cross the Belarus border into Lithuania, he also explained he suspected a leak within the company, that said, Jack and Ingrid waited in the park, Jack was getting worried, he had no idea who the leak was, he knew he could trust Sally but who did she have to consult to make things happen? That call alone was risky, it seemed whenever Jack made a move the Russians were on him in a flash.

Jack turned to Ingrid, "What's this all about?" She replied, "I can't tell you, if we get caught they will torture you to find out what you know and who you've told, so it's better if you don't know," Jack then thought about Ingrid, "Won't they torture you?" "No" she said, they already know I know, they'll either take me back to Russia or kill me, but they'll torture you to find out how far it's gone, either way we're both dead!"

"I think we had better get off this bench" said Jack, Ingrid asked why, Jack explained he couldn't trust anyone and the company knew exactly where they were, they moved, not far, just stood by a tree from where they could see the bench, it had been several hours since Sally called when an old white Lada car pulled into the car park, a man got out and walked over to the bench, Jack watched as the man casually looked around then he sat down on the bench, he made a call, then a few minutes later Jack's phone rang again, it was Sally, She said "Jack, hand the package over to the man on the bench, he will give you papers to get yourself across the border, we will have a car there for you tonight," with that the phone went dead.

Jack quickly explained to Ingrid that she was to go with the other guy, she refused, "No, I stay with you or I don't go at all!" she protested, "OK said Jack, wait here," Ingrid moved behind the tree as Jack walked towards the man on the bench, he was about twenty feet away when a shot rang out and the man on the bench fell sideways, he had been shot, Jack ran to him, ducking low and as fast as he could searched the man's pockets, he found a brown envelope, a wallet, a phone and some keys, taking them Jack ran back to Ingrid, there were two men running across the park in their direction, Jack and Ingrid ran towards the White Lada in the car park.

As soon as they reached it the men stopped and ran back the way they had just come from, Jack opened the doors and yelled "Get in!" Ingrid hadn't closed the door when Jack reversed at speed turning the car on a sixpence and with tyres screeching took off down the road. Jack could see the shooters in his mirror, they had a much faster car than the beat up old Lada Jack was driving, luckily it was one of the most common cars on the road there and they all seemed to be white, he mingled with the traffic trying to get the shooters to follow someone else, Jack turned off the main road into a maze of back streets, then into a huge car park, parked in a bay and they both got out of the car and hid behind an old wooden booth where the car park attendant pretended he was doing some work.

The shooters were driving slowly up and down the rows of parked cars, once they had passed the wooden shed Jack and Ingrid ran into a shopping precinct, it was packed, a great place to lose yourself, they sat down in a coffee shop and ordered a coffee each.

Jack opened the envelope, inside he found papers which would get him across the border but nothing for Ingrid, the wallet had a little cash, a company card, and the guy's identity card and driving license, there was also a photo of who Jack assumed were his wife and three children, he thought about them for a moment and felt thankful he didn't have any kids, or as far as he knew anyway, all this stuff and still no way of getting Ingrid across the border, how had they been found? It was looking more and more like a leak within the company, surely not Sally? She was the last person Jack would suspect, who had she talked to? It was a puzzle Jack had to work out, why did the Russians want Ingrid so bad?

They drank their coffee, Ingrid said "Do you think it's safe to go back to the car?" Jack thought about it then decided not, they must have found the car in the mall car park by now, and they'll probably be staking it out. Jack looked at the dead guy's phone, it was a company phone and had the usual entries in the contacts list, he thought about calling mother from it but what if that phone had been compromised, he knew mother or father wouldn't be at base, they are the local contacts to where the phone was issued but they are also obliged to liaise with the company on all issues so Jack thought if he could persuade mother that headquarters was not to be trusted, but how could he do that, mother wouldn't trust him, not knowing who he was and calling from a local operatives phone shortly after he'd been killed, it was all very suspect.

Jack accepted they were on their own, at least for the time being. Finally something dropped into place, Jack led Ingrid out of the café and into the main shopping mall, he was looking around, then he suddenly changed direction he said to Ingrid, "I need you to get that girl to talk to us somewhere quiet," he pointed to a woman in the crowd, Ingrid spoke to the girl in Russian and she walked with them back to the café, Ingrid whispered to Jack, "this is it, she wants to stay somewhere public, you can't blame her," Jack whispered back, "find out where her loyalties are," there was a conversation between the two women, at one point the woman looked shocked and Jack got quite nervous, all she had to do was start screaming or shouting and the game was up, she didn't, in fact she seemed to be coming around quite nicely, Ingrid arranged a meet in the park in thirty minutes, swore the girl to secrecy and the girl headed off.

Ingrid turned to Jack and said "What are you up to?" Jack just smiled "I have a plan, he said, we will need some money," given that the Russians were aware Jack and Ingrid were in Pastavy Jack decided to get what he could from a cash point, the trouble was any company card transactions would be immediately noticed but it was a chance he had to take, Ingrid waited around the corner, Jack inserted the card and withdrew a wad of cash, he was quite surprised it worked at all, quickly the two of them ran through narrow streets and back alleys to get away from the area without being spotted.

Chapter Twenty one
Saskia

About three in the afternoon Jack and Ingrid arrived at the park and sitting on the bench where the other operative had been killed earlier that day was the girl from the shopping mall, She looked reasonably similar to Ingrid which is why Jack chose her, he explained the deal, Ingrid translated, the girl who's name was Saskia would receive the money Jack had just withdrawn in exchange for Saskia's documents, identification card and passport, she would need to apply for a visa which would take about two weeks, she would get half the money now and the other half when the task was complete.

Ingrid would call her with the location where the rest of the cash was hidden, then Saskia was to report she had been robbed in order to cover herself, by then Jack and Ingrid should be across the border,

To Saskia this was a lot of money and she seemed keen, the only problem now was where to stay for two or so weeks.

Saskia was given the number of the pay and go phone Jack had bought previously so she could call when it was all ready. Of course there was a risk that she would just keep the first payment and vanish but that was a chance they had to take.

As they were about to part company Saskia said something to Ingrid, Jack looked at them and said "What?" Ingrid told Jack that Saskia had offered to put them up at her place, Jack thought about that and despite being very risky he agreed as he couldn't think of an alternative, this girl was turning out to be something of a blessing, it seemed.

It was quite a walk to Saskia's place, and it wasn't very big it was not much more than a bed-sit, one bed and it's own bathroom but it was warm and dry, Saskia left to fetch the visa application form, this was a very nervous time for Jack and Ingrid, they wondered whether or not Saskia would return alone or with the authorities, she was still a stranger but looking around the room she needed the money. Late afternoon and there was a key in the door, Jack and Ingrid stood there holding their breath, half expecting to be looking down the barrel of a gun at any moment, it was such a relief when Saskia came in, she had shopping and the all important paperwork.

After filling in the form and gathering all the supporting documentation Saskia started cooking, it was too late to take the forms to the post office to send off, the food smelled great, Jack was starving, they all sat down to eat, the girls on the bed and Jack in the only chair, this was what he expected the sleeping arrangements would be but a chair is better than being outside in the cold.

Saskia didn't speak any English so the conversation that night was pretty much between the two girls who seemed to be getting on great. It was late and time to turn in. There was no privacy except perhaps the small bathroom but both of the girls got undressed in front of Jack, Ingrid had explained to Saskia that she had no nightclothes, Saskia said she didn't wear anything anyway, of course Jack couldn't understand what was being said so he was quite surprised when they both got into bed together naked, Jack stripped down to his boxers and got under a blanket in the chair, Ingrid said to Jack, "Saskia says you cant sleep like that, get in here with us", Jack certainly wasn't going to complain about that and wasted no time in climbing in alongside Ingrid.

It was about four in the morning when Jack opened an eye, he could feel movement in the bed, in the dimly lit room it was hard to see what was going on but then Ingrid let out one of her quiet moans, she was trying not to wake Jack but he knew what that sound meant, suspecting Ingrid was either dreaming or discreetly touching herself he rolled over on his side and tried to get to sleep again, it was then he felt something touching him, he put his hand under the covers to find a hand on his cock, Jack was getting hard thinking about Ingrid's hand on him but she was the one making the moaning sounds, what was going on? Only after feeling about under the covers did he realize what was happening, Saskia had her face up between Ingrid's thighs and was eating her pussy, Ingrid realizing Jack was awake had grabbed hold of his cock and was stroking him as best she could whilst wriggling about in absolute ecstasy as Saskia expertly licked and sucked her.

Jack was getting very horny, not just because Ingrid was stroking him but the thought of Saskia going down on Ingrid was a dream come true, he wondered if he was going to get some of Saskia too, but then thought maybe she's just into girls, and decided not to blow it by being pushy. Ingrid was getting very worked up, so much so that she could no longer deal with Jack, so he just laid there enjoying the show, albeit in the dark, Ingrid's breathing was getting faster and deeper, her breasts were heaving up and down, Jack could feel her entire body next to him moving in rhythm with Saskia's tongue until she muttered something in Russian, Jack knew she was cumming and in a big way, he felt a little inadequate that he had not managed to excite Ingrid quite that much.

Jack was feeling left out as Ingrid threw herself on top of Saskia, they were now eating each other, two women in bed totally naked next to him and going at it like it was the end of the world and

Jack just lay there watching with his hand on his cock, a car drove past and the headlights lit up the room enough for Jack to see Saskia laying on her back next to him with her face glistening where she was covered in Ingrid's juices, she was tasting Ingrid's wet pussy above her while Ingrid worked hers, it wasn't long before Saskia gave out a sound which told Jack she was there too, this excited Ingrid who then licked Saskia slower she seemed to like this, Ingrid could tell Saskia was getting sensitive but didn't stop, instead she licked her very lightly which seemed to get Saskia going for a second time, she was talking quietly and intensely in Russian and then it happened, Saskia went as rigid as a board, Jack could feel her stiffen up right next to him, he was sure he could hear Ingrid lapping up Saskia's cum as she erupted for the second time.

Totally exhausted the two girls lay next to each other breathing heavily, the breathing subsided and Jack thought he could hear them tenderly kissing each other or was that just wishful thinking?

Morning, and everyone was awake, traffic was getting busy outside, Saskia was getting dressed, she had to work, Ingrid once again asked her not to breathe a word to anyone, Saskia left for work, Jack and Ingrid were in the room alone, Jack smiling said "Did you enjoy yourself last night?" Ingrid not sure how to take that asked "Why?

Was it a problem for you?" Jack still smiling said "No not at all, I enjoyed it very much," Ingrid smiled and said "I need to sleep," Jack agreed and they both drifted off. It was difficult to sleep during the day, the road outside was noisy and the blinds didn't stop the sun very much, but the biggest reason was the worry, this place had only one route of escape, the door, "I hope she doesn't talk to anyone about us" said Jack, Ingrid said she trusted Saskia, she seemed to be genuine and as Jack knew, the girls had become very good friends.
Just after four Saskia returned home, Ingrid was already cooking a meal for the three of them, as she came in through the door she gave Ingrid that look, the look that says last night was great and I want more, the girls talked for a while, Jack was feeling like a spare part but their lives depended on Saskia so he put his emotions aside, this was going to be a tough couple of weeks imprisoned in this overcrowded room and playing gooseberry to the girls.
Second day at Saskia's and Jack decided to try to find the leak, he left Ingrid in the room and went for a walk, once a good distance away and in a quiet spot Jack called mother on the dead guy's phone, There was an answer, a woman, she asked "Who is this?" Jack replied "It's password Truffles" she then said sounding quite surprised "Hello my boy, do you want to meet up?" Jack said yes and arranged to meet at the bus stop, he gave her the exact location, Jack then watched

the bus stop from the coffee shop across the road, after about ten minutes a car drove slowly past the bus stop, Jack could see a woman inside, she was looking around, he waited a while, the car drove off followed by a call, Jack answered the phone, it was mother, "What happened?" she asked, Sorry said Jack, "I got delayed, can we meet tomorrow?" "of course" said mother, Jack waited a while, he saw her coming back down the road and drove straight past the bus stop, Jack was trying to find out if she was alone or being shadowed, he wasn't quite sure how but the first step was to see if she would actually answer and then if she would turn up, Jack pulled the sim card and battery out of the phone, put all three items in his pocket and left.

He was being cautious because he had no idea what anyone was up to, was he being set up, was there a leak and if so who was it, The following day Jack called mother again, this time he arranged the meet to be at the café in the shopping mall where he and Ingrid had gone previously when they were being chased. This was good as it was very public, Jack made his way across town, he sat at the same table and waited, he didn't have to wait long, a woman sat down opposite him, She was very smartly dressed, a beige suit Jacket and skirt, her hair was up, Jack thought she looked a bit like Audrey Hepburn, she said "I wonder if they sell truffles here?" That was all Jack needed, the key word.

"What's going on?" He asked, the woman spoke quietly "Where's the package?" She said, Jack simply replied "safe," then she asked, "What do you want?" Jack said "I just want to do my job but it seems we have a leak somewhere, every move I make someone is there trying to kill me," the woman thought about that for a moment, then she said, "Possibly but who knows your every move?" "I think they have access to company cards, they seem to be wherever I use mine" said Jack, the woman looked at him and said "you are not alone, several agents have been eliminated over the past few weeks on unrelated jobs, the only way they could follow the cards is if they had access to all the company cards, but how?" Jack paused then said "How did you pay for your coffee just now?" She replied "with my card of course" it was the moment it all fell into place, Jack began cautiously looking around, everyone looked suspicious, every time someone put a hand in a bag or pocket Jack half expected to see them pull a gun out.

"We have to get out of here" said Jack, they stood up and casually left the café whilst remaining vigilant, nothing, no one following, no one doing anything out of the ordinary, maybe they hadn't been in the café long enough for the bad guys to get there.

Jack and mother walked to the car park, "That's me, over there" She said pointing to a red mini, Jack was still looking around as they approached the car, mother went to push the button on the key fob, Jack put his hand over it and said "stop! When did you buy fuel?" On the way here, that's why I was a few minutes late" she said, Jack looked under the car and sure enough there it was, a bomb.

He explained as they quickly walked away "you used your card to buy fuel, yes? There is cctv at the garage and your registration number is on the system and on your receipt?" She quickly pulled the receipt from her bag "oh my god, yes, it is" she said, Jack went on, "you then used your card in the coffee shop, you see they would know where you'd parked, they had your car details so there was no need to come inside to the café" She looked shocked, "So I'm a target too?" "It looks like everyone in the company is" said Jack, "But where are they getting the card details from? There must be a leak back home!" He said.

They walked for a while up and down quiet streets, Jack told her she would have to vanish, she suggested they all stick together but Jack said that'd make one target instead of many, mother said she had an exit strategy and the two parted company.

Jack wasn't much wiser as to who the leak was, he found it hard to believe it would be any of the staff at work, each of them only had enough information to do their job, no one knew all the facts. He was now thinking that maybe he was the target not Ingrid, but maybe they both were, and maybe it wasn't the Russians chasing them, maybe it was some other organization, or possibly both, this was big.

Jack got back to Saskia's place to find Ingrid standing holding a frying pan, she almost hit him with it as he walked in, he instinctively sidestepped and grabbed the pan, "what are you doing?" He said, Ingrid replied "I was so scared, I've been here on my own most of the day imagining all sorts of things, I'm so glad you're back," she was quite upset, Jack sat her down and explained what he'd learned.

They still had some time to go before the visa was due to arrive and they were getting bored sitting in this one room apartment, Ingrid said she wished they could go out for dinner or something, anything, just a change of scenery, but it was too risky, anyway they'd probably be turned away, their clothes weren't exactly dining out standard and they had no spare cash, Jack however had cravings of his own, it had been over a week of sharing a bed with two naked women who only seem interested in each other, what a situation.

The next day Jack thought they will need a car to cross the border, if anything was to go wrong they would have no chance of escape on foot, so he went back once again to the shopping mall car park, to his surprise it was still there, Jack

checked over the old white Lada looking for bombs, trackers, anything out of the ordinary, when he was satisfied he drove it away and parked a few streets away from Saskia's.
Jack felt quite at ease going out and about, they weren't looking for a man alone, they were looking for a couple, but even so he was always on his guard.

When Jack returned to Saskia's she was there, she had picked up the post and the visa was among it, Saskia was going to miss her nights with Ingrid but there was one more as it was decided to try to get across the border in the morning, that way they would have the best part of a day to get some distance down.

It was early evening, they had all eaten dinner and were settling down for yet another night of Russian language TV, they were all laid side by side on the bed when Saskia said something to Ingrid, Ingrid laughed, Jack said "come on, share the joke?" Ingrid said, it's not a joke, Saskia asked if you'd like to play tonight as it's your last night here and you didn't seem interested before, that's why she didn't ask you," Jack sat up "What! I've been in hell listening to you two every night and not being invited," he said,

Chapter Twenty two
Threesome

Ingrid for the first time in bright light started kissing Saskia on the mouth, deep passionate kisses with tongues, Jack was almost drooling as he watched them go at it, buttons were being undone with great efficiency, clothes were getting thrown away and it wasn't long before the girls were putting on one hell of a show for Jack, He could feel his hard cock trying to burst out of his jeans, he had to undo them, so he took them off along with everything else.

The three of them were all naked on the bed and Saskia was on the pillows with her arms outstretched across the headboard, her long slender legs were as far apart as she could get them, Ingrid had her face right up between them, licking her and driving her crazy, Jack saw an opportunity, he moved in behind Ingrid, she was head down on Saskia and her little round butt was up, Jack tasted her, she was so sweet, and already very wet, he got up and put his erect cock against Ingrid's wet pussy, then slowly and gently pushed into her just a little, she was busy so he gave her it all, Both of the girls were making all the right noises as Jack thrust in and out of Ingrid, but he wanted Saskia, He'd had Ingrid already and was craving some new territory, she was there, Ingrid had brought Saskia to an intense orgasm, she was trying not to cry out as she

shook from head to toe. Ingrid had now stopped eating her and was giving out a moan every time Jack slammed his hard cock deep inside her, then Saskia lined up right next to Ingrid, it was an invitation for Jack to enter her, he withdrew from Ingrid and slid easily into Saskia's dripping wet pussy.
Jack was alternating between the two, the girls were holding hands as he pleased them both fairly and equally, Jack was sweating, as were the girls, "there's nothing as sexy as sweaty bodies" Jack thought, Saskia moved, she flipped over onto her back with her legs up on Jack's shoulders, her butt hanging just over the bottom of the bed, Jack was loving being inside her she was wet, very wet and he could feel her juice on his balls as they slapped against her, Ingrid had climbed onto Saskia's face and was close to orgasm, she leaned forward and Kissed Jack deeply on the mouth as Saskia made her cum.

Jack had never done this before but always dreamed of, a threesome with two sexy women who were into each other.
They were all exhausted, Jack was the only one not finished but he was being polite and waiting till the girls had theirs, they were all laying flat on the bed resting and for the first time Jack was in the middle.
Saskia and Ingrid looked across Jack to each other, smiled then got up on their hands and knees either side of him, Jack thought he had

died and gone to heaven as they took it in turns to suck his cock, sometimes one would suck the tip as the other licked the shaft and then as they met they would kiss each other, Jack wanted to cum, he was getting close, he wanted to cum inside a pussy, he knew Ingrid wouldn't do that but Saskia seized the moment and climbed on top of him, she was riding him hard, Ingrid was watching with a huge smile on her face,
Saskia was getting tired so she laid back on the bed, legs outstretched she invited Jack between them, it wasn't long after that when Jack was overwhelmed by the urge to fill her with his hot fluid, one enormous push as far up inside her as he could get and he could feel it spurting from him, as waves of excitement kept him pushing and pushing like he was trying to get his balls in too.
This was the best experience of Jack's life, so far.

Exhausted they all slept soundly and as the sun rose lighting up the room Jack climbed out of bed, the girls woke up as he did, Ingrid got up and made coffee, Saskia stayed in bed, she had to go to work in a couple of hours but Jack and Ingrid should be gone by then.

Jack couldn't take the bag of guns with them as they would surely be found at the checkpoint so he left them with Saskia, she was asked to hand them in saying she'd found the bag at the park, whether she did or not was her decision, the hand gun Jack had would have to go with them, it was a risk they had to take, if anything went wrong they didn't want to be totally defenseless.

It was time, Saskia was up now and getting dressed, she had a tear in her eye as they said their goodbyes as did Ingrid, the two girls promised to stay in touch once this was all over, as for Jack he had another port of call if or when he was sent to Belarus again.

Jack fetched the car and parked it around the corner, he then taped the hand gun under the dashboard with duct tape, where he could reach it if he had to and they set off for the border, Ingrid checked all their papers were in order, she was a little worried about the photo as Saskia had different hair but Jack assured her it will help if anything, they were similar looking, so much so they could have been sisters so there shouldn't be a problem.

The checkpoint was not much to look at, it was a quiet minor road and a couple of small buildings and two barriers, as far as Jack could see there were only two or maybe three guards, he pulled up at the barrier, Jack was used to this sort of tension, Ingrid looked a little nervous, "Stay calm" he said quietly as they stopped, a guard asked for papers which Jack handed over, the guard took them inside, another one appeared, he stood by the car, holding his machine gun at the ready, several minutes later another one appeared, he beckoned Jack to pop the boot, Jack obliged, they were searching the boot and looking under the car with a mirror on a stick,

Ingrid was getting twitchy, "Why is this taking so long?" she whispered, Jack replied quietly, "they always try to make you sweat in case you're hiding something, just keep cool," one of the guards asked Jack and Ingrid to step out of the car, he then had a brief look around inside, opening the glove box, checking over the sun visors, Jack was worried he would find the gun so as a distraction he started walking towards the hut where the first guard had gone with their papers, the guy searching the car stepped out and called Jack to come back. That was enough to stop the search, it must have been a few minutes later although it felt like hours, the first guard returned with the documents and they were allowed to continue.
As they cleared the second barrier the bell on the hut started ringing, one of the guards picked up a phone which was on the wall, then he started waving frantically at the other two, they all ran after Jack and Ingrid but it was pointless, Jack accelerated and they were over the line into Lithuania.

Worried that the authorities may be alerted in Lithuania Jack said "we're not out of the woods yet, although it really does depend on who's chasing us," Ingrid said "It's the Russians, isn't it?" "I don't Know, if it was just the Russians there are so many things that don't add up so we still need to be very careful," replied Jack, they were sitting on the local speed limit so they didn't attract the attention of the local cops whilst trying to get as far as they could as quickly as they could.

About seven hours later they reached Klaipeda, a port on the Baltic sea, Jack was amazed they had driven straight through Lithuania without a single incident, even after stopping to refuel, for that they had chosen a run down, old back road garage not equipped with cctv and they had paid in cash.

That night was spent in a cheap somewhat shabby hotel, Jack booked up for a few nights but that was the last of the cash with maybe enough to get some food, Jack knew he couldn't use his company card, it would have been too risky, Suddenly like a light bulb switching on he had an idea, he called Carol, he asked her to post him his personal bank card, gave her the hotel address and then all he had to do was wait, no one could have any idea where they were as they had been careful not to leave a trail so Jack was feeling quite secure.

Chapter Twenty three
The Docks

They would have to spend the next few days finding a way to get to the next point on their escape route, he knew once in an EU country he'd be able to travel distances without border checks but getting there was not easy, the war in the Ukraine and the constant migration of refugees both from there and from the middle east meant many borders had been tightened up.

The following morning Jack went down to the docks, he watched the loading procedures, he saw the crews coming and going, there had to be a way of getting on a ship, neither he or Ingrid had the correct documents.

Getting into a container would have been stupid although Jack did consider it for a moment.
On the second day he was approached by a man who asked what he was doing, Jack had to take a chance at some point so he said "I have to get on a ship, can you help?
The man smiled and said sure, why not, he was an American, Jack was somewhat relieved he seemed to have stumbled across someone who was friendly, it made a change from people trying to kill him.
"Where do you want to go?" Asked the man, Jack said "Anywhere as long as it's EU or UK, the guy laughed, "It must be your lucky day

buddy, we're leaving in two days, I can get you on board, the captain is a decent guy but you'll be expected to pull your weight, what can you do?" Jack suddenly added "There's two of us," "Two of you eh? Well that's gonna cost ya buddy" replied the man, "How much?" said Jack, the man thought about it, "Two grand" he said. Jack took a moment, "where can you get me to?" he said, the man replied, we're stopping at Copenhagen, Rotterdam and London, so take your pick buddy," Jack couldn't believe his luck, He went back to the hotel and told Ingrid what he'd done, She was impressed if not a little reserved, things so far hadn't always gone to plan.

The following morning Jack's card arrived in the post, he then realized he wouldn't be able to draw two thousand from the cash point and banks usually need a bit of notice, not only that, his passport had an alias on it and his bank card was in his name, it was all falling apart.

It was getting dark, he only had one more day to get the cash together, Jack saw a sign, it read pawnbrokers and cheques cashed, "That's got to be worth a try" he thought, inside the shop was a tough looking man sitting behind a desk, this guy looked as if he'd been carved up, beaten up and put back together several times with glue, he had scars everywhere and only one ear, Jack was a bit hesitant but explained he needed cash and could do a bank transfer in exchange, the guy looked at Jack suspiciously, "Who's after you?" he asked, thinking the man may be cautious of getting involved in something, Jack made up an excuse, "I need to buy a car and the seller will only accept cash" he said, the man looked him up and down and then said, I'll ask you one more time, lie to me again and you can get the fuck out of my shop, Who's after you?" "OK," said Jack "but you won't believe it," "Try me" said the man, Jack explained without too much detail what had happened.

A deal was struck, Jack transferred the money and the man gave him the cash, it was quite expensive, Jack had to pay three thousand to get two but he was sure he'd be reimbursed by the company when this was all over.

The following morning Jack and Ingrid met the American sailor by the harbour gates, Jack flashed the rolls of notes at him and they went into a warehouse, Jack and Ingrid were shown a large crate and told to get in, the American said "I can't walk you on, we're all getting our papers checked but you'll get on board OK this way and I'll let you out once we hit the open waters, Jack agreed, "The money?" said the American, holding out his hand, "When we're at sea" replied Jack, the American knew it was in Jack's pocket so said "Fair enough buddy" and screwed the lid on the crate with Jack and Ingrid inside.

It was dark in the crate, there were air holes and a bottle of water, This wasn't the first time he'd been transported this way, Jack thought back to Cairo and when he was inside Sophia's trunk, but of course he was alone in there, now there were two of them in the box, Jack wondered if it would be possible to have Ingrid in such a small space, but thought it wouldn't be much fun.

They were beginning to think they had been left behind, it had been ages, then at last voices could be heard, had they been discovered? Jack could hear instructions being shouted then all of a sudden the box fell flat on the floor, Ingrid let out a little cry as she banged her head on the wooden crate, luckily the noise outside masked it, then they were being lifted, it must have been a crane they seemed to go up and swing around for some minutes before landing unceremoniously the right way up, it went dark, there were heavy metallic sounds and then peace.

All was quiet except for the gentle vibration and the distant hum of the ships engines but no way of telling whether or not they were moving.
It had been several hours since their box had been loaded when there was an increase in the noise of the engines and a slight sensation of movement, Jack thought they must be under way, they were both getting cramp but it was another hour or two before any signs of life could be heard,

eventually there was light as the box was opened. The American was there alone, "Come on" he said, captain wants to see you, I'm Mike by the way,"
Mike led the pair up stairs after stairs and corridors until finally they reached the bridge, they were standing in the corridor when Mike brought Jerry the captain out,

Jerry held out his hand and Jack passed the two rolls of notes over, "Two thousand dollars?" he said, Jack suddenly realized it had cost him more yet again said "No, British pounds," Jerry smiled and said "even better as he put one roll in his pocket and handed the other to Mike, "You do know how much trouble I'd be in if you get caught on my ship?" Jerry said to Jack, who replied, We do appreciate this and once we get back I can make sure you don't get any repercussions," Jerry then looked at Mike and said, "Get them to work Mike."

Mike took Ingrid to the galley and put her to work cooking and cleaning for the crew, Jack was on general duties around the ship, cleaning and maintenance, he was shown what where and how.

Jack and Ingrid were given their own cabin, it was small but livable, fold down bunk beds on the wall which didn't please Jack too much but at least it was reasonably comfortable, Jack was sick of grey paint, it seems that's all he'd done since they got on board, anyway he'd paid his passage so why work too, but he couldn't complain, he was on his way home.

They were on the last leg of their journey it would take about thirty six hours to get to London and they were already twelve hours into it, the first two stops had been easy, no one came on board to inspect or check papers so Jack and Ingrid didn't have to get back in the box, London however would be a different story, they had to get out of the docks without going through any checks, Jack would have been OK but Ingrid was on a Russian passport.

Chapter Twenty four
Home soil

The coastline was visible, Jack put away his paintbrush, he went to see Jerry, "How do you plan to get ashore?" asked Jerry, Jack didn't really have an answer to this, he hadn't thought that far ahead, "I'll look for an opportunity along the way" he said, Jerry asked "can you two swim?" Jack thought he was joking and laughed "yes" he said, "you are kidding?" Jerry said "Look, we'll be going past Canvey Island, I can't stop the ship but I can get you close to the Jetty," Jack thought about that, "OK but how do we get off the ship?" "I'll have the crew steps lowered as we go past said Jerry,"

The ship slowed as it would normally, rivers have a speed limit and they were now on the Thames, the crew steps had already been lowered and Jack could see the refinery at Canvey island, he and Ingrid made their way down the steps, the Jetty was only about twenty feet off the side so as they approached Jerry had the engines stopped so they cruised past without the propellers sucking Jack and Ingrid under and dicing them up, at that moment they jumped and swam for it, Mike who was standing at the top of the steps called on his radio to start the props once Jack and Ingrid were clear.

No one had seen them and the Jetty was clear, soaking wet they dragged themselves out of the water and squelched as fast as they could along the boardwalk to dry land. It was only when they reached the refinery they heard a shout, "Oi you! What do you think you're doing? This is a secure area!" It was a security guard, Jack had to think on his feet but at least he could speak the language this time, "Sorry mate, we just fell off my mate's boat," he said, an excuse which would explain their appearance, the security guard laughed as he escorted them out through the main gate.

It felt great to be back on home soil, Jack had to find somewhere safe for Ingrid, it wasn't safe to take her to the old corn exchange until he knew who was to be trusted there, so he booked her into a hotel using his personal card.

Jack sat in the café opposite work with a cup of coffee and watched the door, nothing seemed out of place, the same people coming and going, he decided to go in, he finished his coffee and crossed the busy main road, nothing felt out of place, once inside the old corn exchange building jack approached security, his card was invalid and two security guards grabbed him, Jack didn't resist, this wasn't that unusual after a mission had gone wrong, they took him to an interview room, sat him down and waited.

Dave Davis entered and sat down, "good morning Jack," he said, Jack replied, Sorry Dave, because of what's happened I can't talk to you," Dave hesitated for a moment, "who do you want to talk to then?" "It has to be Mr Gordon" said Jack, looking surprised and with a laugh Dave said "You want to talk to the department head?" Jack said "Yes, I'm not discussing anything with anyone else", Dave got up and as he was leaving the room he turned his head and said "I'll ask the question but don't hold your breath"
It was only about fifteen minutes later when Mr Gordon walked into the room, "leave me alone with Jack, and turn that camera off" he said pointing up to the corner of the room,

Dave and the other guard left the room, the red light on the camera went out and Mr Gordon said "Hello Jack, What's going on?" Jack replied "I believe we have a rat in the house sir, my card has been compromised and it's not just mine," Mr Gordon paused and then said, "yes I know, we are working on it, but why wouldn't you talk to Dave?" Jack said "I have no idea who to trust," I thought I could trust Sally, but whoever is behind this knew about my call with her, and Sal is someone I would normally trust with my life." Mr Gordon said "What happened to Ingrid Roskov?" Jack hesitated for a moment, then said "I have her in a safe house," "Which one?" Mr Gordon asked but then added "oh, OK I understand, probably for the best she stays there for now at least."

Jack found it hard to believe it was anyone in the company, everyone seemed so loyal and trustworthy, of course there was always the possibility that someone was being blackmailed or got at in some way but then the system would have picked up on unauthorized emails or other computer traffic, even the phones were programmed to listen for key words.

Then the penny dropped, what if it was the system? Everything ran through an external government secure server, that would hold card details and movements, even mission details, it was the only place everything came together but it's location was secret, no one in the company knew where it was, it was operated by a government agency and was supposed to be impenetrable.

Time was of the essence, the longer this went on the more people it put at risk so Jack had to find it and fast.

Chapter Twenty five
Tim

He had been back for almost a day and although he only lived a few miles away he hadn't even had time to call Carol to tell her he was home, Jack was desperately trying to locate this server,

There was a room on the third floor where a geeky bloke worked, Jack had heard about him because the guys would bring their own laptops in to get him to fix them, But Jack couldn't think of his name, he went to see Sally and asked her, she knew who the guy was because he had sorted out her phone after she got a virus on it, Sally called the guy on the internal phone system, asked him to come down, His name was Tim. A few minutes later the elevator door opened and Tim stepped out, "come with me," said Jack, Tim followed Jack outside, across the road and into the café.

Jack bought Tim a coffee. "I hear you know your way around computers?" Said Jack, Tim, looking suspicious said "I'm not doing anything illegal," Jack then said, it's for the company, I can't tell you the details but I need to know where the external server is located, can you find it?"

"Probably, but I want it from the top, to be frank I don't know you or what you're up to," said Tim, Jack smiled and said "Of course, that's the answer I wanted to hear," they finished their coffee and went back to work, after a call from Jack Mr Gordon met him on the third floor and between them got Tim to find the server, they stood over him as he brought up a map on his screen and with the help of a program he installed they watched as the location of the server lit up on the map. "One more thing" said Jack, Mr Gordon looked concerned as Jack asked Tim "Can you find the leak?" "Leak? What sort of leak?" Asked Tim, Jack gave him a quick rundown of what had been going on, "I can try" said Tim, "but it may take some time," Mr Gordon said "do what you can son, but time is something we don't have."

Jack left the office and headed out, he bought a pay and go phone and a sim from a local shop, he then, making sure he wasn't being followed went to the hotel where Ingrid was staying, Jack handed her the phone, "no one knows you are here, it looks like we have a security breach so you'll need to stay here for a while, if you need anything my number is in the phone, don't call anyone else," Ingrid agreed, "will I see you again Jack?" she asked, "I'm not sure" he replied, "I hope so but under better circumstances," with that he left.

An hour or so later Jack's phone rang, it was Tim, he went to talk and Jack said "Shhh not over the phone Tim, I'll come in."

Fifteen minutes later Jack was in the office, Tim was smiling, feeling very proud of himself, "I found it," he said "It's another server, our secure server was hacked and all the traffic was diverted through an outside one, which meant everyone still got their data but so did the extra server, "Where is it?" asked Jack, "I don't know yet" said Tim, but I do know where it was sending the data, I sent a packet of fake but believable data and followed it, it goes to all over the world, must be hundreds of locations, I have a print out of all the addresses" Tim handed the list to Jack, then said, "Would you like me to cut off the leak?" Jack thought about it then said, "no, not just yet, we may be able to use this to our advantage," Mr Gordon arrived, Jack had called him as he was entering the building.

Jack looked down the list, "we need to get everyone briefed in person and off grid cards and phones issued" he said, then he spotted an address on the list, I'll take this one, I'm curious about it, If any of these addresses change Tim I want you to call the agent who's going to it, nothing about this operation goes through channels!"

Jack set off, he boarded a plane to Warsaw, then just as previously he hired a car, and set off on the same route, no problems, no one following, eventually Jack arrived at Mogilev, he booked into a hotel then went to the same nightclub where he had seen Nikki talking to the suspicious looking men around the table at the end of the room, it was late, the club would be closing soon and Jack was still looking for the men, then he spotted Nikki at the bar, she was talking to the barman in a way that said she knew him.

Jack wandered over and sat at the bar right next to her, she looked surprised and was more than a little cautious as Jack said "hello", he bought her a drink and told her that business had kept him in the area, Jack guessed Nikki was involved in this because it was at the café in Minsk where he had first met her, why was she there? It was at the same place he remembered seeing two men walking away from his car, he also remembered Nikki searching his wallet in the hotel, it was all falling into place,
Jack had his story all worked out, it was quite possible that Nikki and her accomplices would believe Jack and Ingrid were unable to get away so they could in theory still be around so Jack concocted his story accordingly.
It seemed highly likely Nikki was up to her sweet little neck in all this so Jack decided to play along for a while.
They spent the remaining hour in the club drinking and dancing, each of them playing the other one along, it was closing time, no sign of the men he was looking for so Jack and Nikki left together, "where are you staying?" asked Jack, Nikki looked him in the eye and said "with you?"

Jack smiled "good answer," he thought, as long as he's there he might as well enjoy it and she may let something slip.

They walked back to the hotel, "I didn't expect to see you again" said Nikki, Jack replied, "I couldn't resist looking for you after last time" Nikki thought "he's like all men he thinks with his cock first," she thought she could use this to her advantage.

Chapter Twenty six
Saving Nikki

They were in the hotel room, Nikki went to the bathroom, Jack was tempted to grab her phone from her bag but didn't know how long she'd be, as it happened not long, Nikki emerged from the bathroom, she was totally naked, Jack could see her clothes laying on the bathroom floor through the open door but was distracted by her long slender legs, his eyes followed them all the way up, this time Nikki was more seductive than playful, she was either very good at acting or not as drunk, either way Jack was going to have her again.

Jack got undressed, he placed his clothes over the back of the chair then laid back naked on the bed, Nikki began touching and fondling his balls, then she stroked his cock which was now rock hard, she lowered her face onto it and licked the length up and down getting him wet before taking it all in her mouth, Jack's cock must have been some way down Nikki's throat and it didn't bother her at all, no gagging, no hesitation, she slid her mouth up and down slowly each time swallowing his cock until his balls were pressing against her soft lips.
As Nikki lifted off Jack's cock there were long strings of saliva still attached, she then got up and straddled him, her tight pussy riding up and down as her hands pressed on to his chest, after a while

she stopped, Nikki reached into her bag and produced a vibrator, she lifted up a little off Jack's cock and inserted the vibrator into her ass, all the way in, as she lowered herself back down he could feel the vibrations inside her pussy, it was something new and very exciting, it wasn't long before Jack shot his cum deep inside Nikki's pussy, the vibrations made the whole thing more intense, he could feel his face going red as he tensed up, Nikki laughed, she knew he was having a good one.

Nikki got up, she went to the bathroom to retrieve the vibrator, when she returned Jack was still laying there smiling, Nikki saw some cum which had settled along his shaft so she licked it off, then she gently sucked him, Jack was getting horny again, Nikki could tell so she continued, gently sucking and licking his sensitive red cock until with a groan Jack came again, Nikki sat up, swallowed and then wiped her face with a tissue from the box by the bed.

Jack was pretending to sleep when Nikki got out of bed, again she searched his clothes, Jack was watching in the dim light, and when he was sure she had his wallet in her hand he hit the light switch. "Hello?" he said, Nikki panicked, she went for her bag but Jack was nearer, he grabbed it, Jack tipped it up on the bed, a small 9mm pistol fell out, Jack picked it up, removed the clip and cleared the one from the chamber, then he

threw it back down on the bed, "Would you like to explain?" He asked.
Nikki was stuck in an awkward situation, she obviously liked Jack even if it was just for sex but now she had exposed herself as the enemy.

She began to cry, Jack thought it was a ploy so he said, "That wont work either, I think you better start talking." Nikki explained that "they made her do it," the classic blame tactic, again Jack wasn't falling for it.

Eventually Nikki gave up, "I can't tell you anything, if they think I have been caught they will kill me," Jack asked "who are "they"?" Again she said, I can't tell you, "get me out of the country to somewhere safe, then I'll tell you what I know she said."

That was exactly what Jack had in mind, get her back to base and let them interrogate her. So once again he was in the situation where he has to get a woman out of Belarus whilst being hunted by the unknown enemy, only this time they didn't know, yet.

Early morning and it began to rain, Jack checked out and took Nikki to her place in Orsha to grab some clothes and papers, he stayed with her every step of the way, Jack was also holding her phone, she had lied to him too many times in the past, he had to be sure she was on the level this time.

Nikki had a whole array of documents and paperwork, multiple passports, it was obvious whoever was running the outfit she worked for was well organized and connected, they got in Jack's car and headed towards the border, Jack thought if he could get to the border before they realized she was gone they may have a good chance of getting away pretty quickly

Nikki didn't have a visa for Poland and it would be quite a delay to get one, company channels were closed so they were on their own. Jack made a run for Brest, there was a border there, but once there they would have to arrange a way across but he already had a plan in mind, Jack arrived at the hotel and checked himself in while Nikki waited in the car, then Jack carried Nikki's bags in and she followed a few minutes later, that way she could keep her passport.

Once inside Jack called Tim on his off grid phone, he photographed Nikki's passport and sent it to Tim, he was on the phone for only a minute or two then hung up, within an hour the phone rang, it was Tim, they spoke briefly and Jack hung up. Nikki was looking worried, she was genuinely scared of what would happen to her if her people caught them, she would be killed for sure, she also had no idea what awaited her where they

were going so neither outcome seemed very appealing.
In the morning Jack and Nikki went to hairdressers and changed her appearance as best they could, Jack thought she still looked hot.

It was still safe to go out and about, Nikki looked remarkably different with her new hairstyle and her people hadn't tried to contact her yet, or at least they hadn't tried to call, Jack still had her phone. That evening they went out to a nice restaurant for a meal, Nikki felt like she was on a date but in reality she knew she was effectively a prisoner, the only thing they discussed over dinner regarding the situation was her role as far as getting together with Jack went, she explained she was to gather whatever information she could, but being with him was something she enjoyed anyway so it wasn't a difficult task.

Jack and Nikki were at the hotel for four nights, each one filled with sexual pleasure and Nikki always had a new trick up her sleeve, on the morning of the fifth day Jack drove Nikki to a field which seemed to be in the middle of nowhere, it was a grass field with sheep in it, they sat on the grass by the gate for about ten minutes, then the sound of an engine, that was followed by a light aircraft flying low, so low it looked as if it was going to take out the trees, then as it crossed over the field the pilot threw a metal tube with a red trailing ribbon out of the window, "Run!" Said Jack, they both raced across the field to retrieve the canister, Jack got there first, then they both ran back to the car and drove to the hotel.

The hotel was big so Nikki's presence wasn't noticed by the staff as they went up to the room together, once inside Jack unscrewed the canister, inside was a rolled up envelope containing Nikki's new passport in another name and a visa valid for ninety days, that's all they needed, it was now about midday so they put the bags in the car and made their way to the border crossing, it was a long bridge with buildings on the far side, there was a bit of a queue so turning round and escaping if they needed to would be a non starter. Jack was always nervous about these border crossings with someone else, his papers were always spot on but this time they had been put together in a rush for Nikki and off grid so Jack didn't know if they'd flag up if checked online.

Once again the guys back at base came through and Jack continued on his way, Nikki looked relieved too but for her there was no going back, they would know for sure she had gone by now.

Jack decided to drive back to the UK, there was no real issue with borders within Europe so he should be able to drive straight through, they arrived at Warsaw and Jack checked them both into a hotel using Nikki's new passport, they felt pretty safe so they went out for a drink and then on to a club. It was always a good plan to mingle among the crowds, hiding in plain sight.

It was their last night together and Nikki made it perfectly obvious she wanted to go out with a bang, literally, Jack considered all this sex at work as part of the job, it was tough but it was for queen and country.

Nikki was laying naked on the bed, she loved it, if she could live life without clothes she would, Jack stood there looking at her long thin body, her long legs, her soft plump lips, her smooth shaven pussy and he was loving everything he was seeing, Nikki was so adventurous Jack never knew what she would do next, he laid on the bed next to her and they were both still for a while, Nikki whispered to him "Did you like my ass? Jack smiled and said he loved that, Nikki said "would you like to do it again? Jack simply and quietly said "yes," then Nikki said "what else would you like to do to me?" Jack couldn't think of anything else, she had already given him everything he could ever want in bed.

Jack was watching English TV as they lay there, then Nikki moved around and began gently licking his balls, Jack was getting aroused, then Nikki got up and went to the dresser, she returned with an elastic band, she then wrapped it around the base of Jack's hard cock, "why?"

He said, she smiled and said "you'll see," and she went back to playing with him, by now Jack had lost interest in the television, Nikki was distracting him, he couldn't see the screen anyway as she had her pussy in his face begging him to eat her, Jack obliged as Nikki sucked his cock, after quite some time Nikki was reaching her orgasm, she was losing rhythm on Jacks cock as she thrust her pussy into his face, her juices were flowing out of her, Jack was drinking her sweet nectar, she stopped sucking Jack and just savoured the moment, she was quiet and still but making cute little sounds of satisfaction, then she moved around she got on her hands and knees, Jack got the message and maneuvered around behind her, her pussy was slippery and soaking wet as he pushed his erection into her, she moaned a little, but after just a few strokes Nikki reached back and relocated Jacks cock into her tight ass, Jack did not complain, he noticed he was getting a bit red but it wasn't bothering him, it was just the elastic band which so far he hadn't understood, Jack pushed his cock deep into Nikki's ass, she loved this, he got faster and faster hammering away like it was a race, she could feel the power in his hips as he slammed into her.

He was sweating, she was crying out with every push and it was then Jack found out what the elastic band was about, as he came with such an intense feeling, he thought his cum was going to exit through Nikki's mouth it was so powerful, he could feel the pressure like a fire hydrant going off and filling her up, she was loving it too, jack was still cumming when Nikki pulled him from her ass and took him in her mouth, she was getting every last drop from him, this really turned Jack on, she just seemed to love the taste of his cum.

They fell asleep in the position they were in at that moment, and lay there until daybreak.

Morning arrived, Jack and Nikki were feeling confident, there was a straight run to Calais ahead and all in relative safety, Jack checked out of the hotel while Nikki threw her bag on the back seat of the car and climbed in, as jack reached the doorstep there was an almighty clattering sound, he looked left towards the front of his hire car which was parked outside and saw the gunfire ripping through it,

Nikki didn't stand a chance, the windscreen was exploding outwards as the bullets tore through the car from behind, there was blood and bits of bone splattered all over the smashed windscreen and out over the front of the car, Jack instinctively ducked back inside the doorway as the shooters car raced past. Stunned he got to his feet and ran out to the car, Nikki was slumped forward being suspended only by her seat belt, she was unrecognizable, she had been hit in the back of the head and the exit wound had blown half her face off.

Jack couldn't wait around, he knew he should be heading home but Jack felt sick, he felt angry and he felt robbed, Nikki didn't deserve to die and Jack would avenge her, he caught a train, his papers were still good for the crossing so he made his way back to Saskia's place, he knocked on her door and she was surprised to see him, of course she didn't speak English but she understood what Jack was asking for as he mimed most of it, she invited him inside then pulled out the bag of guns he had left there from under the bed. He threw the bag up onto the bed and sorted through it, taking out a couple of pistols and a nice rifle with telescopic sights fitted, that one was in it's own hard case, Jack threw the bag over his shoulder and left, he went straight into town and hired another car and set off. That evening Jack staked out the night club in Horki, from the top level of the multi storey car park he was in a position to see who comes and goes but far enough away not to look suspicious, he saw three men come outside, they were talking, smoking and laughing, Jack recognized them as the men around the table Nikki had been talking to.
Leaving the car where it was Jack walked down the road to the nightclub, once inside he made his way to the table where the three men were, they stopped talking and looked at Jack, obviously

they knew who he was, one of them reached towards his pocket, Jack said "tut tut" as he pulled out the pistol he was holding under his jacket, the man stopped, one of them in a strong Russian accent said to Jack, "you are a dead man, just like your bitch, dead!" that saved Jack asking the question, he backed off without saying a word, he was still walking backwards when he reached the dance floor, then he momentarily lost himself in the crowd.

Chapter Twenty seven
Payback

Jack came out of the front door with such speed and force he knocked the doorman over, he obviously had no idea Jack was behind him or Jack would have never been able to shift this enormous man, the doorman got to his feet as the three men from inside ran out into the street, Jack was gone, he could see the three men from the corner he had ducked around as they stood in the street shouting angrily at the doorman who had no idea what was going on.

Once again Jack was up on the car park but this time he'd found a quiet spot and had the rifle sights lined up at the front door of the club, it was only twenty minutes later the three men appeared outside again, Jack lined up on one of them, gently squeezed the trigger and watched as the bullet tore it's way through the guy's chest, he hit the ground, one of the others ran back inside the club as did the doorman and the other one who was already out in the road ran towards the car park where Jack was.

Jack carefully and calmly packed the rifle back in it's case and got down behind his car, it didn't take much guesswork to figure out he would be on the top level and not many minutes later the guy from the club appeared, he was sneaking around the cars with his gun in his hand, Jack was laying on the ground, he waited until the guy got close then from under the car he shot his ankle out, he went down and Jack fired several more shots at him, Jack saw the blood on the floor and the gun no longer in the guy's hand so he walked around and just to make sure put another one in his head.

It was time to move, no doubt they would have called for reinforcements by now, Jack got into his car but before he could set off he heard tyres screeching, obviously they were on their way up, Jack drove to the end of the car park, pulled into the last bay then forward so he was in the aisle, behind him was the empty bay, to his left was the wall, and to his right the aisle where the bad guys would hopefully appear, as soon as he was in position Jack rolled down the passenger window and began firing at the oncoming range rover, he hit the windscreen at least twice, the car was coming at him fast, another volley from Jack's pistol smashed through the range rover's windscreen, it was accelerating hard towards him, Jack held his nerve, his car was in reverse, he had his foot on the clutch and at the very last moment while still firing Jack shot backwards into the parking bay.

The range rover hit the wall, smashing the barrier as it plunged over the side, there was a loud bang as it hit the concrete six floors below, Jack looked over the edge to see the car on its roof and on fire, he then calmly stepped back into his car and drove off.

Satisfied he had taken his revenge Jack drove all the way back to Saskia's, it was now the early hours of the morning, he woke her up, despite being tired she was still pleased to see him on the doorstep, Jack put the guns back in the holdall and slid it back under the bed, Saskia made coffee and they sat together, Jack was using a translator program on his phone to talk to her, obviously he couldn't tell her anything work related, he did tell her Ingrid was safe and well, Saskia typed into the translator "Do you want me?" Jack replied "want?" as if he didn't know, she typed in again "do you want to fuck?" Jack replied, I need to sleep, Saskia then made a little sign with a sad face and pretending to wipe away a tear.
Jack being Jack would have loved to have her again but he was dog tired and really needed to rest.

When Jack woke, Saskia had already left for work, he got up and went to the bathroom, then he noticed the goodbye note she had left him in the form of a lipstick kiss on his cock, Jack smiled, he grabbed the bag of guns from under the bed, and walked a few streets away to where he had left the car, still nervous he checked it before driving off.

There was a river just before the check point so Jack threw the bag of guns in, he couldn't risk being caught with them and didn't want Saskia to be either so it was better this way.

The rest of the journey was uneventful, he dropped the hire car off with a transport company to return it for him, it was the first hire car he had managed to return in one piece albeit with a few bullet holes in the side from the car park fight. Jack went home, Carol was pleased to see him, he had been away for ages this time, he spent the night at home then the following morning he went into the old corn exchange building where he was immediately summoned to his line manager's office, as soon as he got in the barrage of shouting began with "Who authorized you to start a fucking war?!" Apparently the shooting at the nightclub and the flying range rover had made the news, seven dead, it said, but it also said it was a suspected gang war.
The rogue server had been severed from the system but no one still knew who was behind all the trouble as there had been no successful captures.

Jack then turned Ingrid in, the system was secure so there was no more risk, she would be given a new identity and housed somewhere nice, Jack still didn't know what her value to the government was but he knew not to ask or he'd have been given the usual need to know answer.

Jack was given three weeks off, the company called it suspension but to Jack it was holiday time.
Carol asked, "fancy going somewhere?" He thought about their trip to Kenya and said "as long as it's in the UK, maybe."
Jack spent a few days clearing up the garden and doing the chores which had built up while he was away, it was nice to relax at home in the evening even if it meant watching the crap Carol likes on the TV.

Chapter Twenty eight
Home

Carol must have known Jack was having other women but she chose to ignore it, he was a needy man and worked away a lot, as long as she never saw it that was fine by her, in fact she had even contemplated bringing in a third party for her and Jack but decided not to because she didn't know how she would feel afterwards.

After two weeks of normality and a week before Jack's suspension was to expire he received a call from work, they said it couldn't be discussed on the phone so Jack had to go straight in, on arrival there was a noticeable amount of activity, he stepped into the elevator and went straight to the fourth floor, the other were all heading into the briefing hall.

Once everyone was seated and settled Mr Gordon took the stage, he started off by greeting everyone and apologizing for calling this urgent meeting, then went on to say, "Tim in I.T. has managed to come up with a file of names whilst interrogating the rogue server they had taken down, these people are suspects in the killing of several agents and the breach of data from the company server, There's a list of names and locations on the board, working in pairs we want these people brought in if possible or interrogated in the field if that's the only other option, any questions?"

Jack raised a hand but before he could speak Mr Gordon said, "Your suspension is lifted Jack."

Everyone scattered, Jack and Sid were paired up and sent to Prague, he checked the board to see if Belarus was on the list, Jack still felt he had a score to settle there for Nikki but it wasn't there. He asked why and was told the names on the list for Belarus were all dead, Jack smiled as he left the building with Sid after collecting their travel documents.
On the plane Jack said to Sid, "have you seen this address?" It didn't mean anything to Sid, but Jack knew what sort of place it was, it seemed whoever was behind this wasn't likely to be a government more likely an organized gang.
The plane touched down and the two men collected the hire car they had waiting for them, they then drove to a hotel near the city centre and checked in, they had two adjoining rooms.

It was about eleven in the evening when Jack knocked on the door between their rooms, Sid opened it and Jack said "Let's go and check out this place shall we?" Sid agreed and they walked to the address they had been given, it was a nightclub, inside there were pole dancers and the whole place looked sleazy, moments after they entered they were approached by two young ladies wearing next to nothing and asked if they'd like some company.

Jack thinking it was good cover and they should act like every other guy in the place agreed and the four of them sat down, Jack with the experience he had gained in Belarus had already drawn cash from a cash point on the way so he didn't have to use the card, he was still cautious even after the leak had been plugged.

Sid was a thin, well dressed man in his mid twenties and was a little shy and embarrassed by the situation, Jack could see Sid was struggling and laughingly commented, "You'll have to fuck one of them tonight to maintain your cover!" Sid looked terrified, he'd never been to a place like it, Jack went to the bar to buy some more drinks, on his return he handed some cash to the girl who was entertaining Sid, she took him by the hand and tried to lead him away, Sid was reluctant but Jack leaned over and said "Don't make a scene," Sid then feeling he had no choice followed the girl to a private room. It was thirty minutes or so later when he returned alone but with a big smile on his face, Jack leaned across and said "Well, what did you find out?" Sid replied "She likes to be tied up," Jack looked amused and said "No stupid, about the people who run this place!" Sid was a little embarrassed and said "Sorry, I didn't know that's what I was supposed to be doing."

They spent all evening in the club and all they saw were scantily dressed hookers and strippers, no sign of any management.

It was early hours when the club closed and the two men walked back to the hotel, "That was fun" said Sid, Jack laughed and said "We're not here to have fun but it looks like we are going to have to become regulars if we're going to get anywhere, even if that means having fun," Sid smiled and they both entered their respective rooms.

In the morning the two men met at breakfast, Sid asked what they were going to do for the day as the club was only open in the evening, Jack said they were going to ask about, to see what they could find out. They finished eating and left for the club, they sat in a café just down the street, it was possible to see anyone coming or going to the club, they sat there drinking coffee for over two hours, nothing, no movement at all, then the waitress asked "Is there anything you guys need help with?" Jack looked up and said, "The club over there?, who owns it?" The girl said "it belongs to the same people who own the one on the square, I don't know their names, I see different people come and go, I work there sometimes," Sid said "You mean?" She said "No, I just serve behind the bar, I don't do that at all," Sid seemed a little disappointed by that, "Why the interest?" She asked looking at Jack, "Oh we're looking at buying a club in the area," the waitress said "I don't think it's up for sale," Jack smiled and said "everything is for sale if the price is right, how can I get to meet the owners?" She smiled and said "I'll find out when they are coming, I'm working there tonight," Jack said they would be there that evening and hopefully see her there.

The men went to the club on the square, there was nowhere to watch from so Jack fetched the car and they sat in there waiting to see if the owners would turn up but again, nothing, the whole thing was starting to seem like a complete waste of time, Sid said "I thought stake outs were supposed to be fun, I'm bored senseless, and one more thing, can I put last night's conquest on expenses?" Jack laughed "yes of course you can but call it fact finding, not fucking!"
Sid laughed and said great, I might do some more fact finding tonight then."

Eventually they went back to the hotel and waited for the club to open.

again they went to the club, the same one as before, the girl from the café was behind the bar and as soon as the guys walked in two girls latched onto them straight away, an hour or so later Jack asked Sid if he was going fact finding, Sid said yes but pointed out a girl he would rather go fact finding with, Jack said "go and ask her, I doubt she'll refuse," Sid didn't need to ask her he hadn't got halfway there when the girl spotted him and walked his way, she simply took him by the arm and led him away.

Chapter Twenty nine
The Meeting

Jack went to the bar, as he was ordering drinks the girl from the café said the men he needed to talk to would be in later that night, so he took his drink and sat down to watch the show.

About one in the morning an elderly grey haired man tapped Jack on the shoulder and said "So you want to buy my club do you?" Jack invited the man to sit down and explained he was looking to buy a club in the area, not specifically this club, the man said "there are only two like this and they are both mine, there's no room in Prague for any more." He may have been knocking on in years but Jack could sense the man had an air of power about him, he was obviously well connected, Jack had now seen his face so he knew who he was dealing with, Jack asked if they could discuss one of the two bars and the man told him in no uncertain terms that neither were for sale at any price, and left, Jack kept one eye on him and one on the naked pole dancer.
The elderly man spoke briefly to a much younger heavy set man at the bar, it was obvious what the topic was as they kept looking across at Jack. Then Sid returned from his second fact finding mission of the evening, "You not going for it?" He asked a pre occupied Jack, Jack said "Oh?

What? Oh, no sorry," realizing Jack wasn't very interested Sid went to get himself another drink, the two men at the bar watched him walk to the bar then they left, Jack followed shortly after, they were on foot, he kept his distance so as not to be spotted, the men walked for quite some time then the elderly man went into an apartment building while the younger of the two got into a car parked in the street and drove off.

Jack watched the apartment building noting which windows lit up, he made a mental note then going inside Jack worked out which apartment it was.
On returning to the club he noticed Sid was sitting engrossed by the performance going on stage, Jack sat down, Sid asked "Where have you been?" Jack casually said "Doing my job, what have you been doing?" Sid told him he had just been watching the show, Jack thought "why me? Why do I get landed with dopey here?" He smiled to himself as he enjoyed the show.

It was closing time, as the guys were leaving the barmaid asked if she could walk with them as she didn't feel safe on the streets at night, She introduced herself as Pepa, Jack said it'd be fine, the guys waited for her, she was only a few minutes then they set off together.

As they approached the hotel, Sid went on ahead and Jack asked Pepa if she would like a drink, he

would then walk her home, she accepted and they went up to Jack's room, needless to say Jack didn't walk Pepa home.
Pepa was a sweet innocent looking young lady of about twenty years old, petite in stature and she seemed quite easy going, Jack asked her what she knew about her boss, she said "it's not just one it's like a company but the man who you were talking to was the man in charge of it all," she said "the staff are all very loyal to him but it's mostly out of fear, he's been known to be quite nasty and he doesn't get his own hands dirty, he uses his heavies for that."

It seemed to Jack this old man was the one they needed to get to, after a while Jack said to Pepa, "would you like me to walk you home now?" She said, "ok, but there's a favour I'd like to ask you if I may" Jack said "ask away," Pepa pointed to the open door to the bathroom, "I see you have a bath, May I? I only have a shower at my place at it's not very good, I haven't had a soak in a proper bath for ages, Jack smiled and said "yes of course you can, he then started running the bath for her, once it was done Pepa went into the bathroom, Jack said "I'll just get you a towel," When Jack returned with the fresh towel Pepa was already in the bath, Jack knocked on the door, "come in," she said and he opened the door, Jack was surprised to see this pretty little thing wasn't at all shy, she lay there in all her naked glory for

Jack to look at and she didn't seem to mind at all that he was standing there staring at her.
"Do you like to share?" Said Pepa, Jack was slightly unsure what she meant by share but he had a pretty good idea she wasn't referring to a packet of crisps.

As soon as she clarified he was invited to join her Jack stripped off, throwing his clothes through to open door into the bedroom, he climbed into the bath with Pepa and she began touching him with her wet soapy hands, of course Jack being Jack he was hard almost immediately, Pepa stood up, she stood over him then holding onto the sides of the bath she slowly lowered herself onto his erect cock which was sticking up out of the water like a periscope on a submarine, as Pepa was riding slowly up and down on Jack's shaft, he grabbed the shower head from the stand on the side of the bath, adjusted the temperature and put the pressure to maximum, then aimed it carefully, Pepa squealed as the powerful jet of water hit her pussy and Jack thought it felt good too, the water in the bath was splashing over the sides and Jack was getting concerned the room below may be getting the water so he pulled the plug out for a while and calmed Pepa down, or at least he tried to, she was so excited and loving every second of it, she stood up in the bath astride Jack and she unscrewed the shower head from the hose then inserted the end of the hose into her pussy, it felt so good as she kept removing it momentarily to let the water flow from her all over Jack, he was loving the show, then she dropped the shower hose into the bath and relieved herself, Jack felt her hot golden shower hit his skin, he had never done anything like this before, Pepa was giggling, Jack found he was getting turned on even more by what she was doing, he reached up and put his hand into the stream, he was tempted to taste but didn't know how she would react and by the time he had decided whether to or not it was over, He picked up the hose and handed it back to her, she began to direct the flow from the hose over her clit but the water was now so high in the bath it was partly going down the overflow but still spilling over the sides whenever either of them moved. Jack pulled the plug out again.

In the morning Sid knocked on the door and walked in to find Pepa still there, sleeping in Jack's bed, Jack was just finishing in the bathroom, they left Pepa where she was and went into Sid's room, Jack said "I found our man last night but he's well protected, I'll make the arrangements," Sid looked sad, he had enjoyed this mission even though he hadn't done anything really to contribute to the work, well yet that is.

When Jack returned to his room Pepa was just stepping into her little lacey panties, Jack stood and watched her dress, he was tempted to stop her but he had work to do and he needed her out of there.

Chapter Thirty
The Abduction

Just after eleven in the morning Jack and Sid were waiting in the car near the old man's apartment, he appeared on his own and headed down the street, he picked up a newspaper and crossed the road, Jack couldn't believe his luck the guy was walking straight towards them, this was going to be easier that expected, as the old man neared the car, Jack stepped out, flashed his gun at the guy and said "Get in," as he stepped into the car he said "have you any idea who you're dealing with?" Jack said nothing, as the old man sat in the back seat, Jack moved him over and got in next to him, holding the gun, Sid drove off.

What they hadn't seen was where the old man was going, he was on his way to a car not far away where two nasty looking heavies were waiting for him, they had seen him being abducted and were now on their tail.
Sid was driving fast, "Where are we going?" he shouted, Jack said "Tocra!" Just follow the signs, the men in the car behind weren't shooting, they were keeping pace but not chasing, Jack figured it was because they had the old man in the car and they didn't want to risk his life. Sid reached Tocra airfield, it was a small field for light

private planes and gliders, "What now?" He shouted, Jack said "Fuck! They're late, keep driving around the field."

Sid kept ahead of their pursuers but they were close and getting too close for comfort, it was just then the chaser's car got hit with a hail of bullets and skidded off the road and into an old wooden shed, Sid looked to his right and a twin engined plane was flying low along side them, the plane landed and Sid pulled up close to it, their hostage was bundled inside and the plane took off again.

Jack said to Sid "well done mate, nice driving," Sid said "Why aren't we on that plane?" Jack explained it was all to do with weight limits, with the pilot, passenger, and the six armed guys on board it would have been too much with them too so they had to make their own way home.
Sid said "So when are we heading home?" "Now" said Jack, "you don't want to stick around for when the shit hits the fan do you?" "I suppose not said Sid", they got into the car and headed for Germany. "Why not the airport?" asked Sid, Jack looked briefly at him and said "If you were the bad guys where would you be looking for us?" Sid nodded as if to say he understood,
"You enjoyed that club, didn't you said Jack" Sid smiled and said "Yeah, I certainly did" Jack said, "fancy stopping off at Amsterdam on the way back?"

Chapter Thirty one
Bull

It was the following summer.
Screaming and shouting could be heard, suspecting something like a terrorist attack, Jack ran towards the commotion, as soon as he turned the corner he was confronted by masses of people screaming and running straight at him. "Great! This is all I need, the only holiday with my wife in three years and this happens!" he thought, as he ducked back inside a doorway.

The panicking crowd stormed by, Jack stepped into the street only to be confronted by two angry bulls, he could see a few people limping in the distance as they had been caught by the beasts. Jack was stumped, he had no idea what to do, this simply wasn't in the training manual.

Just then a hand reached out and grabbed him, it was his wife, she was laughing, there were now a few men in the street herding the bulls away, Carol was still laughing as she explained, "they always do this here at this time of year, it's called running the bull, it's an old Spanish tradition".

They walked back to the hotel, Jack was a little embarrassed, he was the secret agent who went on complicated rescue missions all over the world and his wife just rescued him from a tradition!

Spain was lovely, it was warm, sunny and for the first time in what seemed to be an eternity, Jack could relax, they spent the rest of the day lying in the sun by the pool. Jack would have preferred a beach location but that would come later, today was Pamplona, tomorrow Madrid and then drive south, they had it all mapped out.

The next morning Jack was up bright and early, he was keen to get going, the staff in the hotel had heard about his unfortunate run in with the bulls and every time a staff member saw him they would make horns with their fingers, scrape their foot on the floor and make mooing sounds. Jack was the only one not amused.

The car loaded and Carol up, they went to get breakfast for the last time in humiliation hotel, Jack asked for cereals and the waiter took great delight in asking if he'd like cow's milk with that, and as they left the restaurant Carol said to the waiter, "bye, we must be mooing on now," which amused him even more.

"Damned unprofessional!" said Jack as he climbed into the car, Carol called him grumpy and said he needed to grow a sense of humour, and off they went.
They stopped at Zaragoza for some lunch, Carol wanted to see some of the architecture there but Jack insisted they had to get going, so on the way

out they got to look at some of the fascinating buildings from the car, neither of them knew what was what but it was all pretty spectacular.

Carol said to Jack, "Look, that man with the camera, wasn't he at our hotel in Pamplona?" Jack glanced at him and said "probably but this is Spain, full of holidaymakers and it's not as if Pamplona is far away."

They walked back to the car and headed off to Madrid, as they drove along Carol said, "wasn't it lovely for your company to give us this fantastic holiday?" Jack knowing there would be a catch said "Yes, wasn't it." Carol picked up her book and said "you don't sound very enthusiastic Jack," he just muttered something about getting something for nothing and continued driving towards Madrid.

The hotel was something else, it was top class luxury, Jack and Carol had a very pleasant suite. As they settled in Jack's phone rang, it was the call he knew would come, he went into the bathroom to take it, then said to Carol, "I need to nip out, won't be long," she didn't seem that bothered, "OK" she said, like he was popping down the shop.

Jack was back within the hour, he put an envelope into the room safe, Carol was getting ready for dinner, Jack said "Where are you going?" She replied "You're taking me out for dinner" Jack said "am I?" then headed for the shower.

After Dinner they walked a while through the back streets, it was very quiet, Carol treasured times like this, she didn't get many as Jack was always somewhere around the world doing his job, the job which he couldn't talk about, she held Jack's hand and wished it could always be like this.

They eventually arrived back at the Hotel, it was one night in the most luxurious hotel in Madrid, after a glass of wine they climbed into the huge double bed and spent hours making love, slowly and passionately.

Bright and early the next morning there was a knock on the door, their luggage was collected and taken to the foyer, they spent about an hour in the restaurant at breakfast, thankfully without any bull jokes this time, then they checked out and headed for the door.

All of a sudden there was a loud boom and the ground shook for a moment, alarms started sounding, including the fire alarm in the hotel, people stopped in their tracks to look around, wondering what had happened, moments later a fire truck arrived, then another and police were everywhere.

A police officer walked over to Jack "Mr Morgan?" he asked, Jack said "Yes, why? What's happened?" The policeman said "Would you come with me please sir." Jack and Carol followed the policeman to an office by reception, they were told Jack's hire car had exploded killing the car park valet, Carol looked Shocked, Jack pretended to be surprised but he was used to things going wrong, they were asked to produce their passports and not leave the country until further notice.

Chapter Thirty two
Kidnap

After the commotion had calmed, Jack said to Carol "You need to go home," She said "How can I? They have my passport!" Jack said nothing, he simply picked up his work phone and made a call, within two hours Carol and Jack's replacement passports arrived by motorcycle courier, Jack put her in a taxi and sent her to the airport.

Jack was trying to figure out why someone would blow up his car in a valet operated car park, maybe it was a warning, maybe they didn't know it was valet operated, or maybe it was an accident, either way this was a time to be alert and take no chances.

A replacement car was delivered and Jack Packed his bags into the car and left the hotel, he wasn't sure what to do next but he knew if he gave whoever it was the slip, he'd be safer so he changed his plans and headed for Gibraltar, he thought best get to British soil, at least he'd be able to blend in and there would be some border control.

It was late when Jack arrived, he hadn't pre booked anywhere and it was the height of the holiday season so everywhere was full, he went to a bar for a drink and to think about his next move.

Jack asked the barman if he knew of any accommodation, he didn't but their conversation was overheard by a woman also sitting at the bar, "I can help," she said, Jack's ears pricked up, "You know of somewhere?" He said, "No" she replied, Jack was puzzled, "then how can you help?" he said, the woman who was in her late forties and looked a bit of a cougar said, "I don't know of anywhere, but I do have room at my place," the barman raised an eyebrow as Jack accepted her offer and bought her a drink.

She introduced herself as Karen and told Jack the story of her divorce and how it led to her moving to Gibraltar, Jack pretended to be interested as he needed her spare room but he was more concerned with the attack on him in Madrid, he was sure it was no accident because it was his car and no one else's, the odds said it was certainly deliberate, he was angry that they had targeted Carol too but thankful she was safe at home or at least on her way.

The bar was closing and Karen got into Jack's car and directed him the short distance to where she lived, he parked around the corner in the next street and they walked up to her apartment on the second floor, Once inside Jack asked where he should put his bag, he only had the one, there was

another but it was in the car. Karen pointed out the bedroom, Jack stepped inside, it was obviously Karen's own bedroom, he said "I can't take your room," she smiled and said, "Do you have a better offer?" then the penny dropped, she was going to share with him,
He really had two choices, play along and sleep comfortable or sleep in the car and be an easy target, he chose to stay, suspecting she would want more than just sleep.

Jack got down to his boxers and climbed into bed, within minutes Karen appeared from the bathroom wearing absolutely nothing, Jack took a discreet look and thought she was pretty fit especially for someone knocking on fifty, just the sight of her shapely figure, ample breasts and masses of black curly pubic hair got him aroused, Jack had no defense, there was no way he could deny wanting her, especially as she pulled back the sheet to see him hard as a rock and pointing at the ceiling.

Karen wrapped her hand around Jack's cock and started slowly stroking, Jack was ready for this, she went to suck him but then stopped, "You don't mind, do you?" she said, Jack smiled and said, "Good grief ! No, help yourself." She did, Karen took him right back deep into her throat, as she lifted off Jack could see long strings of saliva between his cock and her lips, then she swallowed his entire cock again, and again, he wondered why she wasn't gagging.

He had the urge and desire to cum in her throat but reconsidered as it would have been rude not to give her hers first, she had after all given him somewhere to sleep, He maneuvered her into a position where she was sitting on his face with her hands holding the headboard, he gently tasted her wet pussy as he gripped her buttocks with both hands, she was rocking back and forth, Jack really didn't need to do much more than stick his tongue out, she was doing all the work.

Karen came quite quickly but very intensely she moaned as she rubbed her clit quite forcefully on Jacks mouth, he could taste her juice, he knew she'd had a good one, she slid back along his body, he could feel her mat of hair moving down his body as she went, Karen sat herself above Jack's waiting erection and lowered herself slowly down, "Don't cum in me" she said, then she proceeded to ride up and down as Jack licked her nipples, her breasts were swinging on his face and moving with her rhythm, then he stopped her, rolled her over onto her back and climbed between her legs, he penetrated her again, slowly pushing deep inside, then faster, and faster, Jack was pounding her like there was no tomorrow,

Karen was wriggling as she wrapped her legs around him, Jack was getting close, he tried to move her legs, he couldn't withdraw, Karen said quietly, "do it, do it, cum in me!" Jack didn't argue, he erupted sending what seemed like a massive amount of his cum deep inside Karen, she held him there long after he had finished, his cock was getting soft and she still kept him prisoner inside her, gripping him with her legs.

After they had recovered, Jack asked "Why did you say not to and then make me cum in you?" she smiled and said "I'm not on birth control," for a moment Jack thought what any man would think about, consequences, but then he would be thousands of miles away and she didn't even know his surname.

Morning arrived and Jack called Carol at home, there was no answer, he then tried her mobile, he got an answer but it wasn't Carol, it was a man's voice, "About time!" The man said, Jack said "Who is this?" The man went on to explain how he and his colleagues had Carol, and if Jack wanted to see her alive again he better be a good boy, and do what he was told.

"What do you want?" said Jack, the voice on the phone said "You have in your possession an envelope, we will exchange your wife for the envelope." Jack had no choice, the man said he would call back with the arrangements later, he made it perfectly clear they would kill Carol if Jack failed to comply.

Jack opened the envelope, it contained a list of names and an SD card, he had to know what was on the card so Jack went to an internet cafe and inserted the card, it was compromising photographs of a prominent politician in the British government, and details of where and when they were taken.

Jack knew it would cause serious repercussions back home, but then if these elected MPs couldn't keep it in their pants it's their own fault. He knew he would probably get fired or even jailed but there was no way Jack was going to let his wife die.

He considered changing the details but they already knew what was there, they just wanted the evidence, Jack had no choice, he put everything back as it was and waited, the call came a short time later, Jack was told to cross the strait and get to Casablanca in Morocco, He went to the Moroccan embassy and secured a visitor visa, it was unbelievably quick and before the day was out he was on the car ferry.

Jack drove towards Casablanca thinking about the movie and wondered if it had changed much, then he pinched himself, of course it had, this was the twenty first century, it's such a shame in these modern times people still fight and do bad shit to each other, surely mankind should be past that by now!

His train of thought was interrupted by his phone ringing, He was told to proceed to the Wharf container terminal and await instructions, as he arrived he noted it was busy, ships being loaded and workers everywhere, he was somewhat relieved it looked like a public place meeting rather than some deserted barn in the middle of nowhere, that would be risky.

Jack was told where to park, as soon as he stopped a woman tapped on the car window beckoning him to open the door, Jack reached over and opened the passenger side and she got in, "Do you have it?" she said, Jack said he had and asked about Carol, the woman said "we have no desire to harm her but you must hand over the envelope"

"Not until I see her," Jack insisted, she said "drive" he started the car and was guided to a yard full of containers, at the quiet far end there was a van, "She is in there" said the woman, Jack weighed up the situation, he saw a lot of risks associated with the current exchange, "Bring her here" he said, the woman agreed and phoned the men in the van, The van approached slowly and two armed men stepped out, one fetched Carol from the back of the van, Jack stepped out of his car.

"How do you want to do this?" one of the men called to Jack, Jack showed the envelope and called back, "One of you bring her here, once she is in my car I will hand you the envelope" then he produced a lighter and said "any tricks and the envelope goes up, it's soaked in petrol," the men chatted among themselves for a moment, they looked worried, "Agreed" said the man, one started walking Carol towards Jack, "Stop!" called Jack, "No guns," the man handed his gun to the other and continued walking Carol to Jack, Jack told the woman to go, she walked quickly towards the van.

Carol was put into Jack's car, Jack handed over the envelope, the man sniffed it, it was soaked in petrol, he then opened and checked it, it seemed OK so he walked away, Guessing they would try to kill him and while the man was still in the line of fire, Jack quickly jumped into his car which was still running and sped off, the dusty area became a cloud as Jack gunned the accelerator and spun the car around, then as he sped off he pressed a button on a remote control and the envelope burst into flames as the guy was holding it.

Jack could see in his mirror the van giving chase but his car was much faster, all he had to do was find a clear road.

Carol was terrified as they sped through the busy streets, on their way out of the city, jack didn't know the area and was relying on the compass in the car to guide them south, "Why south?" carol shouted, "we need to go north" Jack was busy trying not to kill anyone and that was hard because the streets were full of pedestrians, almost bringing them to a stop at times, he eventually said "They know we need to go north,"

They hit the N11 and that gave Jack the opportunity to get some distance down, Jack floored it, it wasn't long before they saw signs for Marrakech, Jack didn't want to be predictable and he didn't think a city would be the safest way to go, he left the main road and proceeded west, surely they'd never be traced out there, by the end of the day they had reached a place called Safi.

They found a cafe and stopped for something to eat and drink, it seemed the heat was off, for now anyway, even Jack had no idea where they were. While sitting in the cafe Carol said "Isn't it about time you told me what this is all about?" Jack looked across the table at her and said "I cant, you know I cant." Carol was not happy, after being taken captive and chased half way around the world she thought she was entitled to an explanation.

Safi was not really what you would call a holiday hot spot so they stood out like a sore thumb, that became a problem as they returned to the car, as they walked into the car park they saw a group of men standing around the car talking, one of them spotted Jack and Carol, the men ran towards them.

Jack and Carol ran through a series of dirty alleyways, there were bins and rubbish everywhere, Jack dragged Carol down behind one of the bins, he grabbed a broken pallet and ripped off one of the boards, it was seconds later when two of the men chasing them ran into the alley, Jack was listening carefully and as soon as he heard their footsteps approach he stood up and swung the board edgeways, catching the first of the men in the throat. As he fell down the second one went bowling over him, Jack was there in a flash, he hit the guy with the board flat side on and it broke, Jack was standing there with a splintered half board in his hand when the guy on the ground went for his gun, Jack stabbed his hand with the sharp jagged end of the broken board, he then grabbed the man's gun and the gun from the other one who was laying on the floor choking.

Jack then said to the one with the bleeding hand "Do you speak English?" the guy nodded, then Jack bellowed at him "I'm supposed to be on my fucking holiday!" he then took Carol by the hand and walked away with their guns in his pockets.

Jack found a hotel, and checked in, of course now they had no luggage, it was too risky to go back to the car, Carol asked "how did they find us?" Jack said it was obviously the car, that's where they were when we came out of the café, I bet the sneaky sods put a tracker on it. Carol then asked "what was in the envelope?" Jack whipped an envelope from inside his jacket, oh just a copy of the papers and the SD card from my camera with the holiday snaps on it," Carol laughed and then remembered some of those were taken in the hotel room "Jack you did delete those naughty ones?" He laughed, "sorry, no time but it's all burnt up now anyway, do SD cards burn?" He asked grinning.

"As long as you're OK, that's all that matters," said Jack, Carol smiled and said, I am now, it's all a bit exciting really isn't it, maybe I should write a book when we get home?" "No, you know you can't do that sweetheart," Jack replied.

The following morning Jack and Carol boarded a bus to Agadir, they then got a flight to Gran Canaria, Carol asked why they weren't going home, Jack told her the expected way home would be via Spain and if the bad guys were chasing them that's where they'd be looking, anyway we were given an all expenses paid holiday so we're going to have an all expenses paid holiday.

They checked into a hotel and Jack called the office, he explained what had happened and asked what they wanted him to do with the package.

A while later Jack's phone rang, it was Amy from the office, she asked Jack if he had seen the contents of the envelope, he admitted he had, but he'd had no choice, He was told to seal the envelope and someone would collect it soon, he was given a password.

Chapter Thirty three
Elise

The following day Jack went to a pre arranged rendezvous to hand over the envelope, what he saw when he got there surprised him, it was the woman from the kidnap handover in Morocco, she even had the password, Jack took her aside and asked her to explain, she said she worked for the company and had been undercover trying to find out who was involved in agents from the company being killed a year earlier, this lot had connections but were not directly involved. Jack said he would have to verify her and he called the office.

The office confirmed she was genuine so Jack handed over the envelope, "He said "If this is just dirt, why not simply destroy it?" She said "I don't know, it's political so I don't get involved" and she left.

Jack and Carol returned to the UK a week later, Jack went into work and was summoned by Mr Gordon, "Hello Jack" he said "I understand you saw the contents of the package?" Jack said, I didn't have much choice," Mr Gordon said "That's OK, but just forget whatever it was you saw, it doesn't exist, OK?" Jack agreed but said "Just one question sir, why would we want that ourselves? Why not destroy it?"

Mr Gordon replied, "OK, but this goes no further, how do you think we keep operating this company with such a generous budget?" Jack gave him a knowing smile and left the office.

Jack was assigned a new job, he was on the agent killer case from a year ago, their agents were being killed off by an unknown organization and it had been a fruitless ongoing operation to find out who and why, Jack himself had been targeted at the time but the killings all seemed to stop once a leak in the company computer system was plugged.

Of all the places Jack didn't want to go he was assigned to Morocco, He landed at Marrakech airport and booked into a hotel, his handler called him within minutes of checking in, his company phone was showing "Mother" on the display so he knew it would be a meet with a local agent.

"Hello son" said the woman on the phone, "Oh, hi mum," said Jack, she replied with "I'll meet you at the Elite café in thirty minutes," Jack headed off straight away, as he entered the café he was waved at by a woman sitting at the far end of the room, he sat down at her table.

There was a coffee waiting for him, just the way he liked it, The woman said "You'll be working with a partner on this job, she'll be here soon,"

Jack had a suspicion who it might be and his suspicion was confirmed shortly after, it was her again, "This is Elise, Jack, I understand you've already met?" said mother, Jack said he had and with that mother said "Elise will bring you up to speed," and she left.
"Where do you want to do this?" said Jack, Elise looked him up and down and said "Up to you Jack," of course at this point Jack thought his luck was in, "My hotel?" he said, she agreed and off they went.

Elise was doing two jobs, she was trying to show Jack the work that had been done so far and at the same time fending him off, Jack fancied a piece of this girl she was tall and slender, dark skinned with black eyes and hair to match, but she wasn't playing.

Elise said, "look, get your mind out of the gutter and help me out here!"
Jack said, "OK, what do you need?" Elise said I don't have a clue where to start, I have photos and some names but no idea where to find them," Jack smiled, "I do, last year I took some of them out, they like to run sleazy clubs, that's where to start looking." That idea lasted less than a minute, Elise said "You won't find any here," Jack thought, then said, True, not legal ones anyway, now who to ask?"

They left the hotel, Jack suddenly had an idea, he hailed a taxi, if anyone would know it'd be a taxi driver.
They climbed in, "Where to?" said the driver, Jack replied "The best strip club in town," The driver seemed to understand and headed out of town, after a few miles of nothing they came across what looked like an old farm building, the taxi pulled over, Jack paid him and both Jack and Elise got out, they walked towards the door, there was a menacing looking gorilla in a suit standing there, Jack said nothing, got his wallet out and handed some cash to the doorman, they were both let straight in, although Elise did get some odd looks.

Once inside there were naked women everywhere, not the usual "buy me a drink" types who welcomed men, they'd usually be wearing something skimpy, these were all totally nude and walking about the place. Jack noted there were quite a few western looking young women working there.

Jack and Elise found a table in a quiet corner, Jack said "Don't you feel uncomfortable in a place like this?" Elise didn't react, she just asked, "should I?" At that moment it all made sense, he wasn't getting anywhere with this girl and she was fine around naked women, she's a lesbian, he thought.

Two of the girls came over and asked Jack and Elise if they'd like some company, One girl, well made up looked about eighteen or so sat herself on Jack's groin and started wriggling her bare ass about, Jack was already hard, she looked him in the eye and said in perfect English, "you're naughty," Elise looked at Jack then at his bulge," she smiled, the other girl seemed a bit nervous of Elise so she just sat at the table., Elise beckoned her to sit on her knee, which she did, then Elise looked at Jack and said "am I naughty too?" Laughing, Jack bought the two girls a drink and then asked them to leave.

Elise was looking around, she didn't recognize anyone from her photos and it would have been too dangerous to ask staff, so they just sat there drinking and watching the show. Elise said "Why don't the police shut this place down? It's not exactly hidden," Jack said "if Belarus was anything to go by, they buy the cops"
When Elise heard Jack say Belarus the penny dropped, "oh, you're the guy who went on a shooting spree, I heard about that!" Jack didn't reply, he just carried on eyeing up the girls.

A complete evening wasted, no sign of anyone on the list, maybe they were in the wrong area, maybe the wrong country, Jack thought maybe give it a couple of nights then call it in as a dead lead, they went back to their hotels.

The following night Elise didn't go to the club, jack drove there on his own, he parked up and went inside, still plenty of girls about but no sign of any management, The young girl he was greeted by the night before came over again, "hello naughty man" she said as she sat on him again, Jack wondered if she ever fucked the clients, maybe he'd find out later.
Jack was buying the drinks so the girl hung around, eventually she made her interest clear, she sat beside him and gently stroked the bulge in his trousers under the table, if Jack was going to interrogate anyone at the club it would be this girl but he had to get her away from there.

"Where do you live?" He asked, the girl said, "I live here," "What here in the building?" asked Jack, she nodded, Jack said, "do you ever go to town?" she looked down and said "I wish," Jack paused and then said "come back with me tonight?" the girl said "I can't, I'm not allowed." Now Jack knew there was something wrong, it was looking like the girls were being kept there against their will, that suggested organized criminals.

Throughout the night he tried to get the girl to talk, eventually she began to avoid him, he could see her looking at him from across the room at times, Jack sat there all evening on his own, still no sign of any of the bosses, he knew they had to be around somewhere, these girls were obviously being controlled and they were afraid.

Jack discussed his suspicions over breakfast with Elise, she agreed it was a lead that needed following, they drove to a nearby place where they could see who came and went during the day, there was very little activity, Jack knew the girls were living there but the only time he saw any of them was when they brought the bins out to the skip.

That night, Jack and Elise went to the club again, this time Jack booked a private show with the young girl he'd been coaxing, she took him upstairs, along a long dimly lit corridor with doors along both sides, then they went into one of the rooms, it was lit by a dim red light, the first thing Jack noticed was the camera on the wall, "not very private," he said pointing to the camera, she looked at him and said "it's for our protection," she didn't seem to be that convinced either.
She told Jack to lie on the bed, he did, then she got on top of him and started rubbing her body all over him, he was aware of his hard cock making his trousers bulge as she pressed her smoothly shaved pussy against him, it was what she referred to as a private dance, Jack was not allowed to touch her. He went to speak, she put a finger across his lips to suggest they were listening, after his time was up he discreetly

handed her a rolled up note wrapped in a condom, she worked naked so there was only one place she could hide it, Jack stood between her and the camera as she pushed it up inside.

This could blow the whole operation and Jack didn't even know her name, but he had a feeling he could trust this girl, he could tell she wanted help.

Chapter Thirty four
Lucy

The club closed, Jack and Elise waited in the car in the car park, about thirty minutes later the girl came out carrying a bag of rubbish, she walked towards the skip, Elise was in the driving seat, "Make it look good" she said as she started the car, they came to a halt by the skip, Jack knew there were cameras everywhere, he jumped out, grabbed the girl, she put up a bit of a struggle, then he bundled her into the back of the car and Elise floored it.

Jack looked back and surprisingly nothing was happening, he had expected to be chased, or at least people to rush out to try and rescue her, but no, all was calm.

She said her name was Lucy, she had been taken from her home in England when she was five, Jack asked "How old are you now Lucy? She said "fifteen," Jack took her hand, "what do you remember about your family?" he said, she looked sad, she said "not much, I remember my mum chasing the car I was in, that's the last thing I remember." Elise said "Where are we going Jack?" He thought for a moment then before he could answer Elise said "Oh shit! The cops!" Jack said, "pull over." Elise stopped the car at the side of the road, Lucy was crying, "don't trust him," she said, he will take me back," Jack stepped out of the car, the cop pushed him against the side of the car and began frisking him.

Jack saw the cop's hand go for his holster and immediately responded with a backwards head butt, breaking the cop's nose, Jack spun round and raised his knee into the cop's groin, he went down, as Jack, Elise and Lucy left, the cop was handcuffed to his steering wheel and his radio smashed, Jack had his gun.

"They know where we're heading!" said Jack, "turn off," Elise took a dirt road off the main highway and headed off into the dark countryside, eventually stopping in a quiet spot miles from anywhere.

"What the hell are we going to do now?" said Elise, Jack thought for a moment, then said "The first thing we need to do is get Lucy out of the country to somewhere safe. They continued on the dirt road until they reached Kettara, a village with nothing much in the way of anything, they turned north on the N7, it was a long winding road which ran through mountains, the landscape was all the same, like driving through the world's biggest quarry.

After some fuel stops and sharing the driving they eventually arrived at El Jadida, a coastal town to the south of Casablanca, Jack said "we need to lose this car, if they've got the police in their pocket you can bet your boots we're on the wanted list for some jumped up charge," Elise agreed, "Jack saw something which gave him an idea, "can you ride a motorcycle?" he asked Elise, "sure, I love bikes," Jack dumped the car in a back alley and using his company card bought two nearly new Motorcycles, he chose BMW as they had to be reliable, Lucy rode pillion with Jack and Elise followed on behind, it wasn't long before Jack spotted a large group of British bikers on tour heading home so they blended in with them.

A few hours later the group arrived at Tangier, Jack met mother, she had been waiting in a street not far from the ferry as arranged, Jack had called for help some time earlier after taking a photo of Lucy and sending it ahead, Jack took off his helmet, left the bike with Elise and walked to the car, mother handed him some documents and Jack walked back to the group.

They followed the bikers onto the ferry, and Lucy's new passport and papers worked perfectly, "We'll need to get some British plates for the bikes if we're going to do the rest of the trip with these guys," said Jack.

Ninety minutes later they were in Gibraltar, the bikers all had their hotels pre booked and Jack had a bigger problem than before, the place was

still booked out, Gibraltar was heaving with tourists.
Getting British plates made up for the bikes was easy, they parked among the other bikers so no one would notice them, even with a description if they knew what they were riding.

They got talking to the bikers who were very helpful, one of the girls who were supposed to be on their tour hadn't made it so they had a bed spare, it would mean sharing a room with two other girls but they were welcome to take it, Elise and Lucy were quite happy to share a single bed. Jack however was stuck, well for a moment he was, then he remembered Karen, he said goodbye to Elise and Lucy and went to find her, the bar would be his first port of call, he thought it might not be a good idea to go to her apartment.

Jack walked into the bar, there she was, sitting in the same place, talking to the same barman, Jack went to the other end of the bar and sent her a drink over, she looked across and saw him, she smiled and called him over, "Hi Karen, how are you?" he said, she smiled as she thought of a response then said "pregnant!, you got me pregnant you bastard!" she said, Jack looked worried, almost panicking, then seeing the terrified look on his face she started laughing, "Gotcha!" she said, the relief jack felt at that moment was like someone had lifted an elephant off his back.

"I suppose you want to try to get me pregnant again?" she said in a slightly drunk manner, Jack smiled and said "I did try not to," Karen still laughing said "I know, anyway if you want to fuck me we better go while I can still stand up,"

Jack wondered if she was like this with everyone, as he helped her home, "I'm not a tart, I don't do this sort of thing you know, not ever" she said, that answered Jack's unspoken question. Karen eventually got the key in the door then collapsed on the bed, Jack being a gentleman undressed her, put her into bed, climbed in next to her and went to sleep.

About six in the morning, Jack was having a wonderful dream, it was the most magnificent blow job he had ever had, he woke up as his cock pulsated and shot his hot cum into Karen's throat, she choked a bit but didn't stop, then Jack watched her as she swallowed it all, Jack said "well that's me done, what about you?" She looked up, licked her lips and said, "that's thank you for putting me to bed," he smiled and knowing he had to get going he headed for the shower.

Karen joined him a few minutes later taking great pleasure in soaping his cock which made him hard again, "I wish….." started Jack, Karen said "shhh" don't worry, I'm happy, I know you have to go".

Jack was loving this part of the trip, being a member of this group of bikers, it was a great experience as they rode together at a steady pace north through Spain, France and eventually England, Jack felt safe as they boarded the euro tunnel train, he wondered if he would be allowed to keep the bike.

Chapter Thirty five
Home

It was late at night when they reached home, Elise had a sister she wanted to stay with, Jack took Lucy to his house, Carol was very pleased to see him and welcomed Lucy, she knew she wouldn't get an explanation so she didn't ask, she just made a room up for her.

The following morning Jack got up to a full English breakfast, Lucy was already at the table tucking into hers, after they had finished Jack took Lucy to work, she was talked to by one of the women interrogators and came up with a lot of useful information, the girls she had been working with were mostly child kidnap victims, so it really started to look like this was a major trafficking operation.

Lucy's parents were located, it had been ten years since Lucy had been taken, Jack had the honour of reuniting them, he took Lucy to her mother's home in Southend on sea, Lucy stayed in the car while Jack knocked the door.

Lucy's mother came to the door, Jack said "Hello, Mrs Jackson?" he asked, "Yes, can I help you?" she replied, Jack paused then said "I have some news about Lucy, may I come in?" The tears were already welling up in her eyes, she had been expecting to hear her little girl was dead for the past ten years and it looked as if that day had come, "Please sit down Mrs Jackson," said Jack, Already thinking the worse and then being asked to sit down, she knew what was coming, she was crying, tears streaming down her face, Jack said "She's been found," Mrs Jackson said "I guessed that is what it would be, have you caught him?" "Him?" asked Jack, "The man who killed her, I saw him you know, I saw him take my little girl!" Jack looked surprised, "But, she's not dead" he said, surprisingly to Jack Mrs Jackson's tears and emotional state got worse, she was now overcome with joy, Jack said "She's here, she's outside in my car, are you ready for this?" Mrs Jackson put her hands either side of Jack's face a kissed him, "Yes oh my god yes" as she stood up, stumbled a bit then went towards the door, she opened the door to find Lucy already on the doorstep, it had been ten years but she knew instantly her ordeal was over, she hugged the girl so tight Lucy cried out.

Jack was smiling all the way back to London, that was the most beautiful thing he had ever seen, he even had a tear in his eye at times.

Jack got back to the office and ten minutes later he was briefing the team on his findings, Jack and Elise were sent to Prague, there seemed to be a lot of activity there and someone else would go to Marrakech, someone who could go to the club and not be recognized, Jack had blown his cover there.

Jack and Elise arrived in Prague, they booked into two rooms in the same hotel, over lunch they discussed their plan of action, Jack said "Oh great, looks like I'm trolling the streets for underage prostitutes then, this place is full of them!" Elise smiled and said "You shouldn't have much trouble finding one then"
"What are you going to do while I'm out soliciting?" said Jack, Elise laughed, Oh I don't know, maybe go for a manicure or a facial." Jack winked at her, "I'd give you a facial!" he said, completely destroying the tone of the conversation, Elise snapped at him "Don't you ever think of anything else?"

They left the hotel, Jack was doubtful about finding his targets during the day, usually street walking was an after dark profession in most places, not here it seemed, he hadn't gone more than a few hundred feet when he saw an obvious contender, she was certainly not underage but may well know some valuable stuff, Jack asked if she spoke English, she didn't but he had a translator on his phone so used that, she took him away from the main road, to a quiet alley, she sat down on a low wall and held out her hand for money, Jack was prepared, he had already drawn out plenty of cash.

Jack handed some notes over, she was more than happy with the amount and went to unzip his trousers, Jack stopped her, he used the translator to say, just talk, no sex.

She didn't seem quite so happy then but went ahead, the longer she talked the more money she wanted.
She did tell him she knew about some young girls working the area but she wasn't prepared to discuss their handlers, they were obviously feared, Jack now knew where to meet the youngsters, all he had to do was get them to talk.

Jack wouldn't find them until the evening so he went back to the hotel room, there was a knock at the door, it was Elise, "Did you score then?" she asked, laughing, Jack smiled and said "be professional will you?"
Elise laughed and said "see, I can be smutty too!"

It was lunch time so they both went to the hotel restaurant together for a nice meal, on the company of course.
Elise had been checking out the local brothels and finding out who the registered owners were, she had sent all her information in to the office and they were running background checks.

Evening came around and once again Jack hit the streets, he went to the place he had been told he would find the youngsters and found nothing, it was quiet, maybe the woman he was talking to earlier had tipped them off.

He had been walking the area when a car stopped, a young woman, not much more than a child, got out, she then walked to the corner and started being very obvious to the passing traffic, Jack walked over to her, She said something, he didn't understand, he asked if she spoke English, she nodded, "You want to fuck?" she said, Jack was surprised by how blunt she was and said, "I want to talk" the girl started to walk away, Jack followed, "I'll pay for your time," he said, the girl kept walking.

She hadn't even asked what he wanted to talk about, he guessed she was under orders not to talk to anyone.

Jack's phone rang, it was Elise, she said "where are you? I'm at a back street club and half these girls look like they should be in school!" Jack took the address and walked there, it was only about fifteen minutes away.

As he entered the door he spotted Elise, she was sitting alone at a table, Jack joined her, she spent the next few minutes discreetly pointing out the young girls, seeing them was one thing, getting them alone was something else, Jack thought about the lengths they had to go to in order to get Lucy out of Marrakech.

Jack said "Maybe I should book a private room, maybe I can get one to talk?" Elise said, "you did it last time, my turn," Jack smiled, go on then, but watch out for cameras."

Elise chose a girl and they went off to a private room, once inside the girl asked Elise for money, she handed over the requested amount then the girl started to undress her, Elise stopped her, Elise was now laying flat on the bed and the young girl went to go down on her, Elise was trying to talk to the girl, but she was unstoppable, she had to do her job, she knew she was being watched,
The girl pulled Elise's panties to one side, Elise stopped her, "come here," the girl crawled up alongside Elise,

Elise knew what she was doing looked sexual to the camera, but she had no intention of exploiting this youngster, but if she hadn't played along with it their cover would have been shot to hell. This girl wasn't talking, Elise said "Kiss my neck" the girl was quite willing and Elise took this opportunity to whisper to the girl, she whispered "I want to help you,"
The girl said nothing but she didn't stop kissing Elise's neck, Elise tried again "meet me somewhere quiet? I'm here to help,"
Again the girl said nothing.

The session came to an end, Elise returned to the table, Jack asked her if she'd had any progress, she said "No, a brick wall, I don't think we're going to get anywhere like this," Jack decided to leave it at that, it was bad enough having to get these girls which may well be underage into private rooms which also put themselves in a difficult position, let alone get them to talk.

Just before closing time the young girl from earlier walked to the table, she handed Elise a drink and a paper napkin, Elise noticed something written on the napkin so discreetly put it in her pocket. The club closed, Jack and Elise had just sat in the car, Jack went to start the engine and Elise put her hand out, "Stop," she said, she pulled the note from her pocket. Elise said "Drive around the back, Jack did, then as they stopped near the rear entrance the door opened, three big men stepped out, then all of a sudden Elise's door was opened and she was dragged out, Jack got out and ran around the car to help her, then everything went black!

When Jack woke up the car was still running, he had the mother of all headaches, his pockets were all pulled inside out where he'd obviously been searched, his wallet lay on the floor a few feet away with the contents spread around it. Jack struggled to his feet, staggered to the front of the car, there was Elise, she was unconscious on the ground, bleeding and battered, Jack felt for his phone, it was gone.

He carefully picked Elise up and put her in the back of the car, She was obviously in pain, she cried out with every movement and every bump in the road. Eventually they arrived at the hospital, Jack pulled up outside with his horn blaring, the staff were there immediately, they took Elise inside and Jack threw the keys to a waiting porter and shouted, "park it for me please mate!" He didn't really care if the guy parked it or left it there, he just needed to be with Elise, once inside jack was pacing up and down the corridor, Elise was being tended to in a room with the door closed, after what seemed like an eternity a nurse came out to see Jack, "Nothing broken, she'll be OK but we want to keep her in for observation. Jack felt relieved, he asked to see her, they said she had been sedated and he could see her tomorrow.

Jack found the porter, collected his keys and gave the guy some cash, he then went to his hotel. He sat there silent, thinking he'd let Elise down, but how was he to know they'd get jumped, the questions were going through his mind, did the girl tell? Probably not, she was very discreet with the note she'd given to Elise, she must have been seen or caught on camera, maybe she was intercepted as she went for the back door, so many questions but only one conclusion, these guys had something to hide.

Chapter Thirty six
Lily

Knowing his cover was blown at the club, Jack decided to try the streets again, there were plenty of working girls but none seemed out of place, he went into a shop, bought a sandwich and a coke, then sat on a wall to eat his lunch, it was then Jack spotted a girl of about fifteen or younger working the corner, he walked over to her, she asked if he was looking for some action, he said "where? Surely not here!" She spoke excellent English, "We can go in there if you like," she said pointing to an overgrown park across the road.

Jack hoped this would be a break so he pretended to be a punter, "How much?" he said, the girl gave him a figure which he agreed to and they went into the park together, when they reached a secluded spot Jack handed over the agreed amount of money and she began to remove her clothing, Jack stopped her, " he said , I just want to talk to you."
He hoped this one would be more forthcoming as there were no cameras about.
"Talk?" she said, "Talk is extra," Jack reached into his pocket and pulled out some more cash, he asked her what her name was, she said "Lily," Jack didn't believe her so he went on to ask her where she was from and how come she is here, why does she do this job and so on, she wasn't

very cooperative, she said "Why? Are you trying to save me?" She laughed, Jack said he was being serious and there was a much better life for her if she would just be honest.

Jack thought to himself he had interrogated hardened criminals easier than this, the girl was defensive to the extreme.

"How about I take you somewhere to eat?" he suggested, she immediately reacted "No! I can't go anywhere," Jack knew then she was being controlled, so he said "I can get you out of this racket, I can get you home or to another country, if you want out"
She thought for a moment then said "What's in it for you?" Jack said, "I just need some information so I can shut this lot down, but only after you're safe." Lily paused for a moment, "what do I get?" she said belligerently, "jack said isn't your freedom and a decent life enough?"

"I want money," said the girl, Jack agreed to talk about it, he said he would see what he could do but he needed the information.

They walked the short distance back to Jack's hotel. Put his and Elise's bags in the car, checked out and collected their passports, the girl said "I don't have a passport" Jack told her not to worry and they drove off, "Where are we going?" Lily asked, Jack replied, "we're getting you away from here but there's something I have to do first."

Jack parked the car at the hospital, keeping the girl by his side he went inside to collect Elise, she was on her feet, her face was a mess, one swollen black eye and loads of bruises, she was walking but obviously in some discomfort.

The three of them climbed into the car, "When do I get my money?" asked the girl, "Soon," said Jack, they drove for an hour or so then Jack pulled into a truck stop.

Jack turned around in his seat, looked at Lily and said "you can have your money when you've told us what we need to know," Lily was still being stubborn and said "How much?" Jack explained how much would depend on what she knows, they all went inside the truck stop for a bite to eat, the truckers were looking at Elise and her injuries, and Jack as if he'd done it, there was quiet mumbling going on, it felt quite uncomfortable.

After eating they returned to the car, Jack went ahead and checked all around and under it, this was becoming a bit of a habit, everything seemed OK so they got in, before moving off Jack said to Lily "We're about to cross into Germany so you better start talking,"

Lily said enough to show Jack and Elise she knew what was going on, Jack still sat there, "Why aren't we going?" asked Lily, at that moment a motorcycle drove into the truck stop car park, pulled up alongside the car and the rider tapped on the window.

Jack opened in a little and an envelope appeared through the gap, the motorcyclist rode away, Jack handed the envelope to Elise then drove off. Elise opened the envelope and inside was a set of documents for Lily, who was now Rachael according to her paperwork.

It was late at night when they reached Frankfurt, Jack booked them all into a hotel, Elise was sharing with Lily for reasons of security and Jack was in an adjoining room.
This was where questions needed to be answered.

Once again Lily was an English girl, she also had been snatched when she was little, but from a hotel in Spain, her abductors had beaten her, kept her isolated and convinced her they would kill her if ever she disobeyed them. She also came up with a number of names, none of which were on the list Elise had, Maybe they were dealing with two separate groups?

Elise boarded a plane for London the following morning taking Lily with her, Jack headed back to Prague.

Although Elise's cover was blown in the club there were still several similar clubs in the area, Jack had to get hold of one of the men on the inside, he going to need some help.
He checked into a hotel, a different one, it always pays to keep on the move, he called mother to arrange a meeting, it was about ten that evening when the meeting took place in a restaurant. Mother said she would make the appropriate arrangements and gave Jack a password.

Chapter Thirty seven
Mill

Jack got back to his hotel about eleven, his bags had been put in his room but there were no towels and after all that traveling he needed a shower, he called room service and a pretty little maid in uniform appeared some fifteen minutes later, as she entered the room their eyes met in a long lingering gaze, the sort of gaze that would have said the same had their tongues met.

"Will there be anything else sir?" She asked, Jack couldn't take his eyes of this woman, she was exactly the type he would go for, pretty, small framed with long legs and to top it off that white maid's apron sent all sorts of kinky thoughts through Jack's mind, French maid scenarios and so on, Jack was still standing there speechless when once again she said "Will there be anything else sir? He couldn't help himself, he had to say "yes" but he had no idea what was next, she glanced down at his bulging trousers and said "Should I run your shower sir?"

Without a moment's hesitation Jack said "Yes, yes, run the shower," the maid went into the bathroom, Jack followed her, He picked up a bottle of shower gel and as she was fiddling with the temperature setting in the cubicle he deliberately reached over her to put the shower gel inside, he was pressing quite firmly against her and she knew he was taking his time.

She turned and they ended up face to face and very close, they both held that position for a while, Jack then blurted "Join me?" She smiled, Jack said "Oh my god! Did I just say that out loud?"

"you did," she said, Jack said, I'm so sorry, what must you think of me?"

She put her hand on his trousers and said "do you really want to know?" Jack smiled, I need a shower," he said, I can help with that," said the maid, they both stripped off their clothes and Jack got in the shower followed by the maid, she soaped him all over, she was obviously enjoying the feel of his muscles as she gently and slowly washed him.

"My name is Mill" She said as she washed him with her soapy hands getting lower and lower on his body, then Jack had a feeling which could only be one thing, his hard cock was now inside her soft mouth, that mouth he had been staring at with her red full lips, he had wanted to kiss since the moment he saw her, he hadn't kissed her but her mouth was doing something much better, the water was streaming over both of them, he looked down at her soaking wet hair as she gently and slowly savoured his cock, her mouth felt so nice as she took as much of his shaft as she could before withdrawing.

Jack pulled her up, he felt he couldn't hold back much longer so he had to stop her at that point, she was standing in front of him in the warm rain of the shower, he kissed her deeply, she responded, her whole body seemed to be involved in this kiss.

They dried themselves, Mill spent a while drying her hair as Jack prepared some drinks, "Won't they miss you?" he called to her, "I finished ten minutes ago" she said.

After drinks they climbed into bed, Jack was tired, he was falling asleep, he didn't want to, he wanted Mill but he was so tired, "would you like me to stay?" she said, Jack was already asleep.

It was about four in the morning when Jack woke up, he was looking at the face of this gorgeous woman sleeping naked alongside him, he composed himself then slowly and carefully slid down in the bed, her legs were already spread apart to a point so Jack moved them a little more, she didn't stir at all, he found her treasure, a smooth shaved haven of paradise, Jack began slowly licking her, he had to stop he was yearning for a taste of her, he pushed his tongue as far as he could into her, she tasted lovely,, he could feel her sticky juice on his lips then went back to licking her, she was still sleeping soundly.

Mill must have been aware of something, maybe she was dreaming because every now and then she would react, a tiny movement, a quiet moan, eventually she woke up a little, she started to react a lot more, moving in rhythm with Jack's licking, she was getting wetter, Jack took a taste every now and then, and all of a sudden she came, she was wriggling and thrusting against his face, Jack inserted a finger, that made her orgasm even better, she was crying out so loud Jack was concerned the guests in the next room may be woken, she was calming down, as she did Jack inserted two fingers into her, when he withdrew them they were wet, he put his fingers in her mouth, Mill sucked them dry.
She took a pillow and rolled onto it, Mill was now laying face down with the pillow under her, this made her little round bum sit up nice and pert,

Jack climbed onto her and put his erect cock inside her wet pussy, she was so wet and slippery, he then put his legs outside hers, effectively closing her up onto his cock, this was tight, he pushed hard until his groin met her firm buttocks, again and again, harder and harder, Mill was getting close again and within a minute she came, this time she was squirting her juice all over the pillow and the sheet, jack could feel her soaking his balls as he continued to pound away at her pussy, he was close, he wanted to cum inside her, but he didn't want to ask the question so at the very last moment he withdrew and watched at he shot his cum all over her ass, he studied it for a moment as it dripped over her anus and headed down towards her pussy.

"I need another shower" he said, Mill agreed but this time they would resist temptation and shower separately.
Mill returned to the bedroom to find Jack sitting in the chair, "What's up? I thought you'd still be in bed," said Mill, Jack laughed and said "It's soaked" as he headed for the bathroom, Mill looked, it was, She said "Sorry about that, it's been a long time for me and I think I must have got carried away."

At just after eight, Mill had already left when Jack's phone rang, it was the call he had been waiting for, Jack packed his bags into the car, checked out of the hotel and headed for the rendezvous point, he arrived to find a van and two cars full of men waiting for him.

Jack was handed a stab vest and a gun, he put the vest on and they all drove to the club, it was closed that time of day, it would be a good guess that most inside would be sleeping, one of the men picked the door lock, as they opened it the alarm started chirping, again another man dealt with that with the help of some fancy hi tech electronics.

They were inside, it was dark, the blinds were all closed, they all had night vision glasses and proceeded quietly to search the building, they needed a live hostage.

After searching the building they found nothing, there was no one there, maybe this one was operated differently to the one in Marrakech, maybe it was two different groups.

"They'll know we're onto them when they return and find someone has been in here, and they will," said Jack, that's easy said one of the men, he went to the bar, opened the till and took the float, another removed the recording equipment from the office so there'd be nothing on camera, and someone else loaded up the booze and cigarettes, they left, leaving the door wide open, as the gadget was removed the alarm sounded and they were gone.

"There you go Jack, they got burgled, simple, anyone fancy a drink?" Said one of the men.

They dropped Jack off at his car and drove away. As Jack headed back to the hotel, he thought what a waste of time and resources that was. Then he had another idea, He opened one of his bags and took out a small metal case, opened that and pulled out what looked like a normal phone charger, only this one had a microphone and transmitter inside, he turned the car around and went back to the club, it was now swarming with police.

There didn't seem to be anyone from the club there, at least not yet, Jack parked up and casually strolled into the building, he went to where he'd seen the boss's office earlier that day, he tapped on the door, there was no answer so he went inside, found a vacant power point and plugged the phone charger in, it was a good spot too, right by the desk.

As he was leaving one of the cops asked "Excuse me, who are you?" Jack pointed to the small metal case he was carrying, "I left it here last night, just come to pick it up, Franco said it was OK," the cop let him pass and Jack went back to his car.

He then switched on what looked like a small radio and after fiddling a bit he could hear what was going on inside, Jack thought he better not stick around the cop might find out there is no Franco, or a staff member may recognize him when they turn up. So he went back to the hotel, luckily they still had available rooms because Jack had checked out that morning thinking he'd be on his way somewhere with a suspect by now.

Jack intended to have a lazy afternoon, there was nothing he could do until the club returned to some sort of normality, so he lay back on the bed, closed his eyes and got some much needed sleep.

He woke up at four thirty, he was hungry, he picked up the phone by the bed and ordered some food, it wasn't long before there was a knock at the door, he called out "Who is it?" "Room service, with your meal," came the reply, Jack thought he recognized the voice, he opened the door to find Mill with a trolley of food for him, she entered the room, Jack walked round behind her and suggestively touched her behind, she said "I can't, I'm working but I finish at twelve if you want me?"
Jack smiled, he lifted the silver platter lid to reveal his burger and fries, he said "I'm looking forward to twelve," Mill smiled as she left the room closing the door behind her.

Chapter Thirty eight
A breakthrough

At about seven that evening Jack drove to the strip club, he parked somewhere away from cameras but close enough for his phone charger bug to be picked up, there was nothing going on for about half an hour then jackpot! Two men had entered the office, Jack heard the chair creak as one sat down, there were raised voices, he listened and wrote notes, "I don't give a fuck, tell him to bring the merchandise here before he delivers it, I want to check!" the other man seemed afraid, he said "He won't be happy!" then the first man shouted at him, "Just fucking do it! Nothing goes past here unless I check it out first!" the other man left, the man in the chair was still muttering after he left.

Jack still had nothing concrete all he knew was something was coming, but when? He had no choice he would have to spend his time bored stupid and getting cramp just sitting quietly in the car, on the poxy car park.

Jack was getting worried, he was alone there, it was a dark desolate place, he needed a gun, he had no idea what to expect. It was eleven thirty, Jack was looking forward to getting back to Mill at the hotel but it wasn't looking hopeful, then a van arrived, it parked by the back door, Jack got out of the car and walked up to get a better look, the driver banged on the club door, a staff member opened the door and the man stepped inside.

Jack saw an opportunity, it was risky but he had to try, he ran to the van and looked through the window in the rear door, inside he could see two young girls, one about eight or nine years old and one a little older, they were tied up, gagged and on the floor, Jack tried the door but it was locked, just then the door to the club opened and two men came out, Jack quickly ducked in between the van and the alley wall, the men opened the van spoke to each other in a language Jack didn't understand then the one went back into the club, the van driver got back into the van and drove away, leaving Jack standing there exposed, he ran back to the car and followed the van at a distance.

The van had been traveling for quite a while when Jack decided it was time to act, he waited until it was out in the countryside and hoping the driver wasn't armed, Jack accelerated, passed the van then slammed on the brakes, the van driver had nowhere to go, he had to stop, then he put it in reverse and drove backwards for a few hundred feet, the van was swerving all over the road, it eventually veered off and hit a tree, the driver got out and ran.

Jack thought, that was easier than expected but then the van driver had no idea what he was facing either.
Jack forced open the one back door which wasn't against the tree, untied the girls and they all ran to the car.

Jack would have liked to take the driver too but he couldn't put these girls in more danger by chasing him, it turns out he didn't need to, Jack was driving back the way he came when he saw the van driver sitting by the road, Jack stopped, he was obviously in trouble, the van driver was in his late sixties, he was scruffy looking, needed a shave, and a bath.
As Jack pulled up along side him he said "help me?" he spoke in broken English but Jack got the basics of what he was saying, he needed to get away, when they found out he had lost their precious cargo he would be a dead man.
Jack searched him for weapons then tied his hands behind his back and sat him in the front seat.

They drove for hours without stopping, Jack was heading for the German border, if he could get them to the office in Frankfurt then maybe they could finally get to the bottom of all this. For a moment Jack's thoughts turned to Mill, she would be waiting for him at the hotel, he couldn't help that, but he was disappointed.

Only stopping for fuel on the way they arrived at Frankfurt the following morning, Jack drove into the underground car park where they were met by security and escorted inside.

In the interview room the girls were telling how they too had been snatched, one from Poland and one from Hungary, the driver however was even more useful, he knew a lot about the organization, he said he was given instructions where to pick up and where to drop off, that was all he did but he knew all the places, or at least the one's he had been going to and from.

The van driver cooperated fully, the alternative would either be a lifetime in prison or death by his employers, neither option was too appealing so he did what he could to save himself.

Jack was remembering the original assignment was to find out who had been responsible for killing his colleagues a year earlier, now it had turned into a trafficking case, funny how one thing leads to another.

Jack was in the canteen having lunch when he felt a hand on his shoulder, a voice from behind said quietly "you saved my life, but I'm still not sleeping with you," It was Elise, she was fully recovered and sat down opposite him at the table.

Jack leaned over to her and said "You are hot, but I wouldn't want a gratitude fuck anyway," he laughed, Elise smiled and said, "I know you, and I know your weakness."

After lunch Jack and Elise went to the interview room, they sat opposite the van driver, he didn't look good, he was going a bit grey in the face, Jack pressed the alarm, the man fell forward onto the table, he was trying to say something, Jack listened as the man whispered, then he collapsed, Jack was pumping his chest and trying to revive him when the paramedics arrived.

Jack asked one of the managers there, "What about the girls?" he said they were being taken care of and would be returned to their families soon, Jack gave a sigh of relief, he was happy someone else would be dealing with that, he felt quite emotional when he returned Lucy to her mother.

Elise walked up to Jack and said "Come on, we need to get going," Jack said "get going?" Yes back to Prague," she said, Jack said "Hold on a minute, who's been doing the leg work while you've been relaxing with your feet up?" Elise smiled and said "You have, but I still outrank you so come on, my hero," she laughed at his expression and they headed for the car park.

Jack went to get into his somewhat tired hire car, Elise stopped him, leave that, it'll get returned, we're using this," she pointed at a big tough looking pickup truck, it was brand new, seriously modified and Jack was dying to get behind the wheel. Elise said, I'm driving as she climbed up into the cab.
"How come we have this monster?" Asked Jack, Elise said "Apparently you're costing the firm too much, because you keep wrecking or losing hire cars!"

Chapter Thirty nine
4X4

They left, the big black shiny truck was certainly getting the attention of the boy racers along the way but Elise resisted the temptation to lose them in a cloud of tyre smoke. Prague lay not far ahead and Jack knowing that his cover was blown and Elise's certainly was, wondered what the plan was, but Elise had all that, she was in charge of the mission.

Jack expected to do the usual stuff, check into a hotel, make inquiries and so on but not this time, they were almost at the club, it was eight thirty and the place had been open for about half an hour, as they passed the car park of the fuel station they were joined by the police who merged in behind them.

This convoy of vehicles surrounded the club, Elise pushed a button on the dashboard and a tray opened below the glove box, on the tray were two automatic pistols and a couple of full clips, Jack grabbed one, put a clip in his belt then passed the other to Elise.

People started exiting the club, the cops used a loudhailer to order them to stay where they were, a couple of shots were fired into the air to reinforce the order, Jack and Elise just stood by the truck as the cops brought out the staff, one of which Elise recognized, he was being held between two cops, She casually strolled over to him, she looked him in the eye and said "Like to hit girls do you?" As she brought her knee up into his groin, he bent over in pain as her knee came up for a second time and hit him in the face, knocking out two teeth, she smiled as they fell into the dirt.

She strolled back over to Jack and said "That's the one I remember from that night." The staff were all being loaded into police vans and taken away, the public had their details taken down and dismissed and finally after an extensive search the club was locked up.

Jack and Elise went to the police station. Interviews were taking place, there were about fifteen suspects in all, the inspector said, best come back tomorrow as they were mostly going off shift and the prisoners will be locked up for the night, so Jack and Elise went to book into a hotel, the same hotel Jack had stayed at previously, they took two rooms with adjoining doors.

Midnight, and Jack was just getting into bed when there was a quiet tap on the door, Jack thought for a moment it was Elise, finally giving it up, but when he opened the door he found Mill standing there, she was in her sexy uniform and asked, "Is there anything you need sir, I have just finished my shift," Jack thought he'd lost this one when he stood her up but here she was, he must be doing something right.

Jack stood aside and Mill entered the room, it was less than five minutes before she was naked and laying in bed waiting for him.

Jack locked the door and Joined Mill, she was in a giggly mood, she was ticklish so jack played on that for a while, then he slid down under the covers and was busy working her clit with his tongue, Mill was in ecstasy as he expertly licked her, she was rigid on the bed, her head tilted back over the pillow so she was looking at the headboard, neither of them were aware of the adjoining door opening and Elise walking into the room, she was wearing a flimsy see through nightdress, she stood by the bed looking at Mill as she gripped the sides of the mattress with clenched fists, Jack was under the sheet on his elbows and knees with his face buried between Mill's thighs.

Elise thought for a moment or two then she put her hand under the sheet, she reached around until she found Jack's cock, he didn't realize it wasn't Mill's hand despite it obviously being too far for her to reach, Elise began stroking him, she was on her knees by the side of the bed, Mill still had no idea she was there and it was a minute or two before Jack finally realized that couldn't be Mill's hand stroking his cock. With one hand jack threw off the sheet, Mill totally ignorant of her surroundings continued as she was, Elise let go of Jack, she moved up towards Mill, Mill still had her eyes tightly closed, Elise Kissed her mouth, softly and lingered there, Mill still hadn't thought how could Jack's face be in two places at once, she was too excited and approaching orgasm to realize or even care, as Elise put her tongue inside Mill's mouth she suddenly opened her eyes.

There was a moment of hesitation as Mill realized this was a woman kissing her, a brief moment of panic, Mill was straight but that was about to change. Mill was so engrossed in the moment she didn't care whether she was being had by man woman or beast, it was just so overwhelming.

Mill got her orgasm, it was spectacular, she was shaking from head to toe, the normally loud orgasm was muffled by Elise's mouth over hers. As the moment passed, Jack got up out of bed, he stood there naked looking at Elise who was slowly removing her tiny nightdress, Jack thought all his birthdays had come at once when Elise climbed on top of Mill and began passionately kissing her mouth again, Mill didn't resist, she was loving this deviation from her norm.

Then Elise turned around getting herself into a sixty nine position over Mill, this pretty little straight waitress was now confronted with Elise's already wet pussy in her face, she hesitated, Elise began licking Mill's pussy, Mill lost all her inhibitions at that point and reciprocated, Jack was still standing, watching, he couldn't believe his eyes or his luck, but he was feeling a bit neglected, he went to the bottom of the bed from where he could see Elise busily eating Mill's pussy. Elise lifted her head and beckoned Jack to take Mill, he climbed up and kneeling on the bed he put his erect cock into Mill's pussy, then Elise took him out with her hand, she took Jack's cock which was soaked in Mill's pussy juice and sucked the full length of his shaft, taking all the nectar in her mouth, Jack was fucking Mill's pussy and Elise's mouth in turn, after a while Jack got up, Elise nudged Mill around so the girls were still in the same position but across the bed, Jack now whilst standing on the floor had access to both ends of both girls, he went to one side of the bed and he could fuck Mill's pussy and Elise's mouth but he'd done that so he went to the other side of the bed and Mill was sucking his cock as he dared to think about Elise's pussy, he did it, he got the prize he had been after for weeks, he pushed his cock deep inside Elise's tight pussy, it was tight too, this girl either refrained a lot or worked out, Jack suspected it was both.

Elise was firm and fit, she had a six pack and visible muscles flexing as she moved in rhythm keeping perfectly in time with Jack, and Mill.

Mill was for the first time in her life satisfying a woman and Elise was indeed being satisfied, Jack was inside Mill as Elise came, coming on Mill's face, Mill could taste her which seemed to encourage Mill to lick her even more, once Jack realized Elise had cum he went around the bed again and immediately rammed his cock hard up inside her, Elise gave out a little squeak as he fucked her pussy hard, and fast, Jack was working towards his, he could feel it welling up, all of a sudden Elise said "Don't you fucking cum in me!" Jack withdrew, the girls both sprung up, they put their faces together and as their tongues touched Jack spurted his cum all over their tongues, mouths, and Mill even got some of it in her eye., Elise had cum dripping from her nose and chin, Mill began licking Elise's face, Elise then did the same to Mill, these girls were eating all of Jack's cum, they were leaving nothing to waste.

Collapsed together on the bed, Elise said to Jack "Happy now?" "Ecstatic!" Replied Jack, Mill said "I need a shower, " she went to the bathroom, Elise got up and said, I'll shower in my room" jack said are you sleeping here with us?" Elise said, "No way, you can have your sticky bedding, I'm going to enjoy my fresh sheets!" Elise left swinging her nightdress in her hand as she went, Jack joined Mill in the shower.

In the morning Jack was woken by his work phone, it was the Frankfurt office with an update on what the girls had said and to tell Jack the driver hadn't regained consciousness and had died before reaching hospital.

Jack was thinking about the last thing the driver had said to him, he had written it down, it didn't make any sense. Just then there was a tap on the adjoining door and Elise walked in, Jack went to say something about last night but she cut him off "Ah ah, ah, don't even think about it, that was a one off!" she said.

They sat down and went through all the information they had, trying to make some sort of sense. Jack spotted something, Casablanca! It was on the driver's list, it was a drop off point. It was where Carol had been taken. Jack put the scrap of paper on the table, the last thing the driver said, it was an eight digit number, he said to Elise, the driver said "Inside 35698271, that's what he said, what the hell does that mean?" said Jack, They studied the driver's statement, "It looks like we have to go back to Casablanca, that's where I was undercover and that's where you turned up, there has to be a connection," said Elise, Jack looked at the map and said "That's one hell of a drive, shall we fly?" Elise pointed out they weren't in a rented car they could just drop off anywhere and all their kit was in the truck, so they would have to drive.

They checked out and set off, by the end of that day they had got to Lyon, it was a trucker's cafe on the side on the main road, there was no accommodation so they would have to get what sleep they could in the truck, all night heavy vehicles were coming and going, it was hard to sleep with all the noise and the headlights lighting up the cab.

Morning came, not soon enough, they went inside the café to get some food but more importantly to freshen up. After as they walked back to the truck Elise had a eureka moment and thumped Jack in the arm, he jumped "What the hell?" he said, Elise pointed at a container truck driving across the car park, "Look!" she said, Jack looked and said "It's a truck, they've been in and out all night, so what?" Elise pointed to the container, "Look stupid, look at that container, what do you see?" Finally the penny dropped, "A number, every container has a number!" They almost ran back to their truck, Jack got into the driver's seat and they left, it was still going to be two days but they needed to get there.

Now there was something of a plan, something to motivate them, some hope of solving this mystery.

"I really need some sleep" said Elise, and within seconds she was gone.

"Where are we?" asked Elise as she woke up, Jack replied, Barcelona will be coming up soon, did you know you snore?" Elise gave him a look and protested "No I don't," Oh you do, and you talk," said Jack, Elise was thoughtful for a moment then asked "What did I say then?" Jack laughed, "I can't tell you, you'll only get embarrassed." Elise was already embarrassed, what had she said that could embarrass her? She decided to leave it at that.

They changed seats, Jack said "If we stop at Valencia we should get there at a decent hour tomorrow," Elise agreed, Jack was soon asleep as Elise took the wheel. It felt like moments later to Jack as the truck stopped at Valencia and he woke up, Elise was on her phone finding a hotel for the night, "Done," she said, Jack took that as hotel booked and asked "Where are we staying?" Elise pointed to a very grand looking building, she parked the truck in the hotel car park, they grabbed their overnight bags and went inside.

The place was as flash on the inside as it was on the out, there was an elevator, Jack looked at the huge marble staircase as he waited for the door to open, above the highly decorative stairs there was an enormous chandelier and above that a paneled ceiling with paintings to rival the Sistine chapel.

The room Elise had booked was just as ostentatious as the rest of the place, Jack said "We can't put this on expenses, it must be horrendously expensive," Elise said "It would be for two rooms but I booked one," jack smiled, she then said "Forget it! I need sleep."

Jack was tired too but he had trouble sleeping that night, he was sharing a bed with Elise, she was as naked as made no difference and he wanted her, despite his hints, nudges and snuggling up to her, she was having none of it, Jack was frustrated, the one thing about Jack was he always wanted what he couldn't have.

Jack went to sleep thinking she may be in a different frame of mind come the morning, he woke up with the sun shining through the window, the temperature was already rising, Jack rolled over to see if Elise wanted to play yet but she wasn't there, the bed was cold, then she emerged, fully dressed, make up done and ready to go, "you getting up?" she said, Jack like a sulking child climbed out of bed and walked slowly to the bathroom, "you said you wanted to get there at a decent hour!" Elise called after him. He soon got over his disappointment, got dressed and headed downstairs, bags in hand.
Late that night they arrived in Casablanca, they'd been held up by traffic, and difficulty getting onto a crossing, it was too late to do anything so Elise booked them into a hotel, two rooms, she

wanted to sleep without Jack poking her all night with his cock.

Jack sat in the hotel bar for a while, Elise went to bed, what a place, there was nothing exciting going on, no eligible young ladies to practice his chat on, and certainly none he would even consider bedding. All in all a disappointing night in, Jack had a couple of drinks then headed up to his room.

Five in the morning and Elise was at Jack's bedside shaking him, Jack, startled, leaped out of bed like it was on fire "What! What? What?" he said in a panic, Elise said "It's five o clock," Jack saw the bright sunshine streaming in through the window, he looked horrified "I've slept all day? Why didn't you wake me?" I am, it's five in the morning" said Elise, Jack went from panic to confused, "Why? Why are you waking me up, it's the middle of the night!" Elise just laughed, as she walked away she said "get your kit on, we have work to do."

Elise drove them to the container yard at the dock, where they had first met, "All we have to do is find that number," she said, Jack slowly turned as he scanned the thousands of containers, stacked high in this huge yard, "It's a needle in a haystack!" he said, Elise had been weighing this up, she knew the layout and said "It has to be on the ground, the van driver would have accessed it, so it has to be at ground level," "good point," said Jack, they began their search in the more remote areas first thinking the bad guys wouldn't want it discovered or accidentally shipped, nothing, they all had numbers but not the number they were looking for.

Chapter Forty
The Container

As they drove back towards the hotel Jack said "Let's not give up on the container theory, it makes sense, but if not at the docks where?" Elise was thinking hard, had she seen a shipping container anywhere else, they always seemed to be at the docks or on trucks.

On the way back to the hotel, Jack took a detour, he wanted to drive buy the illegal strip club just outside Casablanca, as they passed by it looked derelict the door was boarded up, it looked as if part of the building had been on fire, Jack thought that was suspicious, they probably expected to get raided after Lucy talked, Jack pulled up on the gravel car park, then he spotted something, around the back, just visible was the corner of a shipping container, he got out, Elise on his heels, they walked to the rear car park and there were four containers stacked two high with steps up to the top ones. Jack checked the number 35698271, it matched one of the bottom ones, there was no lock on any of them so Jack opened the door.

The container had been ransacked, there was rubbish everywhere, Jack picked up some pieces of wood and held them together, "This was a bed frame," he said, Elise pointed out a stack of six dirty old worn mattresses stacked against the back wall, there were also ropes, plastic water bottles and a bucket among the rubbish.

This had obviously been where either the girls who worked here slept or it was a way station for kidnapped kids.
They checked the other containers, they were still intact, no rubbish, they were simply set up like dormitories, bunk beds and signs of habitation, but these three had not been smashed up, it didn't take long to realize these containers were both accommodation for the girls who worked in the club and the one with the number match was where the freshly snatched kids were kept.

That would explain the fire in the main building and destroying evidence in the container, it was also why Lucy had said she couldn't go anywhere, she was obviously locked in when she wasn't working.

Elise was taking photographs and making notes, they heard a car on the gravel, it stopped by the truck, then it drove round to where Jack and Elise were, it was a local cop, he stepped out with his gun drawn, he called something in Arabic, Jack said "English?" then the cop said, "put your hands up and walk to me,"

Jack and Elise did as requested, the cop said "What are you doing? This is private property and under investigation" Elise answered "We are

Interpol" Jack looked puzzled, how was she going to pull this one off, the cop demanded to see some identification, Elise slowly reached into her pocket and pulled out a small leather wallet, flicked it open and showed the cop, satisfied, he holstered his gun, he did look quite relieved.

Elise asked the cop what had happened, he explained the owners of the club had set fire to the office and left, they also broke up the container, he didn't know if there was anyone being held in there at the time but it was obvious someone or maybe more than one had been at some point.

Elise and Jack were back at the hotel having dinner, Elise said "well looks like we're back to square one then" Jack agreed, then he said "Just a minute, if they were doing this here maybe it's the same setup at other clubs?" "Possibly," said Elise "but the other clubs don't seem to have connections with this one," Jack then said "Oh but the one in Prague does, it was the van driver there who put us onto this one so they have to be the same mob!"
Elise looked satisfied with that and said "So it's back to Prague then!"

Early morning and Jack and Elise met for breakfast, Jack said "before we go I think we should go down to the police station and see what they have, if they'll share," Else agreed it was a good idea so after breakfast they went.

On the way Jack asked Elise "Where did you get that Interpol I.D. from?" She laughed, you mean you don't have one? That could have been difficult yesterday, Just ask for one,"

They arrived at the police station and after introducing themselves were taken to see the case officer, the police were surprisingly cooperative, they had some remnants of partially burnt papers, a list of names and a book full of addresses, Elise asked if she could take copies, the officer said "no need, they've gone, the place is shut down, our investigation is over, you can take the lot," Elise and Jack boxed everything up, put it in the truck and left.

As they were heading out of the city Jack suggested they stop and go through the stuff in the box, Elise agreed so they pulled into a car park, the address book contained hundreds of locations, each one with a date and a number by it, the addresses were all over Europe and the UK, some were even in Russia.

It was a maze, a jigsaw of information which meant very little on it's own, Elise held up one of the burnt remnants, she said "There's a partial address here and guess where?" Jack said "Prague?" Elise said "Correct, give that man a coconut!" The address was indeed in Prague but not the club, which is what Jack thought it would be, but it did confirm Prague was the next place they needed to be.

So they hit the road again, Jack was driving, Elise was scouring the addresses in the book, "There's one here in southern Spain, let's swing by and take a look?" she said, Jack agreed. By the end of the day they'd reached Nerja, it was a holiday resort type of town, the address was up in the mountains, they decided to book into a hotel first as they wouldn't be going any further that day, they checked in and went to a café a hundred meters or so up the road, it was a nice place, English food, English staff, very friendly. A place called Ruskins. They stopped there for some food then went back to the hotel, the hotel wasn't what they were used to, it was very basic, the beds uncomfortable, the balcony was just about big enough to sit on and the view of the car park and bins left quite a lot to be desired. Jack did notice the pool, it was about as big as a puddle but then who needs a pool with the beach five minutes away.

After getting changed, there was still a few hours daylight so Jack and Elise went to the beach, it was a well earned couple of hours relaxation, Jack was eyeing up the girls on the beach, nothing really caught his eye but after an hour he turned his attention to Elise, her long slender

body stretched out on the lounger, beads of sweat trickling off her dark skin, he remembered their one night together with Mill, just then two girls walked past and started giggling, Jack looked round, puzzled then Elise said calmly "You need a cold shower," He looked down to see his shorts bulging from looking at Elise,
She obviously saw him, she must have had one eye open.

As the sun went down they picked up their towels and headed back to the hotel, they had to share a room as it was holiday season and there was only one available but it was a twin room so Elise thought at least she'd get some sleep, Jack was quite disappointed because he knew Elise wouldn't play and who's he going to get into bed with another woman in the room.

The hotel didn't have any proper facilities so they went to Ruskins for breakfast, this place never seemed to close, while there Elise asked one of the staff about the address, she was told the manageress lived in the mountains and she's ask her to come over, she did, within a couple of minutes, she said the address didn't mean anything to her, she had lived in the village for many years and it wasn't familiar, she said it could be a yard or and industrial unit, but that would be outside the village.

Breakfast concluded Jack and Elise drove up the narrow stony road into the mountains, through the village and eventually came across the place, it was an industrial unit, very run down, there were a couple of old abandoned vehicles there, a falling down barn and one shipping container, the place was deserted, Elise looked at the shipping container, Jack fetched a pair of bolt cutters from the truck and took off the padlock, as they opened the door there was a disgusting smell, and flies filled the unit, Thinking the worse, Jack covered his nose and mouth with his sleeve and pulled the door wide open.

Inside there were four knocked up wooden bunks, again empty water bottles and a half full bucket of feces and urine, again it was where people had been kept, and recently too, the bucket hadn't yet dried out and the heat inside was unbearable. But at least there wasn't a corpse as Jack had first suspected.

The question was had they run or was this just a transition period?
Back in the truck Elise studied the dates, she looked at the map and worked out it was a route, from container to container or address, the dates were travel times apart so here today, tomorrows date somewhere else a day's drive away, they'd got a whole network of stopovers set up.

The problem was the dates were all historical so there was no way of telling if or when each container would be used again.

There were no other local addresses in the book, each address was a day's drive from the next, so it was definitely a network.

The problem now was this one had been compromised, Jack had cut the lock off so they would know someone had been here, was this unit now unusable? And why hadn't anyone emptied that bucket, it made no sense to leave it because the next time it was opened it would have been like this, unbreathable disgusting stench, one thing these captives were to their captors was valuable, they came to the conclusion that this one had been abandoned, but why?

The next address was somewhere near Santander in the north of Spain so they decided to stay another night and head off in the morning it was a good eight hour drive, so for the rest of the day they could spend on the beach at Nerja, Elise seemed to like the place, it was touristy but not like Benidorm there was something peaceful about it.
Jack wasn't too happy about sharing a room with Elise, the sun, heat and sweaty bodies

everywhere was making him horny and although he didn't mind being watched, a young lady wouldn't be too thrilled about having Elise as an audience.

The following morning they set off for Santander, Jack thought, why would they choose Santander? Maybe because there's a ferry service from Plymouth but that wouldn't make sense, anyone being taken against their will could easily attract attention on the ferry, and there was always the risk of a vehicle search.

As they drove into Toledo, Jack saw an ancient and impressive castle, he thought to himself how lucky he was having a job which took him around the world to see such magnificent things, they stopped for some lunch, Jack said to Else "What are the odds that the next one has been abandoned too?" She said, "we have to look, it could mean the difference between cracking this or not, anyway more importantly we may save someone's life." Jack agreed, he seemed to be getting motivated now, they were only about four or five hours out.

The sun was beating down and the air con in the truck was a godsend, The roads were good, they'd had no trouble so far, things were looking positive, Santander was now only six kilometers ahead, Jack turned off the main road, the sat nav was taking them cross country, the dusty back roads were so dry there was a huge cloud behind them as they went, Elise said "we should be about there now," then all of a sudden ahead on this rarely used track another cloud of dust, that had to be another vehicle ahead, who would guess they'd see anyone else in this barren place, Jack stayed well back as they caught up, he wouldn't see anything if he got into the dust cloud, the vehicle ahead turned into a fenced off yard, "this is the place," said Elise, Jack stopped before the gate, "Why are you stopping?" Asked Elise, Jack said "That could be our target ahead, there's nothing else here so where else would that van be going?" Jack pressed the button to open the gun drawer, Elise took out the two hand guns and checked them, far off across the yard the van had stopped, a man was forcibly removing a young girl from the back of the van and dragging her to a shipping container, then another and another, he then locked the door and got back into his van, that was the point at which Jack floored the accelerator in the truck, guns drawn Jack and Elise were heading straight for the van which was heading for the only exit, the gate.

Jack swung the truck around across the gate, they both jumped out and pointed their guns at the van's windscreen, it didn't slow, it had nowhere to go, Jack fired a warning shot into the air, the driver realizing he was about to get killed stopped, he put his hands out through the window.

Jack kept his gun on him as he walked to the driver's side window, "Don't move," warned Jack, Elise ran over and tied the man's hands together with cable ties.
Jack then dragged him out, was laying face down in the dirt as Jack searched him for weapons, nothing, nothing in the van's cab either.
After securing his ankles together with cable ties, Jack opened the back of the van to find cages, like dog cages these girls had been locked in for their journey.

Jack cut the ties on the man's ankles and roughly pushed him into one of the cramped cages in the back of the van, once secured Elise opened the container, the three girls were all early teens, they were rough looking, like they'd been to hell and back, one girl even had a black eye.

"What are we going to do with him?" Asked Jack, Hold on a minute replied Elise, she was looking at her phone, then she said "there's a ferry to Plymouth at eleven tomorrow, we can use that," Jack agreed but it still left all night to wait, they were heading into town, the plan was to get a hotel so the girls could get something to eat drink and clean up, the man would be taken to the police station and accommodated in the cells for the night.

The only road out was the dusty track they'd come in on, Elise led the way in the truck with the girls while Jack drove the cage van with the prisoner in the back, they were probably about half way when another van, identical to the first came the other way, Elise told the girls to get down, she then pulled over to give the other van room to pass, Jack pulled in behind Elise, there was nowhere to hide the van.

They passed by, then as soon as the other van driver realized there was something up he turned around and gave chase, this one was armed, he had his arm out the window firing at the van Jack was driving, Jack could hear banging as the bullets hit the back of the van, he was surprised the guy could even see him through the dust, Elise was long gone, she had to get the three girls out of there, Jack was holding the gunman up deliberately so she could get away, another hit, this one went through the van, through the bulkhead and hit the interior mirror, Jack couldn't see any escape so he slowed a bit more, the other van was catching him fast, as soon as Jack hit proper tarmac he slammed on the brakes, the other van smashed hard into the back of Jack's van.

Jack jumped out, ran back to the gunman who was trapped, his face covered in blood, Jack thought that was game over but then he produced his gun, before he could get a shot off Jack slammed two bullets into his face. He opened the back of the gunman's van and in there in another of these dog cages, he found a small child, she was crying and terrified, she was only about seven years old, Jack got her out of the cage and put her into the cab of his van, he then pulled forward, as he moved, the back which was smashed in by the other van opened, or what was left of it, inside he found his prisoner, he'd been hit several times, at least one of the shots was fatal.

With the door tied shut with a piece of rope, Jack drove the remains of the van onward, leaving the dead gunman in his van as he was.

The girl was still crying, Jack tried to calm her but she was inconsolable. He called Elise "Where are you?" he said, she replied "At the police station, are you far out?" Jack told her his prisoner had ceased breathing due to lead poisoning and his mate was the same, he heard her pass the message on to the police officer, Jack met the police car on the main road as the van creaked rattled and screeched along slowly, he then delivered the van including the corpse to the police station while the police car proceeded to see the other one.

Jack then put the little girl into the truck with Elise to take to the hotel, he waited at the police station until the other van had been recovered to the pound, he then went to the hotel.

Chapter Forty one
Ambush

Jack and Elise made a plan, Jack would go back to the yard in the truck, Elise would walk the girls onto the ferry in the morning to be met at the other end, Elise was worried Jack's plan was risky, they needed a whistle blower, that meant taking one of the gang alive, there would obviously be a collection at the container the next day, probably in the morning and Jack planned to surprise them.

Jack made a call, he then took the truck and went back to the container, once there he pulled the heavy gun from inside the back of the truck, it was a fifty calibre fully automatic machine gun, Jack sat it on it's stand inside the container, got a couple of boxes of ammo and then hid the truck behind the container.

He waited, and waited, almost falling asleep at times, at least the kidnappers had left him a good supply of bottled water and a bucket to piss in.

Daylight started to appear around the door and through the vents, Jack knew the next drop point would be a day away because of the information in the book, so they'd have to show soon,
Sure enough they did, it sounded like several vehicles, then a lot of talking, someone opened the container door, he didn't seem to question the

fact it wasn't locked, as soon as he saw jack sitting there behind that massive gun he froze, Jack put his finger to his lip as if to say be quiet, then beckoned him in, the man walked in, then Jack signaled him to stand to one side, he did, then a group of men busily talking among themselves casually strolled in, they stopped in their tracks as Jack said "Hi," they stood there, frozen and staring at Jack sitting there behind his huge gun.

Jack then said "Guns on the floor please gentlemen," they all did exactly as instructed, there were still more voices outside, "Who speaks English?" said Jack, one of the men carefully lifted his hand like he was in school, Jack threw a bundle of cable ties over, "You go and fetch the others, don't do anything stupid or you'll all end up as mincemeat, and you lot, tie each other up, they seemed to understand that and began applying the cable ties, luckily there didn't seem to be any heroes among them, not yet anyway, as soon as the five men inside the container had tied each other up there was the sound of tyres spinning on the loose gravel, a van appeared by the container doors, the passenger was firing at Jack, he obviously didn't care about his mates standing in the way, a few shots and the van made it's way out but the container was lined up perfectly with the gate so Jack had the perfect firing line, provided this lot got out of the way, the second Jack cocked the gun, they all dived on the floor,

Jack opened fire on the fleeing van, the noise from this big gun was deafening inside the metal container, the van didn't make it to the gate, the fifty cal peppered it, punching huge holes through it like it was made of paper. The noise stopped, the men on the floor were terrified and making some strange whimpering sounds.

Jack took his ear plugs out, threw them on the floor and holding his hand gun, checked his five prisoners were all tied up securely then still holding his hand gun he carried the heavy machine gun outside and locked the men inside the container, the phone call he had made from the hotel before he set off was to put the local cops on their toes, and when he heard the vans arrive he had sent the signal, obviously the cops were some distance behind.

Jack dismantled the fifty cal and re packed it into his truck, the cops arrived a few minutes later and loaded up the bad guys.
One of the cops who looked inside the shot up van could be seen on his hands and knees, throwing up after seeing the men in the cab, or what was left of them.
everyone left, once on the road, Jack got the shakes, he sighed a breath of relief, he couldn't believe he'd pulled that off but then again who's

going to argue with a huge machine gun staring them in the face?

The local cops were very helpful, they even let Jack interview the prisoners while they looked the other way, there were three vans with four drop points, Jack now had the addresses where the girls were about to be taken to, they were all about a days drive away so they still had time to prepare a trap. Two were close together, which didn't go along with the day apart scenario in the book. The police were asked to detain the prisoners without any paperwork, it was a national security issue and they would be collected later that day, "Jack said, to put it simply, once they are collected, they were never here," the cops were a little unsure about this but then fully cooperated when they were offered a nice unofficial boost to their budget.

Elise was still in England but would be returning soon, Jack called in the addresses and asked to take the two closest together himself, they were both in France, Jack arranged to hook up with Elise in Marseille.

Jack loaded his stuff into the truck and headed off on his eight or nine hour journey.
Jack arrived at Marseille, booked into a hotel to get some much needed rest. It was about six thirty when there was a loud knocking on his door, Jack leaped out of bed, grabbed his robe

and opened the door, Elise was standing there "I've been trying to wake you for ages," she said, Jack explained how he had driven all night and only closed his eyes a few hours ago.

"Well get dressed! We have work to do," said Elise, Jack mumbled as he made his way to the bathroom, Elise made some coffee. Ten minutes later Jack emerged, he sat down with Elise on the balcony, "What have you got?" she said, Jack explained about the one day timing and the address book, and how this one didn't fall into the pattern as it was two stops close together.

After a bite to eat they both set off to the address, it was a long narrow country lane going up into the mountains, at the end there was a metal gate and behind that a big house, Jack backed the truck away, turned around and parked a way back down the lane, "What's up? I though he was expecting a visit? Said Elise, "Yes" said Jack "but they're expecting a grey van and we're in a black four by four, we need to switch vehicles" Elise thought for a moment, "maybe not, maybe because this is an unusual stop, they could be just expecting a delivery," she said, Jack agreed but insisted they take a look around first to get the lay of the land.

They hid the truck in among the trees and made their way on foot towards the house. It was quiet, it looked deserted except for a car sitting on the drive, the gardens were barely maintained except for one, one that had recently been dug over, it looked odd among the weeds and rocks, they snooped around for a while, then the car drove off.

Chapter Forty two
Celebrity

Jack ran back to the truck and grabbed a shovel, they climbed over the fence and started digging up the garden, it didn't take long, down a little way and the shovel hit something which wasn't just dry dust and soil, Jack got onto his knees and started pulling the earth away with his hands, little fingers appeared followed by a small hand, a child's hand, Jack kept digging, eventually recovering a child of about eight or nine years old, a girl, she was naked and obviously hadn't been in the ground very long, Elise had to walk away, she was so upset, tears were streaming down her face.

Jack refilled the hole, "We can't just leave here there!" cried Elise, Jack said, it's only for now, I need to look around, they sneaked quietly to the back of the house, looked through the windows, everything looked normal, then Elise called Jack, she had found a barred window at ground level, they cleared away the dust as much as they could then looking in there was a bed, there were ropes tied to the frame, it looked like a child's bedroom, there were dolls and books scattered around, Jack said, "we need to get inside," They were just heading towards the house when the car came back, they couldn't see it but it could be heard on the loose gravel, it was too far to the perimeter fence to escape without being seen , so they took cover in the back garden, A man passed a nearby window inside the house, Jack turned to Elise and said "I know that face," he had to think for a while then the penny dropped, he blurted out "That's Mickey Monto!" Elise said "What? The singer?" Jack nodded.

There was no sign of him leaving again so the only answer was to bluff it out, Jack went to the door at the side of the house and knocked loudly, Elise remained hidden in the back garden.

Mickey Monto came to the door, Jack said "I have a delivery for you," without hesitation Mickey Monto said, "Good, where is it?" Jack replied, "soon, I need to find out what happened to the last one, we have to make sure we're not at risk by the goods winding up in the wrong hands," Mickey said "Fair enough, it's been disposed of, it seems the item wasn't up to the job, that's why I ordered a new one but there won't be any talking or falling into the wrong hands, I can guarantee that," Jack said "Disposed of?" Mickey pointed to the back garden, "Yea, I buried it," with that Jack lunged forward, bringing his knee up hard into Mickey's groin, then punched him hard in the face, Mickey's nose broke sending a flood of blood spraying up the wall and then all down his shirt and pooling on the floor, Mickey was out like a light in a heap on the floor, Jack shouted for Elise, she immediately came running in.

"Bluff!" she said, "Do you have any idea of how much trouble we're going to be in if he gets off?"

Jack tied Mickey up and left him where he lay in the hallway, he and Elise then went down the stairs to the cellar room they could see from outside, Jack opened the door, it was obviously where the girl had been held, there were all kinds of sexual toys and equipment including a blood stained whip, ropes and restraints, Jack had a mental picture of what had been going on it that room, it made him feel sick, Elise was waiting outside the door, she had no desire to see the horrors inside. Jack came rushing out of the room, obviously very angry, Elise grabbed him. "If you kill him the press will be all over it, him being a celebrity and all!"
Jack agreed, he still wanted to batter the living daylights of the scumbag but he had to control his temper.

They then searched the rest of the house, there was a digital camera just sitting there on the kitchen table, Jack picked it up and scrolled through some of the photos, he looked horrified, Elise asked him what it was, Jack said "You don't want to know, you really don't want to know, he put the camera down.

"We need to call the police," said Elise, Jack said, "we can't, not yet, we have to get to the second drop point before this gets out or there'll be no point." They put Mickey in the truck, well more of kicked him all the way to the truck then shoved him roughly inside, Elise took the camera and locked up the house before leaving, just twenty minutes later they reached the second drop, it was an old warehouse near the docks, the doors were wide open, Jack drove past, there were two men inside the warehouse obviously waiting for the drop off which was now running late, Jack parked nearby, took a gun and said to Elise, "You need to stay here with that piece of shit, I'll deal with this."

Jack walked back to the warehouse, in through the open doors and up to the two men, he hadn't got a plan, he was just winging it, "Hi" said Jack, "Where is she?" said one of the men, "Jack replied "There's been a delay, nothing to worry about, she'll be here soon," one of the men looked shifty, he said "I don't know your face, who are you?" Jack replied, "you know who I am, and stop referring to the package as her, you don't know who's listening," the other guy nudged him, as if to say "shut up," Jack said it's going to be a while yet, so I'll see you later," he turned to walk away then one of the men said "When?" Jack replied, "soon, just wait here," as he was nearing the doors a grey van came screeching into the building, the two men thought it was their delivery,

Jack stopped and turned around, the van stopped by the two men, there was a bit of a panic going on then the three of them opened fir on Jack, he was now ducked down behind a steel digger bucket, firing back but it was three against one, Jack was pinned down, to get to the door meant crossing the exposed area.

He really thought his number was up, then all of a sudden there was a screeching of tyres and Elise appeared in the truck across the doorway, no sooner had she stopped when the fifty caliber opened fire, she'd got it from the back and put it on the passenger seat with the barrel protruding from the open side window, the noise was deafening, the grey van was no shelter for the three men, the bullets just ripped straight through it. One was hit, his arm had been blown clean off at the elbow, at that point they threw their guns out, the two men came out with their hands on their heads, the van driver was on the floor screaming and bleeding.

Elise stayed where she was and kept the big gun trained on the two men while Jack grabbed a bunch of cable ties from the back, he first put one tightly around the wounded guy's arm to stop him bleeding to death, then he restrained the other two, not many minutes later the police arrived in force, the gunfire had been reported.

Once the police were on the scene, Jack grabbed Mickey from the truck and roughly dragged him out, he fell to the ground as he exited the truck and Jack accidentally kicked him in the groin, the police took him into custody, Jack and Elise along with a few of the police officers searched the warehouse, there were dog cages but nothing else so they all went to the police station.

Jack was shown into an interrogation room, shortly after Mickey was brought in and sat down, he had acquired a black eye and several cuts and bruises since Jack last saw him, "are they treating you well?" Jack asked him, Mickey gave a smirk but remained silent, Jack then said "They're gonna love you in prison, there are some pretty nasty types in there who'd love a celebrity bitch!" said Jack, Mickey then responded with "Ok, OK, what do you want?" Jack smiled, "Nothing, absolutely nothing, I just thought I'd let you know what's in store," Mickey certainly didn't look happy, at this point he was begging, he'd have sold his mother to get out of this mess, Jack said "cooperate and the judge might go a bit easier on you, but to be honest nobody likes a nonce!"

Mickey was spouting names like he'd swallowed a phone book, he told Jack how it all worked, where he kept all his contact details and when he finished singing like a canary Jack said to the police officer by the door "Book him on first degree murder, and offences under trafficking and sexual offences, also put him down as resisting arrest and being uncooperative!"

Mickey protested saying Jack had made a deal, Jack turned to the police officer and said "Really?, Did you hear anything about a deal?" the police officer shook his head, then Mickey was dragged away by two others, he was still screaming and protesting.

Meanwhile Elise was questioning one of the men from the warehouse, she was writing notes as Jack entered the room, he looked at Elise, then at the policeman who was sitting next to her, then he said "You can charge him with trafficking and accessory to the murder of the child!" Immediately the man started arguing that the murder was nothing to do with him, Jack knowing the man had been held in isolation then said

"Your mate has told us everything, he said it was all down to you and you knew about the little girl getting murdered and you covered it up!" The man thinking his mate had squealed then decided to talk, he said he knew nothing about it and his friend was the boss of the whole operation, he had only been there to oversee the handover and make sure the job was being done properly as there had been a few problems recently, he was obviously referring to the intervention of Jack and Elise at certain establishments. This guy was almost in tears, he thought he was being stitched up and the real ringleader was getting away with it.

The statements were coming thick and thin, these guys had turned on each other with venom, Jack left the room while Elise wrote everything down, he got himself a coffee and then went to interview the one he now believed was the boss, this one wasn't playing, Jack told him they already had enough evidence to put him away for life but this guy was not talking.

Jack told the cops to charge him with trafficking and left the room, it had been a long couple of days, Jack was shattered, he went back to the hotel in the hope of getting some sleep.
He had barely dropped off when he felt a sensation under the sheet, it was a feeling Jack knew only too well, it was the soft stroking of a mouth, he opened his eyes to find
Elise, naked and on her knees by the bed, head under the covers working Jack's shaft with long slow deep strokes, he could feel her lips on his balls, that could only mean one thing, his now erect cock was right back in her throat, she didn't gag or resist she just kept on swallowing all of his manhood, she was being so gentle, Jack was surprised he had actually woken up, he had to watch, he ripped off the sheet, switched on the bedside lamp and feasted his eyes on Elise's face as she devoured every inch of him, over and over.

Jack couldn't help himself, despite desperately wanting her pussy, this was just too much to handle and at the moment she took him all the way in, he erupted, squirting his hot cum deep into her throat, she didn't stop, she gulped as she swallowed then just kept on slowly and gently sliding her mouth up and down his shaft until his erection subsided, then Elise climbed into bed beside him and they both slept.

In the morning Jack rolled over thinking he may finish what had started the night before but all he found was a cold mattress, Elise had been up for ages and was packing stuff into the truck, Jack got up, showered, dressed and headed down for breakfast, Elise was nowhere in sight, Jack ordered a full English, for a moment he looked at the huge pile of bacon, sausages. fried mushrooms and the slice of fried bread and thought about a heart attack then dismissed that and got stuck in.

Feeling stuffed he returned to his room where he found Elise packing his bag, "What's going on?" he asked, Elise said "Come on, we have to get going, I want to get home."

They were on the road ten minutes later, Elise was in an exceptionally good mood, music blasting and singing as they headed north, Jack shouted over the music "Why are you so happy?" Elise just shouted back, "We completed the job and I feel good about it," Jack thought for a moment, then said "There are still other parts to this!" Elise turned down the music just long enough to say " We got the big boss, the other are being taken down and I got a promotion, what's left to do?" Jack said nothing, he just felt like they could have done more but like she said it was over, it just didn't feel like it was, Jack turned Elise's music back up, knowing he'd have to drive later he snuggled up in the corner of the seat and closed his eyes.

Chapter Forty three
The chase

"You're so boring!" shouted Elise, Jack ignored her, they were moving fast heading up the motorway when all of a sudden there was a bang, glass shattered everywhere, Elise screamed as the truck swerved onto the hard shoulder, Jack was wide awake and alert, there was range rover ahead of them backing down the hard shoulder towards them at speed, Elise pushed the button, the drawer sprung open in the dashboard and Jack grabbed a gun, she drove forward towards the range rover as Jack fired at it through the open window, there was a huge bang as the vehicles collided, the rear window of the range rover shattered as the rear door was punched in by the truck's nudge bars and winch.

Elise slammed the truck into reverse and floored it, the range rover was a mess, the door all but came off as the truck pulled back, then she drove back onto the motorway, Jack put another couple of shots into the range rover cab as they passed, traffic had come to a standstill, that gave Elise a clear road ahead, The range rover was still operational despite having it's rear end stoved in and it was once again giving chase, Jack opened the small window between the cab and the cargo area and climbed through, he opened the lift up window at the back of the truck to find the land rover right behind them, they were now catching up with traffic again so that would slow them down and put others at risk, the passenger in the range rover had been shot but the ever determined driver had an arm out of the window and was shooting, Jack felt it as a bullet whistled past his ear.

They were now in traffic and Elise was swerving the truck in and out of lanes to find a way through, Jack was firing at the range rover windscreen but every time he took aim the truck would swerve again, they passed a junction and the range rover was joined by two of the grey vans which seemed to be the choice of vehicle for the bad guys.
There was no way Jack was going to take any of them out with the hand gun while they were swerving about all over the place.

Elise was keeping up a good speed and managing to cut off the bad guys as they tried to come along side, Jack dropped the tinted rear window of the truck then opened the case which had the fifty cal inside, there was no time to set it up properly on the stand so Jack picked it up Rambo style, then found he didn't have a free hand to open the window again, "Whatever!" he thought as he fired through the glass, the bullets ripped the range rover to pieces, sending it crashing into the barrier then cart wheeling into a field, by now the traffic behind had stopped so apart from the cars Elise was passing there were only the two vans behind.

The van drivers had seen what had happened to the range rover and had both managed to get either side of the truck out of Jack's line of fire, Elise found herself boxed it, there was an eighteen wheeler in front and these vans on either side, then the eighteen wheeler passed another heavy goods vehicle, Elise stayed hard on it's tail, that in turn forced one of the vans back, the moment it reappeared in Jack's view he opened fire, he saw the driver panic as Jack's fifty cal came into view, the van driver veered off to one side, hit a car and barrel rolled along the motorway.

The other van however was alongside and the passenger was taking pot shots at Elise, she had taken to jabbing the brakes and accelerating to stop them getting a stable target, this worked but Jack was unable to keep a footing in the back, he sat down on a suitcase and guessing where the van would be he opened fire, ripping open the side of the truck as the bullets made their way, there was an enormous bang as the van sideswiped the truck, Elise was turning across the vans path, trying to slow it or force it up against the barrier, she slammed the truck into four wheel drive and both vehicles began to slow, through the rip in the side of the truck, Jack could see the grey van, then he spotted the wheel, he aimed the fifty cal and fired, hoping to hit the tyre, he did and not only the tyre the big gun smashed the alloy wheel, the van came to a smoking stop against the barrier, Elise steered away from it and carried on up the motorway.

Jack dropped the hot smoking machine gun to the floor and climbed back into the cab through the small window, "Job done is it?" he said, Elise didn't answer, Jack noticed she wasn't sitting upright, then she pulled her hand out from her side, there was blood, Elise had been hit.

The truck came to a stop, Jack had a quick look at the wound, put some wadding in place and said "Hold this hard, " he got into the driver seat and headed to the nearest Hospital, Elise was rushed straight into theatre, Jack waited, pacing up and down like an expectant father, two hours passed, then three, the time seemed to drag as he waited for news, dreading what it may be.

Eventually someone arrived, she sat down next to Jack and said "She'll be fine, the bullet is out, she's lost a lot of blood and we'll have to keep her in for a while," Jack felt relieved, "Can I see her?" he said, the nurse said "Yes but she is still sedated and we haven't told her she's lost the baby yet," Jack looked shocked, "Baby? What baby?" he said, then the nurse, looking surprised said "You didn't know she was pregnant?" "No" said Jack, the nurse said "maybe she doesn't know either it was very early days" Jack suddenly had a dilemma, does he tell Elise, or should he say nothing.

Jack went into the room, Elise was awake but still a bit sleepy and confused, she didn't mention any pregnancy so Jack decided to leave it at that. He couldn't help wondering if it was his or not.

Jack decided to stay and wait for Elise, normal procedure would have been to carry on and let the company get her home but Jack was staying regardless, he walked out through the hospital main entrance and saw the truck, or what was left of it, there were so many bullet holes, so much collision damage it was hard to believe anyone inside could have survived, but they did and surprisingly so did the truck, Jack climbed in and the engine fired into life at the turn of the key.

They were at Avignon, Jack booked into a hotel as close to the hospital as he could find, he hid the truck as they were obviously being targeted. That evening Jack hit the bar in the hotel, he had a few drinks, then a few more, by the end of the evening he was just about on his knees.

The sunshine came bursting through the window, Jack woke up with the headache from hell, he really didn't remember going to bed, he rolled over to find a woman in his bed, surely nothing happened, he was absolutely plastered the night

before, not that she wasn't pretty, she was, Jack staggered still half asleep to the bathroom, then he looked for his case, it wasn't there, he needed to change his clothes, the woman started to stir, Jack wondered what her reaction to finding him there would be, was she as drunk as him last night? Would she remember anything?
She opened her eyes, "Oh, good morning," she said, that was something of a relief, she hadn't screamed, Jack said "good morning," he continued looking for his case, he checked under the bed, in the wardrobe, then it suddenly dawned on him, that wasn't his room"

He was still trying to rewind his memory to last night but the whole lot had been erased, who was the woman, would she be offended when he couldn't name her? She spoke "How do you feel Jack?" Jack just looked blank, "Like a train hit me," he said, the woman laughed as she climbed out of bed, "I'm not surprised, she said, you did put a few away last night, I'm Lotti by the way,"

She went to the bathroom, Jack thought about getting dressed and sneaking out but that'd be rude, she returned, "Don't worry, nothing happened" she said, Jack said "I'd only worry that I'd missed it," Lotti laughed, Jack said "Why am I in your room?" Lotti wasn't at all surprised, "because you had no idea which was your room and I was nearly as drunk as you so we crashed out here," Jack looked down at himself and said

"But I'm naked?" "That was your choice," said Lotti.

Jack was more than a little embarrassed as he left her room, he was mostly dressed, enough to get away with, he went to his room and headed for the shower.

Within an hour he was at the hospital, Elise was wide awake and alert despite being in some pain, the first thing she said as Jack entered the room was "Well? Where are my grapes?" Jack laughed, "I didn't have time," he said, Jack asked "How long are they keeping you in for?" Elise said " I don't know but I guess it'll be a few days, aren't you supposed to be in England?" Jack smiled, Yes, supposed to be but I thought you might need a lift."

He spent most of the day with Elise, they got to know each other a lot better than all the time they had worked together, Jack was still there when a doctor came in to give Elise her pain killers, he started to fill the syringe from a bottle he took from his pocket, He asked Jack to wait outside, while he administered the treatment, Jack was suspicious, he went to leave but as his hand touched the door handle he changed his mind.

Jack glanced at the doctor's identity. card hanging on his coat, then he grabbed the syringe, immediately the doctor reacted by trying to hit

Jack but Jack was too quick for him and fended off his punch, the syringe flew up in the air and landed on the bed, Jack restrained the doctor, holding his throat as he pinned him against the wall, Jack held out a hand and Elise put the syringe in it, Jack stuck the needle into the doctor's neck and said "What the fuck is going on?"

The doctor refused to speak, Jack said, "OK let's give you some of this painkiller then!" he then pleaded "Stop! Please, don't! I'll talk, just don't do that." Jack said "start talking then! The guy did, he said he was under orders to eliminate Elise because she had killed the boss's son, Jack said "Who's the boss?" the guy said, "If I tell you, I'm a dead man," Jack said "You're a dead man if you don't, the only difference is I'm here with this needle in your neck, right now!" The guy saw the logic in that and gave Jack a name. A nurse arrived to administer the real painkillers, tablets this time, she dropped her tray as she saw Jack with the needle in the guy's neck, ran out and called for security.

Two security guards arrived within a minute and a police officer who just happened to be talking to them at the time, Jack removed the syringe and the man was taken away.

Once Jack and Elise were alone again she asked "How did you know?" Jack said "Since when do doctors administer painkillers? It's always a nurse," Elise was relieved, she said she would never have guessed and would be dead now if not for Jack, he shrugged and said it was in his job description. At the end of the day Jack noticed the police had set a guard by the door.

At the bar in the hotel Jack spotted Lotti, "Hi," he said, she looked round and replied "Hi yourself" he smiled, in the daylight she was really quite pretty, "Fancy some food?" said Jack, Lotti didn't even think about it "Yes, I'm starving," she said, they went to a local Italian Lotti knew about, He said "It's quite strange how the French in the south speak better English that those in the north" Lotti said, "in the north it's more of wont than cant.

Chapter Forty four
Struck out

They spent the evening in the restaurant eating and drinking, in moderation this time, then walked back to the hotel, on the way they walked past the truck, Lotti commented "Wow! Look at that! Do you think someone has done that for effect?" Jack simply said "Yes, probably" not acknowledging it was his truck. They arrived at the hotel, Jack invited Lotti up for a nightcap, she agreed and they both went to Jack's room, it wasn't long before Jack started getting personal with Lotti, it was in his nature, she resisted his moves saying "I'm not that sort of girl, sorry." Jack was surprised, he rarely failed to charm a woman into bed but Lotti was becoming a challenge, "But we have slept together," said Jack, Lotti smiled and said "Slept yes, but that's it I'm afraid," they chatted for a while and eventually Lotti said goodnight and with a kiss on the cheek, she left. Jack was stunned, he really thought Lotti was a done deal.

In the hospital with Elise the following morning, Elise said "I still can't think who I was supposed to have killed and I've never heard the name Antonio Soto," Jack said "sounds Italian, maybe mob, and you don't recall anything?" No, nothing," she said. Jack went outside and made a call to base, then he returned to Elise's room, "Apparently Antonio Soto is known as a Sicilian don, his son went missing presumed dead last year in Rome," Elise thought about that, "I was in Rome last year but I didn't kill anyone, it wasn't even mob related, I was working on this case, y'know, our agents being killed," she said, Jack said "it looks like they're going to keep coming unless this is sorted, I'm going to see if I can get clearance to go there."

Jack left, later that day he was on a plane to Rome. He had been provided with an address where he could find Antonio Soto and Jack would be hopefully going to talk to him the next day, meanwhile he hired a car and checked into a hotel. The place was expensive, it looked expensive, marble floors, huge oak staircase, fabulous chandeliers but it was just for one night, Jack felt a little out of place in all this luxury, it's the sort of thing Elise would swing on expenses, Jack didn't really care for the elegant lifestyle, it was just the first hotel he'd spotted.

The dining room was like a scene from the past, the place was full of elegantly dressed people some in tuxedos, the ladies were sporting jewelry the like you'd expect to find hidden away in vaults, Jack thought a professional thief could make millions here.

There was no way Jack was going to eat alone in that restaurant, he would look like a loser, so he decided to find a companion.

That was more difficult than he envisaged, where was he going to find someone who was elegant, classy but didn't make him look like a tramp, Jack gave up, he came up with a better plan, there was a McDonald's not far away, he'd skip dinner and go there instead.

Chapter Forty five
Mafia boss

The following morning Jack went to the address he had been given, getting onto the drive through the huge iron gates was like trying to get to the White house openly carrying a weapon, security was all over him, they search his car, searched him and only when they were completely satisfied they let Jack through the gate, once Jack stopped outside the house, he was told where to park and escorted by three huge men into the house, there he was searched again before being taken into a large lavishly decorated room.

"Mr Soto will be here soon" said one of the men as he and another left, the third man remained standing to attention by the door, It seemed like hours before Mr Soto entered the room, Jack stood up but Mr Soto casually signaled him to sit, this atmosphere of life in jeopardy seemed to ease and Mr Soto was really quite friendly and casual in his manner.

Feeling somewhat at ease now Jack asked "Why are you trying to kill Elise?" Mr Soto said "Why are you asking a question you already know the answer to?" Jack paused, he wondered for a moment how Mr Soto knew Jack already had that information, the silence was deafening, then Jack spoke again "She didn't do it, I promise you she didn't," Jack expected Mr Soto to get angry, after all it was a very intimate subject but he didn't, he calmly replied, then Tell me, Jack, who did?"

"I don't know replied Jack but it certainly wasn't Elise, May I ask where you got your information?"
At that moment Mr Soto said something to the man by the door in Italian and the man left, a few moments later a staff member, a very pretty Italian woman wearing a maid's outfit entered the room pushing a trolley, she poured Jack a cup of tea, "You do like tea? Well you must do, you're English," said Mr Soto, Jack smiled as he took the cup.

There was a general and quite informal conversation in progress, Mr Soto asked Jack about his life, and does it rain all the time in England, this went on for close to an hour, Jack was wondering if anything was going to be said about the attack on Elise but decided to go along with this small talk, he didn't want to upset one of the most dangerous men in Sicily.

Jack was toying with the idea of excusing himself and leaving, this was going nowhere, then the door opened, in came the guy who had been guarding the door and with him was another man, a smaller man, Jack knew his face, he had seen him before and just couldn't place him, he thought about all the clubs he and Elise had visited and the people they'd seen, absolutely nothing was coming back to him but he definitely knew the guy's face and he recognized Jack because as soon as he saw him he went white and tried to turn away.

Mr Soto said, Jack, this is the man who saw you're colleague gun down my boy in cold blood, "That's right isn't it Nico?" the guy replied "Yes don," but there were nerves in his voice, if only Jack could place him.
Just then Jack's phone rang, it was work, he could tell by the ring tone, he didn't answer it but that alone was enough to jog his memory, the guy he recognized worked for the firm, Jack had seen him around the building!

"You trust this guy do you?" he asked Mr Soto, he replied yes of course Nico has been in my employment for many years, not wanting to blow the guy's cover until he knew what was going on Jack turned to Nico and said, You're absolutely sure it was Elise?" Jack said it in a way that told Nico he had been rumbled, Nico thought for a moment then said "It was dark, I suppose I could be mistaken," Mr Soto's face changed, he got angry, he shouted "Get this idiot out of my sight!" the big guy took Nico out of the room.

Mr Soto said "How can I ever apologize? There is no way I would have authorized any kind of action if I wasn't totally convinced, which of course now I am not," Jack gave a sigh of relief, "Thank you," he said. Jack was invited to stay for dinner but he made an excuse and left.

Jack headed straight back to Elise, when he finally arrived it was next day Elise was putting up a fight in hospital, she wanted to leave but the staff said it wasn't time, when Elise saw Jack enter the room she calmed down a little, "Well?" she asked, Jack told her the heat was off but there was a double agent involved, Elise said "We're not spies, we don't do double agents!" Jack laughed, "I recognized one of ours, he was on Soto's payroll, we need to get back to London as soon as possible.

Elise discharged herself from hospital and they both headed for the airport.

Sitting on the plane, Elise asked Jack "Do you think Soto is involved in the trafficking?" Jack immediately said "No, not a chance " How can you be so sure?" she said, Jack replied, I've met him, I really don't think he's the sort of man to get involved in that sort of thing, he may be a gangster but he seems to have standards."

Elise got comfortable, her wound was still bleeding so Jack went and got some tissues. "Oh you do care about me then" said Elise, Jack laughed, "Care? I just don't want the cleaning bill from the airline!"

Elise ignored him and tried to sleep.

Back at home life returned to normal, the two of them were given some time off, Jack was mowing the lawn, it was hot and sunny, all of a sudden there was a loud bang, Jack jumped off the mower and dived to the ground behind the stone garden wall, just as Carol came out of the front door with a cold beer for him, she watched as the sit on lawnmower crashed into the greenhouse and Jack carefully peered over the wall into the street.

As soon as he saw Carol standing there he shouted "Get down!" Carol laughed, "What on earth for?" she said, Jack shouted "didn't you hear that gun shot?" Again she laughed, "You've been watching too much television, that was Gerald's old motorbike next door, it's been making that infernal noise every day when he starts it up, he has been round to apologize but you wouldn't know that as you're never here."

Jack was feeling quite foolish now, he got up and tried to make a joke of it.
That evening they sat watching the news on TV, about fifteen minutes or so into the program it was reported that an Englishman had been found in Sicily murdered in what appeared to be an execution style shot to the head, the police suspect he may have been involved in organized

crime, Jack muttered, "I bet I know who that is." Carol said "What's that dear?" "Oh Nothing" replied Jack "Just it's Sicily, it's bound to be mafia isn't it?"

**The end
(or is it?)**

Printed in Great Britain
by Amazon